ROGER COUNT AEROWAFFEN . . . provider of the exquisite and unique amusements to the ever-increasing appetites of the Pleasure Crew, elite society of the habitat Grand Sphere. They called him the Panda—and never dreamed of his greater, far more important role.

UWALK WENN . . . the master rickshaw dancer and master of the Grand Sphere's highest form of self defense. Even he will not learn of Aerowaffen's true aims until it is almost too late.

ELEGANZA . . . the most beautiful and passionate queen of the Pleasure Crew. Now one of her deadly games threatens to destroy Aerowaffen and his plans.

NOHFRO POCK . . . police chief from Earth. One false move on his part could spark revolution, one right move could make his career.

SPENCER LEGRANGE . . . the ruler of Earth's Corporation, exploiter of habitat worlds. His goal is to become the economic slave-lord of space. And only one man can stop him . . .

D1706561

The Centrifugal Rickshaw Dancer

WILLIAM JOHN WATKINS

POPULAR LIBRARY

An Imprint of Warner Books, Inc.

A Warner Communications Company

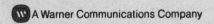

For Kyadda, Dede, and Tayne, who brought summer
with them,
and for Tommy and Ret, who are
in our thoughts more than they know.

Chapter One

The centrifugal rickshaw came down the inner slope of Iron Mountain with a rush reserved for racing. The white blocks of bachelor units and the blue, red, green, and yellow modules of family-housing clusters flashed by on both sides of the road. On the lawns in front of them, reclining people waved while others pointed and shouted from fountained pools. Children ran to the edge of the road to see the back of the rickshaw as it flashed by. Some of them even sang a snatch of rickshaw song after it, but their voices were lost in the rush of wind that blew back from the rickshaw as it flew down the hill.

UWalk Wenn was out at the end of the forks, working the momentum from side to side with a little fluid motion that looked like a dance. Normally, he would have been sitting back at the root of the forks, tilting the eccentric flywheel from orbit to orbit just by moving his hips, but he was looking for real speed and the forks were a lever he could use to work the momentum of the flywheel with.

Using the downhill momentum of the rickshaw's weight, he could make it tear along at a speed that would have left most passengers white with fear. But the bearded mountain in the middle of the longseat only smiled and leaned forward to add to the momentum.

What he added was considerable. The centrifugal rickshaw was large, but except for the flywheel, it was all allumalloy and it was lighter even than UWalk Wenn. The man on the longseat outweighed it by a hundred pounds. A man his size would be a nightmare of a passenger normally. All that weight shifting around over the box where the eccentric flywheel tilted and rolled to keep the rickshaw going was a handicap only the best rickshaw dancer could take in stride. Some clumsy tourist from Corporation Earthside flopping around the longseat would have shifted the center of gravity like a game of chance and even a master like UWalk Wenn would have had to work to keep the flywheel rolling forward of the center of gravity.

But the elegant bear in his formal pleasuresuit was almost as good as another pair of legs. He shifted his weight gracefully just a split second behind UWalk Wenn, and he moved with a grace that the rickshaw dancer thought remarkable in a man that size. It crossed UWalk Wenn's mind that if he had to have an amateur for a passenger in the LeGrange League Annual Centrifugal Rickshaw Races, he would not have been able to find a better one. To move that well, a man would almost have had to have danced the flywheel himself at some time.

It seemed unlikely. Few rickshaw dancers were really big; the strength-to-drag ratio was usually too great to make it efficient. A big man like the passenger could get more momentum in the initial run, but few of them could shift all that weight rapidly enough to make the flywheel's momentum carry most of the burden.

There were a few, of course, who made up for their lack of maneuverability by dropping back between the forks and running the rickshaw back up to speed again every so often, but for the most part, rickshaw dancers were built like UWalk Wenn—well muscled but spare and on the smallish side, like a good medium-weight wrestler.

Still, the passenger moved as if he might have earned a

good living at the trade if he ever turned his mind to it. Probably he could have turned a small fortune with the backing of some race hustler who could run side bets outside the track when the League races were being run. With a man that size on the longseat, the best-known hustler in the League could have gotten takers for his money.

UWalk Wenn did not use his skill in that way, but he was a Grander, born and raised, and he would bet anything he had on the most preposterous proposition if it did not involve rickshaw dancing. There was only one other thing on which he would not wager, and that was a contest involving electric-cane defense. He was a master of that art as well, and he approached both with a mystical reverence that was at the center of everything he did. They had a common flow of movement that stilled the mind while it trained the body.

But there were differences. When he was matching his energy perfectly with the momentum of the flywheel, he was at peace. The perfect motions of electric-cane defense made him ecstatic. One entranced, the other aroused. One dealt with the forces within, the other with forces from without. Nevertheless, it was a point of religious conviction with him that the peace of rickshaw dancing was the only correct foundation for electric-cane defense.

UWalk Wenn trained all his students in the rickshaw for three years before he would even let them begin the movements of the Defense. Only when they could move their own center of gravity fast enough and smoothly enough to keep the flywheel working the rickshaw did he consider them ready to lift a cane. Not all rickshaw dancers were formidable caners, but most could hold their own against the much larger and more powerful adversaries of the LeGrange Police. UWalk Wenn's students were a match for anyone. He wondered how well his passenger would fare with the cane he carried.

He had seen members of the Pleasure Crew handle a cane with murderous ferocity, but not one of the Old Elite fought with more skill than courage. And even their courage was tainted with an insatiable desire for pleasure, like everything else they did. The most industrious of them performed nothing in the way of useful labor. Their grandparents had been in the business of making fortunes; the Pleasure Crew was in the business of spending them. Few of them were good at anything that was not a game, and most abandoned anything that became the least bit tedious. The specter of boredom drove them incessantly. It made them all more than a little insane. Some made their madness work for them through the cane, and those who excelled at electric-cane defense did so from an unquenchable fury rather than any love of form and discipline.

The number who had the capacity for toil necessary to learn electric-cane defense from UWalk Wenn was small enough to count on one hand. And he had made all of those dance rickshaw for days on end despite their station. Not until he had driven them to the breaking point would he even consider admitting them for true study. If the man in the rickshaw had learned electric-cane defense, it was not from UWalk Wenn. But he moved well enough to have learned it from one of Wenn's better pupils. There was something about the way he moved on the longseat, making the shortest turn carry his weight to the other side of the flywheel's center of gravity, that made UWalk suspect he had stuffed that bulk down between the forks of a rickshaw as part of his training.

It made him curious, and he began to work his way back along the forks where conversation would be easier. Up on the longseat, conversation would have been effortless, but keeping the rickshaw moving from there was difficult and dangerous work. Working his momentum in close to that of a passenger was risky for all but the best rickshaw dancers, and it took a journeyman to work even the root of the forks without a loss of speed or an accident.

Moving up to the shortseat increased the chance of a crash by a hundred percent, and only a Fool or a reckless extortionist would move up on the longseat with his passenger.

UWalk moved to the root of the forks. The man greeted

his movement with a scowl. "That where you work your tips?" he said.

UWalk smiled to himself. It was the question of a man who could sing rickshaw, a language of multiple meanings, innuendos, puns, and private jokes. It was a dialect that kept the mind in motion like the shifting equilibrium of the rickshaw. Few dancers could converse in it and not let the center of gravity slip too close to disaster. On the face of it, the man was asking if he was skilled enough to work the tips of the forks from so far back. But there was a second meaning just as likely.

Any rickshaw dancer who found himself transporting an Exec from Corporation might work his way back toward the root until the rickshaw started to become frighteningly unstable. When the fare demanded he move back out on the forks where he could control the rickshaw better, the dancer would complain that it would cut his speed and lessen his fare. It was a subtle game of extortion, but so common that any game of intimidation was called "working your rickshaw." If the dancer made the rickshaw wobble enough, a coward would pay a sizable bribe to get him to slow down or go back out toward the tips of the forks. By working back near the root, a dancer was working the "tips" he could squeeze out of a passenger.

UWalk took the accusation with a smile. "Best place to weight the wheel," he said. His own answer was a pun as well. On one hand it meant that he was in the best position to wait for the flywheel to start to lose its momentum. But to another rickshaw dancer, it meant he was in the best place to test a passenger's courage and make him do most of the work at the same time. A frightened passenger would squirm around on the longseat, putting energy into the flywheel and allowing the dancer to do almost nothing but add a small amount of counterbalance to maintain control.

The man picked up the intended intimidation immediately. "Well, you're working your rickshaw," he said. Then he went UWalk one better. "Why not wait here?" he said and shifted his bulk sharply to the side to make a space on the longseat.

In doing so, he threw the flywheel into a wobble anyone but UWalk Wenn would have had to dive out on the forks to set right again. If he had not moved so expertly earlier, UWalk might have thought the man was just another Fool from Earthside offering the seat without knowing how dangerous it was, but there was no doubt in his mind that it was a challenge. The big man shifted his weight to the wrong side of the flywheel's center of gravity. It gave UWalk no choice but to come up on the longseat or swallow his pride and go back out to the tips.

"A man should work his own rickshaw," he said. It was a Grander folk saying, but it also meant he knew exactly what the big man was doing. The man threw his head back and his great booming laugh made the rickshaw quiver. It was enough to make a poor rickshaw dancer lose control and even a good one lose momentum. But UWalk did neither. With a subtle shift of his weight, he channeled the wobble into the flywheel and the rickshaw picked up speed.

"Come sit," the man said. "Have a talk."

UWalk stayed where he was. "With who?" he said. It was another inside joke. To a rickshaw dancer, it meant the man's tricks were so amateurish that there might as well have been no one on the seat at all.

The big man conceded the point by taking the question at face value. "Roger Count Aerowaffen," he said and leaned forward with a smile and bow that upset the flywheel as much as a solid kick. But UWalk had anticipated it, and there was not even a wobble in the cart. The man sat back with a smile. "Have a seat," he said. UWalk bounced twice on the forks to increase the momentum and made the three-stage climb to the longseat in one easy motion.

The big man pretended to shift out of his way to give him room, but he was really giving the flywheel a counterspin that would have sapped the rickshaw's momentum if UWalk had not shifted his own weight perfectly to balance it. UWalk sat himself on the longseat so that the flywheel spun and wobbled directly beneath them. The smallest failure to adjust from that position would set up a wobble that would lead to a crash. The threat of instant destruction hung in the balance between them.

It was a test of courage UWalk usually applied to his students, sitting with them on the longseat and singing rickshaw with them as if they were not hurtling along at breakneck speed. He would tip the equilibrium out of kilter now and again to see how well they could restore it and how far they would let it go toward imminent destruction before they were forced to take control. It amused him to have someone try to turn the tables.

As UWalk took his seat, the big man sneezed and threw the whole of his bulk at the worst possible angle. It should have sent them flying out of control. But UWalk simply leaned partway behind the man as he bobbed forward and then slid back as he sat back up. The net effect was to keep the rickshaw moving without a wobble. By shifting himself a little, he fed the force of the shift into the flywheel and set them spinning ahead faster than before but no more out of control. The roadway flew under the rickshaw in a continuous blur.

The man sat back in his seat and it was UWalk's turn. "Save those for the uphill," he said. The Count laughed again, but his laugh froze in this throat as UWalk stood up. The tips of the forks shot straight up and the rickshaw careened toward the side of the road. UWalk stood calmly waiting for the crash. The Count flung himself back and forth on the longseat trying to right them or at least slow them down, but nothing he did had any effect. He leaned forward and prepared to jump as the edge of the wheel passed over the borderline of the road.

But at the last possible instant, UWalk bent his knees and shifted his weight to one foot. The forks jerked back down and the rickshaw swerved back to the center of the roadway without even losing momentum. The Count let out a sigh of relief and sat back again. His voice had only a tiny quaver when he spoke. "Master UWalk Wenn, I presume."

Chapter Two

The difference in gravity between Earthside and the Grand Sphere was not great, but it was enough to make Nohfro Pock feel overweight and sluggish. It put him in a bad humor, and he was not in a good humor to begin with. The trip Down was no pleasure for a Grander, and Nohfro had been stationed in the Grand Sphere long enough to find it almost as uncomfortable a trip as a native Grander would. Dealing with Stefan Standard, Spencer LeGrange's Chief Exec, didn't make him any happier, and the fact that he didn't even know what the meeting was about, except that it was too sensitive to trust even to coded communication between Earthside and the Sphere, made him even less happy.

The little gold fist in the middle of his forehead seemed to clench the skin beneath it in a steadily tightening grip. The insignia of his rank was hardly a layer of skin deep, and yet there were times when it felt like it went all the way into his brain. Undoubtedly behavioral engineers had designed it to feel like that, a kind of subtle reminder that the Corporation was entitled to squeeze him in the palm of its hand just as he was entitled to squeeze any of the colonials in his. He never looked into the face of Old Spence, even on the forty-foot hologram in CORPQ, without feeling it tighten.

Still, it had taken him a long time to get that gold fist, and it felt better at its worst than the old white one he had started with as a raw recruit. The years had seen it go from white to blue to red to bronze to silver and finally to the gold of Executive Commander of the LeGrange Police on the Grand Sphere, the largest police contingent off the Earth. The pay was large, the power was greater. He no longer cared that it was not the Earthside post he had sought earlier in his career. He had acclimatized, and he had almost come to enjoy the continual battle it took to maintain any kind of security in the face of a world where everybody was working some sort of intrigue of his own. It was, he often thought, a paranoid's paradise; somebody really *was* plotting against him all the time.

Intrigue was something anybody in the LeGrange Police could count on anywhere in the six habitats that made up the LeGrange League of Stationary Satellites, but in the Grand Sphere there were plots within plots, intimidations within intimidations. Even a Blue had to be tough to last there more than a few months, and to have risen to gold there and to have maintained it for almost a decade was something that took as much intelligence as it did strength. The achievement made him smile to himself, and the little fist seemed to loosen its grasp.

The walls of the waiting room looked like pastel smoke. Their color changed from one muted tone to another, swirling slowly up from floor to ceiling. It was meant to be restful. Nohfro Pock did not find it so. The walls had changed colors perhaps a dozen times while he waited; it was far longer than he deserved to wait. Executive Administrator Stefan Standard was not his superior. If Standard was Old Spence's right hand, Nohfro Pock was certainly his left. Security was no less important than Finance to the founder of the corporation that controlled the world. Old Spence had almost as many enemies as money; it made a man like Nohfro Pock a very valuable commodity.

The wait was an insult, and the insult was intended; he and Standard had been at each other's throats for years. Nohfro Pock paced as he waited. There were four blue rectangles in the red mesh of the floor where Aireclines, variable columns of upforced air, would support him in any posture he found restful, but he preferred to remain standing. When he paced, the tight, soft fabric of his uniform rippled where his body rippled. His body was large, even by the standards of the LeGrange Police, and the shape of his permanently denuded head gave him the look of a missile. The pacing made him look like one that was about to detonate.

He waited with a mixture of anger and disgust, the two emotions Standard called up in him most often. Both were tinged just a little by fear. People of less power than Pock had good reason to fear Standard without reservation. Pock had reason to be wary of him at least under any circumstances, but on his home ground he could be even more treacherous than usual. A powerful man with great weaknesses was always a danger, and Standard's weaknesses were legion. Pock had seen them firsthand the first time Standard had come to the Grand Sphere. Before that, they had been rivals; after it, they were enemies.

It had been Pock's job to guide and protect Standard on a diplomatic tour of the Pleasure Crew, the third-generation elite of the Grand Sphere. He had given him all the usual tourist warnings about trying to keep up with the nearly insane pursuit of pleasure that was a way of life for the Pleasure Crew. What was considered debauch Earthside was a light warm-up for the elite of the Grand Sphere, but no amount of discreet warning ever seemed able to convince an Exec that no Earthsider could keep up with it.

Pock had warned him specifically against mixing DeeBee with sex. The psychological costs of direct stimulation of the pleasure centers of the brain were high enough, but when coupled with the power of the body's own orgasmic response in the brain, they were exorbitant. In particularly susceptible persons, the experience was instantly addictive; in everybody, it was addictive sooner or later. He stressed that point, as he did with every Exec their first time Up, and Standard had even seemed to take it to heart. It had taken Eleganza almost five minutes to make him forget every word of it. After that, Nohfro had lost him in the general rout and did not find him again until after the message had come through that Spencer LeGrange wanted to see him immediately in the communications chamber at CORPQ. His memory of the ride back to Corporation Headquarters in the Grand Sphere never failed to reassert itself whenever he had to deal with Standard.

Nohfro Pock sat in the center of the longseat trying to hold the Exec steady. Standard lolled and giggled with dangerous disequilibrium. His pleasuresuit was on halfway wrong; the thigh display crackled with flashes of insane color, unable to make proper contact with the terminals in his skin to replay the sensations of his first Grand Fling. His eyes were foggy with the Glow, the hazy waves of resurgent pleasure and intoxication that followed for hours a period of intense stimulation of the brain's pleasure centers. He was too waggled to stay upright, and Pock had to struggle to keep him from lurching from side to side and throwing the rickshaw dancer off the forks.

UWalk Wenn stayed discreetly out near the end of the forks, keeping the momentum down and counterbalancing the erratic shifts of his passengers. Whenever the obviously OverDone Exec lurched to one side, Wenn seemed to struggle manfully to right the rickshaw's momentum, and from time to time he went out to the very tip of the forks to keep them from shooting skyward. In actuality, he could have kept the forks down with a minimum of effort, even up on the longseat, but there was no point in letting his passengers know that. Even the LeGrange Police were not above giving a sizable tip for a difficult job well done.

Besides, he had ferried enough Execs and their police chaperons to know that moving back within eavesdropping distance of the longseat would draw an angry complaint and a series of threats and curses. He could hear well enough where he was, and there was no information worth gathering from them anyway. He already knew more than they did from what he had seen around the fountains while he was waiting to transport them back to CORPQ again.

What he knew, he put into rickshaw song, and it went out over the road that whizzed beneath them and was taken up by other rickshaw dancers on its way to its ultimate destination. It did not worry him that the Executive Commander of the LeGrange Police could hear every word of it. The ears it was meant for would understand it in a far different context. The Police paid no attention to such childish singsong rhythms anyway. All rickshaw song to them was semi-obscene doggerel at best, and gibberish at worst. He sang without fear of being completely understood. "He be DeeBee, Slick and Slide, Elle took he tongue-o, tickee for a ride."

Nohfro Pock smiled at the lyric. He thought it meant that Standard, suffering the disorientation of DeeBee, had been unable to perform adequately during the orgy, and that Eleganza had found a more appropriate way for an Exec to participate. It did not occur to him that it could mean that Eleganza, having loosened his tongue with DeeBee, had made him pay for the exquisite ride she had given him by foolishly telling her Corporation secrets.

To Pock, Stefan Standard was just another Fool up from Earthside, one more in a long line of pathetic bureaucrats he'd been burdened with. He was looking forward with relish to presenting him in that state to the justifiably outraged hologram of Spencer LeGrange. He'd seen that forty-foot hologram of Old Spence's head, solid as life, verbally devour Execs who couldn't present a coherent report of their progress, and he was looking forward to seeing it done to Standard.

The Exec on the seat beside him, lolling and laughing and almost pitching the rickshaw off the flatway, had blocked him more than once in his dealings with Old Spence, and he had a justifiable revenge coming. He thought of little else on the long downhill run to CORPQ, except when Standard's hilarity threatened to throw the rickshaw out of control and kill them all. He thought intermittently of taking the risk that Standard would remember it all in the morning and punching the Exec in the side of the head a couple of times. But he remembered the rickshaw dancer on the forks and restrained himself. It remained a passing fantasy except when, in the throes of a particularly vivid hallucination, Standard nuzzled close to him, giving little cries of surrender to overwhelming passion. But even then he did not shove the Exec out of the rickshaw to his death, as he wished, but merely held him at arm's length and waited for a subtler revenge.

The rickshaw slowed mercifully as it went up the little hill near the entrance to CORPQ, and even Standard's startled flailing of arms at finding himself flying along at breakneck speed in a totally unfamiliar place he had no memory of coming to could not throw the momentum of the rickshaw dangerously out of control. Nohfro Pock worried as he helped Standard down from the longseat that he might regain enough of his wits to conceal most of his condition from the eyes of Spencer LeGrange. But he need not have concerned himself. By the time the main wallway had unclouded to give them entrance, Standard was as disoriented and foolish as he had been most of the trip. He even turned and gave Wenn a grandiose wave of dismissal as the little rickshaw dancer began jogging between the forks to get the rickshaw up to speed for his trip back up toward the fountains of the Pleasure Crew.

When Pock finally got him to the communications chamber and they stood waiting for the enormous image of Spencer LeGrange to form before them in all its fury, Standard was standing unsteadily with his head back and his mouth wide open in the midst of some unimaginable reverie. Nohfro Pock waited with suppressed glee as Old Spence's image formed. He never stood in front of that enormous head, with its wavy white hair and dark, cold eyes, without a sobering chill, and it was no different now just because he would not be the main target of Old Spence's impatience.

The head looked down at them like two mice. The mouth opened as if it were about to devour them. The eyebrows lowered in a scowl and the eyes peered down at the disreputable figure Pock held erect by the back of his pleasuresuit like some subdued felon. Old Spence's eyes shifted to Pock, and when he spoke, the voice seemed artificially large, even for the size of the image. "Is that *my* Chief Executive Administrator in charge of Finance and General Operations?!" He made it sound as if Pock were trying to pass off an impostor. Pock nodded gravely.

"The one you were supposed to escort on a diplomatic mission for the Corporation?!" The sarcasm made Pock shudder. He saw his moment crumble like a man watching a gallows he has constructed collapsing upon him from the weight of its intended victim. It had not occurred to him that he would be held responsible for Standard's foolishness. He cursed quietly to himself. He should have known better than to expect justice. The great threat of Old Spence was that he was always so unpredictable. The voice rose with menace. "Is this what you call security?!" The words boomed out over him. Pock shook his head, but Old Spence was not satisfied. "Well?!"

Pock's voice cracked like a suspect's under interrogation. "Nosir."

The enormous eyes swept back to Standard. For a moment they looked as if they intended to burn him to ash where he stood. "Well, Standard, what have you got to report?"

The Exec jerked his shoulders and pulled free of Pock's grasp. For a moment he seemed about to present a coherent and rational explanation for his having led the Executive Commander of the LeGrange Police to believe that he was under the influence of DeeBee, which in fact Spencer LeGrange had authorized as part of his gift to Eleganza. But at the last instant, another irrepressible wave of the Glow broke over him and swept him away. He did that

*little sliding dance the Pleasure Crew use to warm up with
or to change position and sang, in an exact mimic of UWalk
Wenn, "He be DeeBee, Slick and Slide, Elle took he tongue-
o, tickee for a ride."*

The giant head lifted and the mouth opened as if to bite
them in two. But instead a great rumbling chuckle washed
over them. The great head shook slowly and ruefully from
side to side, as if it too had stood where Standard was
standing in some almost forgotten memory. "Well," it said,
"give my regards to Eleganza." And the head was gone.
Pock breathed a sigh of relief for them both. Standard fell
flat on his face.

They had been mortal enemies ever since. Still, compared
with the sheer deviousness of the Grand Sphere, Standard's
intrigues were simple as a push & punch. For all his power,
Standard was a relative amateur. That Pock's advancement
was thwarted from time to time by Standard's jealousy and
sheer incompetence annoyed him, and the gravity only made
it worse. He was annoyed at being made to wait, and he was
annoyed at being annoyed. The gold fist tightened its grasp
in the center of his forehead again, and he relaxed it by
imagining that Standard was some Grander he'd caught in a
roust. He was busily banging away at Standard's head in his
mind when the wallway between the waiting room and
Standard's office unfogged and he saw Standard waving him
impatiently in from an Airecline near the window.

He stood and straightened his uniform and brushed a spot
of dust from its slick black surface near the center of his
chest. He ran a hand over the smoothness of his head. There
was a thin film of sweat that surprised and annoyed him. It
was just the effect of gravity, he assured himself, but he
knew Standard would interpret it differently and he hated
giving him that advantage. The Exec waved him forward
again impatiently.

Pock marched toward him, but he took his time. He
passed through the wallway without a buzz; his cane had
been left in the ID room. There was no need for it there

anyway. On the Grand Sphere he would have felt naked without it, but Earthside the real danger came from information, or the lack of it. The wallway had barely clouded behind him when Standard spoke. "Speed it up, Pock. We're very busy here."

Nohfro let it pass. Standard always seemed to think his time was worth as much as Spencer LeGrange's. If they had been back on the Sphere, Pock might have been amused by it, but the little shading of gravity kept it from being funny. Standard folded his arms across his chest and settled back into the Airecline at a sharp angle. He looked like a praying mantis. Nohfro never saw him without thinking that he could make a better man out of spare parts. Standard was tall enough, but puny, and not in any lean, athletic way, but soft without being fat. There was a kind of weakness to his frame, and he had that wasted look to him.

He wore a green formalsuit, with a dozen touch-command sensors down the front of each side of his chest. They looked like medals, but they were really a series of interfaces with the Corporation's dozens of data banks. He had readout strips on the inside of each wrist, and a hand-sized plate monitor on his right thigh. Something in full color was playing on it. It was a skinner, a replay of the sensations recorded by a pleasuresuit, although without a pleasuresuit to recreate all those sensations, it was little better than a common hologram. It was playing back the movements of some wetwoman doing the slidey-slidey with none other than Standard himself.

It took Pock a moment to realize that it was Eleganza, as she had been on Standard's first trip to the Grand Sphere. He wasn't surprised. If anything, she was even more alluring now, but that first time had been an awakening for Standard. It had been two years or more, but the Pleasure Crew still asked when "Slick" was coming back, and even Eleganza asked about him once in a while. They thought he was amusing. Pock thought he was pathetic.

What did surprise him was that Standard had obviously forgotten to turn it off. That kind of short-term memory loss was common among DeeBees. Direct stimulation of the pleasure centers had its costs as well as its rewards, but DeeBee was hard to come by without official sanction, and a slip that big would indicate more than occasional use. In the Sphere he would have wondered if Standard was setting him up to believe he had a weakness he didn't, but Earthside that didn't seem as likely.

Still, it was more likely than it was that anybody that close to Old Spence could get away with an addiction for any length of time, unless, of course, Old Spence was manipulating it. The one thing he'd learned in his time in the Sphere was that Old Spence didn't miss much and he didn't miss *anything* that was under his nose. It made him wonder if maybe Old Spence was slipping a little. But then he thought maybe it was just that he himself had been in the Sphere too long, where everything was a plot within a subterfuge within an intrigue within a hoax.

Standard raised his thigh nonchalantly and touched the screen, which went foggy. Nohfro pretended not to notice it. There was something puzzlingly wrong about it, something more than just Standard forgetting to turn off a harmless little diversion he'd engaged in to lessen the stress of his day, but he couldn't figure out what it was, and Standard didn't give him much chance to ponder it. "We believe there's going to be an uprising in the League." The way he said it made the "we" sound like "Spencer and I."

Pock stifled his surprise. "Which one?"

"All of them! Catchcage, Hardcore, the Big and Little Wheels, Henson's Tube, and the Grand Sphere. All six of them! All together, all at the same time!" Standard made it sound as if it were happening even as they talked.

It was a ridiculous idea, even on the face of it. A League-wide uprising was impossible. Everything worked against it. Within the Grand Sphere alone, there were enough factions to make cohesive action unthinkable. Moreover, nobody had ever known the six habitats to agree on *any* subject, let alone act together, and anything less than a perfectly coordinated attack would be suicide. Certainly there was a generalized animosity toward Corporation and a not unreasonable hatred of the LeGrange Police, and it was true that the old grievances sometimes led to minor riots on Catchcage and Hardcore, but Standard was talking about an insurrection, and nothing less than total commitment by all the habitats would be required for that.

Even if all the others could work together, and even if there were some force to coordinate them, it wouldn't matter unless the Grand Sphere could be unified, and Pock was certain that could never happen. It went entirely against Grander character. Granders were as individual a lot as could be imagined, and every one of them was working his own rickshaw, generally at Corporation expense. Stealing from Corporation was a way of life in the Grand Sphere; everything in Grander culture was predicated on it. Without the LeGrange Corporation, there would be nobody to swindle except each other. The sport would go out of their lives. A successful uprising was not possible; even a concerted effort was out of the question. Nohfro Pock was certain of it. He gave Standard a look of withering contempt. "DeeBee dreams," he said.

Standard's tone was equally sarcastic. "You should read your own field reports more carefully," he said.

"What about them?"

"Everything! People in the wrong places. Messages that don't sound right. A lot of traffic between habitats."

Pock gave him a look that demanded something more convincing.

Standard smiled. "No fights in Hardcore."

Pock scowled. There were *always* fights in Hardcore. The last of the Obees lived in its irregular mass of old dormitory hulls and renovated cargo containers, the hardy Original Builders, who'd lasted through half a century of lethal risks "laying up structure." Even for third-generation Obees, a good fight was a daily recreation. Obees punched one another for sport, profit, and a release of tension. The only time they didn't fight was when they were fighting the LeGrange Police, or getting ready to. "Hardcore's not the whole League," he said. His voice accused Standard of panic. "Even a full-scale riot there is a long, long way from a revolution."

Standard scowled at the word as if it were treason, but he was stubbornly insistent. "Everything. A League-wide insurrection," he said. There was an arrogance to his tone that implied that *he* knew things Pock and the Police did not.

Pock shook his head. "Look," he said, "for an insurrection, you need all six habitats." He spoke slowly, as if explaining the obvious to a child. "That means you need the Grand Sphere. You can't have the Grand Sphere without the Pleasure Crew." He looked at Standard as if the argument were clearly irrefutable. Standard made no objection. Pock drove his point home with a question. "What could possibly unify the six habitats and make rebels out of the Pleasure Crew?" He was certain there was no answer.

Standard smiled triumphantly. "The Universal Tickler."

The answer was so ridiculous Pock laughed out loud. Of all the bogus paraphernalia a Fool fresh Up from Earthside could buy in the Grand Sphere, the Universal Tickler was the most worthless. Most of those sold to outrageously gullible Earthsiders were blue dots about the size and thickness of a fingernail, just like the Corporation apparatus for delivering DeeBee. Stuck in the middle of the forehead an inch above the eyebrows, it was supposed to provide the only unauthorized form of DeeBee available anywhere.

Generators that size were commonplace, but the blue dot was supposed to contain a device that would map the incredibly intricate pattern of pleasure centers in an individual's brain as well as project a field to stimulate them. Any kind of field would do—electrical, microwave, magnetic, even acoustic. But to be successful, such a field would have to focus its entire matrix of tiny energy points, each smaller than a human hair, at the exact location of millions of equally small pleasure centers. It was the equivalent of trying to project a three-dimensional map of the galaxy on to an area the size of the brain and having all of the points of light line up *exactly* with the location of the stars. Even the Corporation with its vast machines could only match up about twenty percent of the locations, and even that could be done only after hours of preliminary mapping and remapping.

A Fool who bought a Universal Tickler was lucky if it did nothing at all. One that projected an energy net of any kind could be a real danger. Most points in the brain were neutral, but there were just as many that could cause excruciating pain as there were ones for ecstasy. A random field would probably stimulate some of the pleasure centers, the same way any map imposed over any other map would have points of common intersection, but a random field was just as likely to accidentally stimulate the agony centers.

If it hit even twenty percent of them, the result would be an experience of pain great enough to cause insanity. More than twenty was like having the brain literally set on fire with a flame that never went out. Anybody with brainburn committed suicide at the earliest possible opportunity. Pock had burned enough brains to know.

And yet despite the risks, there was hardly a Grander above the age of nine that hadn't sold a Universal Tickler to somebody. The reason was simple. Access to direct stimulation of the pleasure centers was rigorously limited. Even Execs, for all their money and power, did not find it easy to come by. Getting it required having a brain map made, and only Corporation had the technology to do it. The map, stored in the Corporation's vast data banks, was permanent, but each generator was constructed to work once and once only. That was the beauty of the system. DeeBee could not be provided en masse, and even a single application required a process too laborious and intricate to be worth trying to counterfeit. Only Corporation could provide it at all, and it did so sparingly.

And for good reason. Direct stimulation of the pleasure centers was enormously addictive. Sometimes only a few uses built up a desire for it that could not be resisted. Its effects were cumulative, and even those who seemed immune to its long-term effects could suddenly find that they had turned the corner and become pathetic addicts who would do anything to get it.

Old Spence used it to get the cooperation of those who could not easily be bought or intimidated, and as a major reward among his Execs, but even Old Spence doled it out very, very sparingly. An addiction was too easy to come by, and at best it left a recurrent residue of stimulation that affected the concentration, the judgment, and the will. DeeBee was an experience only the few could have, and even Standard's exposure at Eleganza's had been provided for her by the Corporation as a sort of diplomatic gesture from one power structure to another.

Still, the Pleasure Crew craved it above all else. The threat of boredom pursued them like the inevitability of death, and DeeBee kept off the boredom better than anything else. The pursuit of unauthorized DeeBee was always fruitless, but anyone who had experienced it often enough to feel the absence of its ecstasy as intolerable pain could run through a fortune in a few months chasing one impossible promise after another. None of them seemed to care that, if not on the first stimulation then on the second or the fifth or the fiftieth, it would carry them to that state where every moment without it was filled with an excruciating longing for more. Only Old Spence's sparing use of it as leverage kept the Pleasure Crew from a general addiction that would make them extinct.

The Universal Tickler would shift the balance of power out of the hands of Spencer LeGrange and the Corporation faster than anything else. Even loyalty was no defense against DeeBee. It was an irresistible addiction, and even an officer overexposed to it could be turned. For that reason alone Pock had avoided it scrupulously, but he knew that within his own forces there were hundreds who would succumb to that kind of bribe. A reusable brain-mapper and generator, and there was no theoretical reason why a generator could not be made indefinitely reusable, represented a genuine threat. In the right hands it could make a revolution not only possible, but given enough time, almost certainly successful. But all that was useless speculation. The Universal Tickler did not exist, except in the minds of gullible Fools like Stefan Standard.

Standard's voice was indignant. "I don't see what's funny about it."

Pock shook his head as if he thought that anybody who let himself use DeeBee would eventually come to believe anything he was told about it. "You don't find that old rickshaw ridiculous?" His voice was incredulous. "It takes fifty technicians and a machine half as big as CORPQ sixteen hours to map even twenty percent of the pleasure centers and another twenty hours to program a dot generator to cast a field to match it, and you think some colonial's been able to pack all that into the same little blue dot the Corporation uses just to generate its field?"

Standard was unruffled. "White," he said.

"What?"

"White. A *white* dot."

"You think the *color* makes any difference?!"

Standard raised an indignant eyebrow. "I'm telling you what it looks like."

"Let me see it."

Standard was hesitant. "We don't have one. But it's been seen." He anticipated Pock's objection. "And tried."

"Who by?"

"Reliable sources."

Pock sneered. "And you believe some DeeBee's Glow fantasy?!" To him anyone who had used DeeBee was an addict with no claim on reality. "I think your brain's going, Slick." He used Standard's Pleasure Crew nickname on purpose.

The fact that it did not get a response worried him. "I'm not the only one who believes it." The implication was clear and sobering—if it was true. Spencer LeGrange wasn't one to believe anything he couldn't verify himself.

"Spencer LeGrange believes it?" he demanded.

Standard hedged. "He believes the consequences are too serious to ignore the possibility that it exists."

Pock felt the fist of his insignia begin to tighten again. Standard's DeeBee dreams wouldn't have been enough to make Old Spence believe that the oldest rickshaw in the Grand Sphere was suddenly within the range of possibility, no matter how much Standard believed it. There had to be more. "What makes him think it's possible?"

Standard looked reluctant. "There have been certain . . ." he hesitated, "near breakthroughs." He made a noncommittal gesture. "New theories."

Pock looked at him uncertainly. "Can *we* do it?"

Standard shook his head. "Not yet," he admitted. "But advances are about to be made. . . ."

Pock shook his head. He'd heard the promise of technicians before. "You can't expect me to believe—"

"You don't have to believe in it. Just *find* it." It sounded like a direct quote from Spencer LeGrange, and Pock weighed it very carefully. Certainly a lot of the best minds had gone Up during the settlement of the League, and many of them were still active and living in the habitats, but it didn't seem likely that they could get the jump on something Corporation had only recently come to believe possible. He had the feeling that there was something Standard wasn't telling him, but he could not guess what it was. One thing was certain. If there was any possibility of the Universal Tickler existing, much as he hated to admit it, Standard was right; it would have to be found and destroyed before it could be widely used.

"Where does he want me to look?" he said finally.

Standard accepted Pock's surrender without comment. "It's on its way to the Grand Sphere. For all we know, it may already be there. You'll have to find out yourself; I can't do all your work for you." He gave Pock no chance to express his rage. "And it's got to be done quietly. Who's your best Ear?"

Pock cursed himself for not throwing Standard out of the rickshaw when he had the chance. The fist squeezed and squeezed. He struggled to find an answer. He had a thousand informers. Everybody in the Grand Sphere sold information to the Corporation. Some of it was even worth the price. Most of it was part of a series of interlocking lies meant to cheat Corporation out of its money. There were fewer than a dozen who could be trusted to provide consistently worthwhile information, but only one who might be trusted with looking for something discreetly. "Wenn," he said finally.

"NOW!"

Pock shook his head. "UWalk Wenn."

"The little rickshaw man?" Pock nodded. "I remember him," Standard said. There was good reason for him to remember. Wenn had saved his life. It had been an ugly incident. Pock remembered it vividly.

Nohfro Pock was out of the rickshaw almost before it stopped. The crowd that had gathered around the fighters separated like water. The two Obees were still slugging away at each other. Neither seemed to bother with blocking punches, and neither of them paid the slightest attention to Pock. Ordinarily he would have let them fight to exhaustion and then stepped in, but Standard had made some snide remark about the power of the Police in the Grand Sphere, and he had an anger that needed to be taken out on somebody. His cane jabbed the first man in the back. The shock stung but did not stop him. He swung again at the other Obee and then turned to throw a fist at Pock. Pock's second jab caught him up under the chin and the force of the shock knocked his head back and toppled him backward.

The second Obee, deprived of his sport, came at him in a fury. Pock sidestepped him easily and tripped him as he went by. The Obee hit flat, like a man who'd been mixing Sleepers and Stings long enough to become a chemical battlefield where the tide of battle flowed one instant toward violent energy and the next toward a sleep verging on hibernation. Pock waited a moment to see which side was going to win. He stuck the cane down an inch from the man's back and waited. The next surge of Stinger might bring him back up to his feet again more of a problem than he was when he went down. The Obee tried to push himself back up and then collapsed. Pock gave him a shock to the base of the brain to make sure he was out, and turned to go back to the rickshaw. What he saw when he did made him wish he had stayed on the longseat.

Standard was standing up in the rickshaw, shouting at a third Obee who was standing at the side of the Wideway. He seemed to be lecturing him on the evils of drug use and senseless violence. The crowd of Granders seemed to think it hilarious. Pock was too far away to stop it when the Obee seemed to take it in his mind that the crowd was laughing at him rather than Standard and started up the rickshaw after his tormentor. Like his friends, he was apparently a visitor come mainly for the variety of chemical and physical delights always available on the Great Wideway, and he climbed unsteadily.

He had only gotten as far as the shortseat, reaching for Standard's throat, before Wenn acted. He was still down between the forks, where he had gone to stop the rickshaw, and he wheeled it around in a tight circle, toppling the Obee off before he could get a hand on Standard. Pock was almost sorry that the man hadn't succeeded. Except for the fact that Standard was his responsibility, he would have enjoyed seeing some Obee give him a Hardcore Greeting.

The Obee came tumbling off and hit on his back, but he rolled over and came up with his cane out. There was a frozen moment when he hung between going back after Standard and going after Wenn, but the rickshaw dancer came out from under the forks and made his mind up for him. It was all over in a blur. The Obee made a lunge, but the rickshaw dancer stepped to the side and blocked the cane shaft with his forearm. He seemed to roll across his shoulders up the man's extended arm and gave him a little prod with his cane behind the ear; the big Obee dropped like an empty cape. His cane toppled from his hand and hit

*with a blinding flash of blue light that made Nohfro Pock
begin to sweat. The blue flash indicated a lethal charge to
the weapon, and an assassination attempt on an Exec riding
with the Commander of the LeGrange Police was going to
be impossible to explain to Spencer LeGrange's satisfaction. Even modifying an electric cane to make that kind of
discharge was a capital offense. Carrying such a weapon
was a capital crime as well for anyone but the LeGrange
Police. It seemed an assassination attempt pure and simple,
with the fight as a diversion to lure Pock away from his
responsibility. The thought of explaining his error to that
huge head made Pock groan inwardly.*

*Standard sat openmouthed on the longseat where he had
fallen when Wenn spun the rickshaw. He stared at the cane
and the dark starburst of burn on the roadway where it had
hit. The understanding of how close he had come to death
made him pale and shaky. But before Pock could get close
enough to do anything, Standard was back on his feet, his
voice cracking with rage and residual fear, shouting,
"Flash him! Flash him!"*

*Wenn only looked up at him blankly. Standard shook his
finger at him as if he were an unruly child. "Flash him! Do
you hear me? Flash him!" He waited for Wenn to turn the
charge of his cane to its maximum and hold its flashpoints
to the back of the man's skull until they charred through
his spinal column. But Wenn refused to move. Pock ran the
last three steps toward him, twisting the top of his cane to
its lethal maximum. Unlike Wenn, he would not have to
stand for minutes waiting for the cumulative effect of the
charge to execute the assassin. A single jab with the
flashpoints to any part of the Obee's body would cause the
same blue flash as the Obee's cane and with the same
deadly effect.*

*The rickshaw dancer bent to pick up the Obee's cane as
Pock reached to apply the fatal touch. But with a short
backward swing of his cane, Wenn knocked Pock's cane
aside. Pock recovered with a wide swing and took a half
step toward Wenn. Their eyes met and held, Wenn did not*

waver, and Pock knew without question that his best lunge would be parried and turned against him. There was a good chance Wenn could even do it so that the lethal force discharged itself against Pock where his insulated uniform would not save him. Without shifting his eyes, Wenn waited for Pock to move. When Pock hesitated, Wenn lifted the Obee's cane toward him, flashpoints first. "Broke," was all he said.

Pock looked closely at the cane. The filament was clearly snapped, the glass around it cracked and splintered. He could see what the crowd could see the moment Wenn held it up; the cane had broken and the break had caused the flash, not some illegal modification. The truth was apparent to all of them. The Obee was no assassin. The flash had been an accident.

Wenn turned and tossed the cane to Standard. The Exec caught it and examined it. He looked around at the face of the crowd. Pock could see the riot Wenn had saved them from waiting for another chance to happen. Even Standard seemed to understand the situation. Flashing the Obee now would certainly turn the crowd into a mob. The prudent thing to do was let things go as they stood.

But things were already too complex for that; the power of Corporation was at stake. The Corporation administered justice. In any of the habitats, that justice was swift and without appeal. To back off completely would have been an embarrassment for both Standard and Corporation. There was a necessity to assert their authority. Even Pock had to reassert himself. Standard sized up the crowd before turning to Pock. "What's the penalty for assaulting an Exec in the Grand Sphere?" He knew the answer as well as Pock. It was the same in every habitat.

"A hand."

Standard nodded. "Then burn and mark him."

Pock's eyes went back to Wenn's. The rickshaw dancer's were clear and emotionless as ever. There was no way to tell whether he had knocked Pock's cane aside to save the Obee or to keep him from starting a riot that would have cost all *three of them their lives. There was no way to tell if he was the loyal servant of Corporation even Spencer LeGrange trusted or just another Grander disguising his hatred of the LeGrange Police behind a useful and practical mask. Pock turned toward the Obee. Wenn ducked back under the forks. If his act had been rebellion, the rebellion was over. It never occurred to Pock that the rebellion was only being deferred.*

Pock twisted the voltage collar of his cane away from lethal and stepped toward the man. He picked up the Obee's hand. It hung limp. He let it flop back and pressed the flashpoints of his cane to the wrist. There was a continuing yellow flash and a steady acrid smoking. He held the cane in place, drawing it slowly across the face of the wrist until the hand stopped twitching, then he let it drop. The dark line of the burn would heal eventually into a black scar. But the hand would never work again. Pock put a toe under the man's shoulder and flipped him over. The arm slapped limply against the ground. The eyes were still closed.

The man's face was square-jawed, with dark, heavy eyebrows, a simple face. The nose, like that of most Obees, was broken and flattened, and there were a few strips of scar tissue under the eye and in the eye-brow, the remnants of some fist ducked or seen too late. Standard's voice was sharp with impatience. "Now mark him!" There was no need for the command; Pock was already moving to do it, and he resented being made to look like an underling. He turned the tip of his cane upward without looking up. He took the center circle out of his ring and mounted it across the flashpoints of his cane.

When he touched it to the man's forehead, there was a small yellow flash and the wisps of gray smoke again. The man's feet kicked a little while it was being done, but he did not regain consciousness. When the cane was pulled away again, it left a small, ineradicable fist, like the one in the middle of Pock's own forehead, except that it was black and upside down and a good deal deeper. It would make

*the man fair game for the Police anywhere in the League,
except possibly at home in Hardcore.*

*Pock waited for the alloy to cool and then fitted it into
his ring again. The crowd had already begun to disperse.
UWalk Wenn was back between the forks of the rickshaw,
waiting for the command to run it back up to speed again.
When he felt Pock's weight on the longseat, he began to
run, and as he ran he sang. Like all rickshaw song, it went
out across the Wideway and found an echo in the voice of
every rickshaw dancer going by. It was a standard lyric,
seemingly unrelated to what had happened. "Hill he go,
round he go, upside down; rickshaw song he be Grander
frown." Eventually, it would echo in Hardcore, in Catchcage, in Henson's Tube. Ears there were listening for every
word.*

Standard nodded his approval. "I suppose he's trustworthy enough." There was every reason to believe it. Even Old
Spence trusted Wenn enough to see to it that an Exec of any
importance that came up to CORPQ rode everywhere
outside the headquarters in Wenn's rickshaw. And certainly
no Exec had ever come to harm under the care of Wenn or
any of his followers, and there had been more than one
dangerous incident to test their loyalty.

"He's a Grander," Pock warned. To him, it was answer
enough. Standard seemed to miss the point.

"I *know* that," he said patronizingly.

"Only a Fool trusts a Grander." Standard didn't recognize it as a Grander saying, and he was completely oblivious
to its shades of meaning. To a Grander, a Fool was anyone
who wasn't a native of the Sphere. But it meant more than
just an outsider; specifically, a Fool was somebody arrogant
enough to think he could pass through the layers and layers
of intrigue and ambiguity even a simple conversation contained, without a Grander guide, or Fool's Tongue, to interpret for him and intercede when his blundering got him into
trouble. No Grander ever said anything that couldn't be
interpreted at least five different ways, and it was easy for a

Fool to say something or miss some shade of meaning that would lead to bloodshed or worse. To a Grander, going without a Fool's Tongue was making a bet you wouldn't need one, and like all bets in the Grand Sphere, if you lost, you paid.

Standard took the insult with an evenness that indicated he hadn't understood it, but was sure he did. It was the certain mark of a Fool. "Allowing for the fact that he's a Grander," he conceded, but there was no indication he considered Wenn anything less than reliable.

Pock shrugged. There was no way of knowing the depth of Wenn's commitment to them. Certainly he and his best pupils made a lucrative living protecting and transporting the Corporation's Best every time they set foot outside CORPQ. But the only certainty with any Grander was that no matter how meticulously he carried out your instructions, he always had an ulterior motive of his own. Pock's answer was almost Grander in its ambiguity. "He needs Corporation to work his rickshaw."

Standard saw only the meaning that without Corporation's business, Wenn's followers would be reduced to dancing their rickshaws for ordinary tourists from Earthside and the other habitats. He didn't catch the underlying meaning that Wenn couldn't be working any deception without the Corporation to work it on. "So you think he'll remain loyal, if only on economic grounds?"

Pock snorted. "I think he'll dance his rickshaw with the wind."

Standard translated for himself. "And we're the wind."

Pock let it pass; it was a ridiculous series of questions anyway. He'd meant that UWalk Wenn or any other Grander couldn't be predicted any more than the changing of the wind. But there was too much to explain to Standard. A whole world of compulsive gamblers was impossible to predict. You never knew what side bets they had going on, and a Grander took a bet more seriously than anything else. They had a fanaticism about it. What he should have told Standard was that if Wenn or the others saw the uprising as a bet, they would back it no matter what its outcome might cost them in legitimate business.

The odds alone would have made it irresistible. A Grander would bet on anything, any time, any stakes, and the greater the odds, the better. No doubt, it came from the type of people who had volunteered to go to the Grand Sphere in the first place—an untested design, an architectural and construction effort unlike anything that had been tried before. The Speculators who came to the original shell when the mortality rate was six in ten among the settlers and nineteen in twenty among the builders had had to be compulsive gamblers to begin with, and the complexity of life in the Grand Sphere had done nothing to lessen those traits. Most Granders bet like a religious obligation.

A bet, any kind of bet, was an act of faith to a Grander, a form of religious devotion. It was impossible to communicate a thing like that to a man like Standard, for whom everything was planning and plotting and a careful scrutiny of the situation and the odds. For Standard, a situation might be complex, a series of manipulations subtle and intricate, but ultimately they resolved themselves into purpose and planning. The Grander concept of Risk was utterly beyond him.

Pock had no great desire to make him understand it anyway. Standard could not conceive of going against impossible odds for the sheer exhilaration of it. Most of what he knew was incommunicable to Standard, even if Pock had wanted to make him understand it. It was something you had to live in the Sphere for years even to acquire a rudimentary conception of.

"It's a good thing Wenn needs us," Standard said. "He'd be invaluable to the insurrection."

Pock's eyebrow went up involuntarily. It was true, of course; any coup in the Grand Sphere would need to control the rickshaws. They were the only means of transporting people rapidly inside the habitat. If the uprising got far enough, the rickshaws would be crucial, but what tightened the fist in his forehead was that Standard realized it. If

Standard knew that much about UWalk Wenn, he must have been recently briefed, and if Old Spence had gone to the trouble to prepare a briefing on possible strategies for a coup in the Grand Sphere, it meant he was taking the threat seriously.

It was a dangerous situation for Pock. Certainly Old Spence had more sources of intelligence than just the LeGrange Police, but that they could collect information even Pock did not possess about what was going on in the habitats of the league opened ramifications which got worse the more he thought about them. At best, it meant his own intelligence network was not what it should have been. Even an attempted uprising which he had known nothing about could cost him his rank. But there were even worse possibilities. If what Spencer LeGrange knew made him serious about the uprising, it meant he thought it might succeed, and if a revolution could succeed, then Pock's pursuit of the Universal Tickler was not just precautionary. It must exist, and if it existed, it would cost him a lot more than his rank unless he found or destroyed it.

Standard's question pulled him away from his dilemma. "What do you know about a man known as Roger Count Aerowaffen?"

Pock gave him a puzzled frown. "The Panda to the Pleasure Crew?" It was what a Grander would have called him. The name fit his size and general appearance, and the fact that the sexual exploits of pandas prior to their extinction had been a source of widespread public interest would have made the name even more appropriate.

Standard corrected him. "You mean panderer?" It was an outdated term. Although no orgy on the Grand Sphere could be quite complete without the inexhaustible participation of its Panda, he did not provide the Pleasure Crew with sex. Any of the traditional pleasures, both chemical and erotic, could be had almost anywhere in the Grand Sphere. What Count Aerowaffen provided was imagination, entertainment, new attractions for the Pleasure Crew to pursue.

Pock shrugged off the correction. "He finds amusement

for them." A man like Aerowaffen could make a more than adequate living just finding new diversions to keep the Pleasure Crew occupied. Like most Granders, if he had a past or a private life, it was vague. He was a minor criminal in a world of minor criminals. Pock had no personal file on him in his mind. Undoubtedly, he could access the Police computer and find out more, but all it would turn up was that he was a hanger-on among the privileged, that he worked his rickshaw continually, and every time he worked it, it changed. He sold variety to the Pleasure Crew. Beyond that, he was of no interest to the LeGrange Police. Although nothing in the Grand Sphere was entirely on the right side of what the Corporation considered the law, he had no major offenses. No political activity.

"Does he provide them with DeeBee?"

Pock snorted as if the question were ridiculous. "Does he work for the Corporation?" There was only one source of DeeBee, and no one knew it better than Standard. "What about him?"

Standard hesitated. Whatever he knew, Pock could expect to get no more from him than was absolutely necessary. "We have reason to believe he's one of them." Pock did not need an identification of "them." The revolution and its planners were becoming more real to him with every passing moment. "We want him closely watched," Standard commanded. "Very closely. Put Wenn on him." He leaned back on the Airecline and touched a sensor on his sleeve. The wallway behind Pock unclouded.

Pock turned to go without another word. He was anxious to get back to the Sphere, and it was not just the gravity that motivated him. Even before he turned, Standard had brushed the plate monitor on his thigh and Eleganza's ecstasies began replaying in his mind, if not through his nervous system. Pock could not figure out what there was about the skinner that bothered him. Some detail was very, very wrong, but whatever it was hovered just beyond his reach. By the time he passed through the wallway, more important worries occupied his mind.

Chapter Three

The rickshaw picked up momentum again and U Walk Wenn sat comfortably across the flywheel from Roger Count Aerowaffen. The Count seemed cured of his compulsion to challenge the master, and they weighted the wheel together so that the movement of the rickshaw down the slope of Iron Mountain toward the valley and the isolated peak that dominated it was smooth and effortless. The conversation was less so; crucially important things needed to be said, but there was no way in the Grand Sphere to say them directly.

"I've had an ear for your rickshaw for a long time," the Count said. It was suitably ambiguous. If the Count were merely a Fool from Earthside, it might have meant that he was a collector of folk music, as a passenger of Wenn's had once been, or that he was a lover of rickshaw song, or that he was congratulating himself on his ability to understand its complexities, or that he was simply patronizing Wenn, as so many Fools did. But Aerowaffen was a Grander, and so it might have meant that he had a network of spies, or Ears, who stole as much information as they could from the network of rickshaw song, or that he listened specifically for Wenn's song because it carried so much information about the Execs of Corporation, or it might even have meant that he was a spy for the LeGrange Police himself, although he would only have intimated such a thing if he expected to follow it with some extreme intimidation.

UWalk Wenn hoped that, instead, it meant that Roger Count Aerowaffen was the man he had been waiting for, the man from the organizers of the Revolution for whom his songs were ultimately intended. But they were both Granders, and nothing could be taken for granted in the Grand Sphere. "Better to dance rickshaw than sing it," he said.

Count Aerowaffen laughed. It was a polite way to tell him to shut up, and it also meant he would do better to work the wheel than talk about it. But to one who had danced rickshaw, it meant that the experience of keeping the flywheel in motion was far more pleasurable than talking about it. Singing rickshaw was a game; dancing rickshaw was an act of religious ecstasy.

The Count slid a little closer to UWalk Wenn and took over more of what little work there was to weighting the flywheel. "You can't lie to the wheel," he said. His movements were small, but they echoed the rhythm of the snatch of rickshaw song he sang. "Hill he go, round he go, upside down; rickshaw song, he be Grander frown." It was the most common rickshaw lyric.

On one level it summed up the life and attitudes of a rickshaw dancer. Inside the Grand Sphere every place was a hill of one sort or another, and because all meridians and wideways traveled the inside of a great ball, the rickshaw life was always a "going round." The "upside down" referred to the curious composition of the habitats in general but the Grand Sphere in particular. Looking straight up anywhere in the Sphere, there was always land directly overhead and people walking like flies on an Earthside ceiling. The gravity of the turning Sphere kept them in place just as the natural gravity of Earth kept its inhabitants stuck on its outside, seemingly upside down in relation to one another. It was a favorite point of Grander philosophy that on Earth gravity kept people standing on diametrically opposite points, in opposition foot to foot through the diameter of their sphere. Thus, especially because they couldn't see that relationship, their heads were directed away from one another and they were always at odds. In the Grand Sphere gravity kept people at diametric points directed *toward* each other, head to head, a point anyone who opened his eyes could see. On Earthside all questions were settled with force, by the marching feet of people opposed foot to foot. In the Grand Sphere all competition was brain to brain, as befitted a people whose heads always pointed in a common direction. Optimistic Grander philosophers pointed out that the interaction of Granders from diametrically opposed points in the Sphere always passed through the Ring, one way or another, so that acts of individually motivated effort were ultimately focused through a single cosmic purpose.

There was another pun to the "upside down." Iron Mountain divided the Sphere into two hemispheres, and although gravity made them both right-side up, one hemisphere was referred to as Upside and the other as Downside. Upside contained the space given to the Original Speculators for sealing the hemispheres and other indispensable services rendered before or during early settlement. Wealthy settlers were given land in the Upside, and those who earned theirs in return for less essential service or could afford only smaller sections of space were given land in the Downside. The gardens of the Pleasure Crew were in the Upside. In the Downside hemisphere lived the Granders who worked their schemes and did their business on the Great Wideway, which ran at a right angle to the Ring and served as both the main route for travel and the center of business and chicanery in the Sphere. Like the rickshaw dancers, most Granders lived on the Downside.

To the consternation of almost everybody but the Granders, in the Upside all hills were referred to as uphills, and in the Downside all hills were called downhills. The distinction bewildered the average visitor almost as much as having land overhead beyond the sky. To anyone from Earthside, uphills inclined and downhills declined. In the Grand Sphere all hills were judged in that regard as either "steep" or "smooth." Those where the rickshaw worked with gravity were smooth, and those where gravity worked against the rickshaw dancer were steep. In the Downside, all hills were downhills, steep ones inclined, and smooth ones declined. Granders usually ended such an explanation by saying, "Downside, all hills are steep." It was both a covert political statement and an intentional attempt at creating further confusion. It was considered a great embarrassment for a Grander to be completely understood by a Fool.

The last part of the lyric, "rickshaw song, he be Grander frown," was generally taken to mean that a rickshaw dancer, who got ahead not by resisting forces like gravity but by subtly altering them, did not waste time frowning over the way things were; he simply turned them to song and let the song in turn add the momentum of adversity to weighting the wheel. It was thought generally to refer to the rickshaw attitude toward life, that a frown never did any good, while a song made the steep hills smooth, which indeed it did by providing a rhythm by which the centrifugal rickshaw dancer could regain equilibrium from a flywheel temporarily thrown out of kilter by natural forces, the lay of the land, or some Fool from Earthside. It was part of the Grander understanding of the line that the flywheel was never wrongly weighted except by Fools from somewhere else who did not know how to balance anything. Anybody who could add their momentum to the ride was welcome on the Grand Sphere. Anybody from Corporation, like gravity, always worked counter to that ride.

But there was a political meaning as well, one which only those engaged in the long, slow process of revolution would understand. Both Wenn and the Count knew that rickshaw song was the smiling face Granders turned to Corporation to cover their hatred. It was a way of remembering forever old grievances, old abuses, old atrocities that would someday be avenged. The Grander smile was a frown turned upside down to meet the circumstances, one that would become right-side up only when Downside had become Upside. But that would not happen until the Great Rickshaw of Revolution had been run up to speed and the final and steepest hill of all had been run to free all Granders from the restrictions of Corporation.

It was an attitude shared throughout the League, in all six habitats, and it was an unexpressed longing among many who had no idea the Revolution was coming. UWalk Wenn had waited a long time for his rickshaw to carry someone who knew the full meaning of that song. Many of those who understood it he had not seen in a decade, some he had never seen, but they weighted the same wheel as he did, and although it might take half a lifetime to run the Great Rickshaw up to its momentum, the run would not last forever and ride would rise over every obstacle in its path. When Count Aerowaffen sang the lyric again, Wenn joined him, their voices and their joint motion adding momentum and stability to the wheel. The rickshaw picked up speed for the steep uphill that was coming.

Count Aerowaffen smiled. "We sing it in Hardcore when we dance our rickshaws." It was a phrase UWalk Wenn had been waiting for. There were no rickshaws in the jungle of old dormitory hulls and converted cargo containers that made up Hardcore. There were no wideways, no meridians, no long open spaces as there were in Henson's Tube and the Toruses, and the Sphere. There was no easy way to get from one place to another in Hardcore; a trip from anywhere to anywhere was a long, twisting walk through narrow, jostling corridors full of angry men looking for an insult. It was a common saying that the only way to get anywhere in Hardcore was to fight your way there.

Not many people visited it, and few who ran afoul of the Obees visited it twice. If there was a center of hatred for Corporation, Hardcore was it. In it, there was no rickshaw philosophy of turning resistance to momentum by shifting position, as there was in the Sphere. In Hardcore, force was met with greater force, and the malevolence of the Corporation was met with rage and hatred. The riots that sometimes broke out there were always bloodily put down by the Corporation, but never without large casualties among the LeGrange Police. When rickshaw was sung there, its music was always the drums of revolution.

Wenn smiled. "There is no Upside in Hardcore." It was a joke as well as a countersign. It meant everybody was equal in Hardcore, which was largely true, since none of the privileged lived there and few visited. Even Corporation did not maintain a presence there, as it did in all other habitats except Catchcage. There was no Upside where the privileged lived because none but the poorest lived there at all, and although over the years some had moved from there to greener spaces in the Big and Little Wheels or Henson's Tube, they remained Corehard at heart, and those who remained in the Core had no illusions about whose foot was, and had always been, on their necks. There was an implied continuation to what Wenn said. "There is no Upside in Hardcore. And after the Great Rickshaw rolls through, there'll be no Upside at all."

It made UWalk Wenn very happy to hear it. He had waited a long time for the Revolution to begin. He and others had worked decades, slowly, quietly, infiltrating even Corporation Earthside in preparation for it. That Aerowaffen was in his rickshaw meant that the time was finally at hand.

Aerowaffen confirmed it. "There's a steep uphill coming," he said. To another passenger it would have seemed simply that he was reminding Wenn that the momentum of their descent from the Iron Mountain was about to be tested by the rising ground of Upside that marked the pools and gardens of the Pleasure Crew. He might only have been saying that the first of the rickshaw's struggles against gravity was about to begin. But to UWalk Wenn it meant that the final struggle was already in motion.

The rickshaw roared across the valley of Upside and began the first sharp incline toward the peaks of the Speculators. As the Iron Mountain swept away into the curve of the inner hull of the Sphere, it formed a valley which the four Original Speculators had divided between them. In each of its four quadrants, another, much smaller mountain had been constructed, and at the top of each sat the palace of an Original Speculator. Of the four, the most luxurious was the palace of Eleganza's grandfather, Virgil Van Vast, but she did not live in it. Like most of her generation, she preferred her own fountains and terraced gardens about a third of the way down from the peak. The Pleasure Crew had no desire to struggle for mountaintops, to battle continually with Corporation. Their sole interest was pleasure, not achievement. Corporation was an annoyance to them, an old nemesis which bothered them now only so far as it restricted their pleasure or made something they wanted for amusement harder to get. Except for DeeBee, they had no real grudge against Corporation at all.

Roger Count Aerowaffen and UWalk Wenn weighted the wheel together as the incline rose beneath the rickshaw, and it seemed to gain speed against the slowing pull of gravity instead of losing it. "The last uphill," Wenn smiled. It could have meant that they were almost to their destination. It meant that it was the last time there would be an Upside of power and privilege in the sky above its equals. It meant the Revolution was at hand. The rickshaw took the incline of Van Vast's Peak as if they were still roaring down the side of Iron Mountain. The Count and UWalk Wenn shifted in unison as they sang, weighting the wheel. The rickshaw shot through the gate of Eleganza's Garden, but they shifted their weight so perfectly that it put a drag on the flywheel and brought the rickshaw to a graceful stop just beyond the central pool. Just before Roger Count Aerowaffen climbed down from the longseat, Wenn asked one last question. "How will you weight the wheel?"

Count Aerowaffen smiled and reached inside the collar of his pleasuresuit. He held up his index finger. On its tip was a small white dot. "With pleasure," he laughed, "with pleasure."

Chapter Four

Eleganza floated easily in the Sauce. It was warm and thick as mercury, but not at all dangerous. Where it had splashed across the smoothness of her golden skin, it made little beads, and in the places where strips of her pleasuresuit had been peeled or torn away in the grip of passion, the beads were smaller and more oval. She had a vague idea that it was a kind of fractured polymer, but like most of the Pleasure Crew, she had no great interest in *how* her pleasures worked, as long as they worked.

Where the liquid bubbled out of the fountains, it shimmered like quicksilver, and where other fountains tossed it in shimmering arcs, it seemed to change colors continuously. A minuscule change in its temperature changed its hue. The beads of it near her navel were a different color from the string of beads along her inner forearm or the back of her hand, and the droplets that rolled down her long leg as she raised it languorously above the surface rippled and twined like a spiraled rainbow.

She liked the fact that the Sauce changed color so often; it kept it from being boring like most other things. Boredom haunted her, drove her, and she dreaded the idea of minutes that dragged on and on, heavy with the tedium of meaninglessness; of hours unbroken even by the faintest glimmer of pleasure. A kind of darkness seemed to hover always behind her, threatening to cast its shadow over everything she did.

She was not alone in her fear any more than she was alone in the pool; her class and kind shared both with her. She loved and hated them, cherished and despised them. They were all selfish and greedy fools whose whims and interests so often conflicted with her own that it made her torment them at times. At times their willfully selfish refusal to follow *her* whims instead of their own led her to punish them in her own way, but she loved them for that as well because even the most petty of her revenges gave her long, uninterrupted stretches of amusement, and even in the slowest and most depressing of times, it gave her something to continue living for.

And when they bent themselves to her will, when they put their force and ingenuity into giving her pleasure, she loved them all with equal fervor. And she was not entirely selfish. When it came to giving and getting the soft, slippery touch, the buck and drive of building ecstasy, she labored with no less frenzy for them than for herself. There was nothing she would not do to see someone agasp in that drowning ecstasy that lifted them all above the sordid tedium of existence. Nothing was beneath her, no effort too great, no act too bizarre, no rapture too intense for her not to coax, squeeze, wring it out of them or herself.

It was a wonderful trait, that absolute devotion to pleasure, and it made her adored, and envied, just as her cruelty made her feared and hated. Of all the Pleasure Crew, she was the best, the most exciting, the most passionate, the most interesting. And if there were those among her kind who, out of jealousy or simple stupidity, did not agree, they kept it to themselves. Even those who, because it gave them something of interest to motivate themselves with, hated her had to admit that she had talent, and imagination, and vitality.

It occurred to her, as she lay blissfully feeling the ebb of her passions slowly retreating in the warm, soft liquid, that there were those who did not worship her, but the Glow made their foolishness tolerable, and her anger too lay panting with exhaustion and would not even lift its head into her consciousness. It was indescribably nice to be in the Grand Sphere, among her own kind. Trips Earthside were always so tedious, so boring, and the extra gravity made her feel bloated and fleshy and out of sorts. And the people there were always so depressing, although she had pleasant enough memories of the DeeBee and Spencer and Stefan.

She loved the keen, clear lure of adventure, the intrigue, the challenge of the game whose tenor she had established with them in return for some of that exquisite stimulation the Corporation so meanly hoarded to its own. It quickened her all over, gave even the floaty serenity of the pool a sharp spice of danger, like a high note sounded just above conscious hearing at the end of a driving crescendo. It was like the aftertrill of the highest and most beautiful note ever heard echoing in the mind long after it leaves the ear. She listened for that trill constantly, and she was so often disappointed. Only the most dangerous games, the most clever intrigues, the most deadly and self-willed adversaries could make her hear it. Or the most dedicated lovers. Or, she was forced to admit to herself, almost *anybody* coming to her in the intense fog of the DeeBee. But in everything, it was the trill of that peak intensity whose ringing she longed for and pursued relentlessly.

Even in the grinding dolor of the trip Down and the trip Up, even in the heavy, slow, monotonous passage of Earthside time itself, she could hear it ringing. It was something even her genes pursued, an insatiable desire, passed down from her ancestors, the Original Speculators, who had conned their fortunes out of the Corporation and thrown themselves passionately into the pursuit of Risk, whatever it was.

It was what made her irresistible among her kind. Her grandfather had gambled for fortunes, risking life and limb to come to the Grand Sphere even before it was completed, and her mother had risked that enormous wealth for position, for status, for rank among golden peers, richer and more reckless than people had ever been. But Eleganza was playing with the destiny of the League itself, the destiny of Earthside, the history of the race. The mere thought of it aroused and satisfied her at the same time. It left her enormously pleased with her game, with herself, and with her playmates.

They were the same playmates her mother and her grandfather had played against. Spencer LeGrange, his age artificially extended even beyond the gift of long and healthy life the habitats gave, was the very same man her grandfather had swindled, the very same her mother had captivated. All the wealth of the Pleasure Crew had ultimately been tricked or tickled out of the hands of Spencer LeGrange. There was no other adversary worthy enough for any of them. Spencer LeGrange had bankrolled the first habitat, had overseen the building of the other five and the power satellites that powered Earthside.

The LeGrange Corporation *was* the planet Earth, from which her kind had leaped toward the moon. No one had more power, no one was better equipped to handle it, no one liked the thrill of the game more than Spencer LeGrange. And, of course, no one could provide better or more complete stimulation of the pleasure centers than the Corporation founded and run by Spencer LeGrange.

Eleganza had no desire to supplant him any more than her grandfather had intended to wipe him out. Like most of the Specs, they wanted only to skim a comfortable fortune and an interesting living from the blood of the Corporation. The sheer tedium Old Spence must have to endure running his endless meetings, watching over the ineptitude of countless underlings, seemed to her more a punishment than anything to strive for, and she had no desire to take it all away from him. She found it far more exciting, and far more interesting, to simply interfere with it from time to time, to nudge its momentum in a new direction, shift the overwhelming force of its organization toward new, unexpected ends.

The thought of running Old Spence in circles, of kicking the momentum of Corporation out of its groove, sent a murmur of delight through her. She squirmed languidly on the surface of the Sauce, and every muscle stretched with delight and self-absorption. She dipped a finger in the liquid and touched the drops to her tongue. They were as sweet and spicy as her excitement that the game was running, and not even *she* could tell what its outcome would be.

It was the way her grandfather must have felt launching up to those unjoinable hemispheres before the Grand Sphere was fully finished, not knowing how it would come out, with the destiny of the whole race hanging in the balance, with wealth beyond imagining to be won, and every moment running at top speed on the thin, sharp edge of extinction. It was what her mother must have felt, that delicious, secret power that could make men dance like first-landing Fools. It made her think of Stefan. There was nothing more amusing than a Fool. Unless it was a Fool trying to please. There was something in the Pleasure Crew that was always taking as it was giving. But Stefan, so serious, so ridiculous, so earnest in his desire, so helpless in the throes of his passion, so complete in his surrender to the DeeBee, Stefan was a playmate to be savored.

All of her kind, everyone on the Sphere was, even in the moment of their most intense surrender, still working their own rickshaw. But Stefan labored more in her behalf than in his own. Her mother was right; it took a Fool to really weight the wheel. And Stefan, without doubt, was a Fool of Fools. The Glow brought him back to her again, the sweating momentum of his passion, the whirling depth of his surrender. It made her laugh, a deep, throaty chuckle that rippled the Sauce around her in little delightful waves that caught the light and turned it into color.

She opened her eyes halfway and lolled her head to one side to watch the ripples she could feel washing away from her skin. All around her the light that always seemed to come from everywhere and nowhere in the Grand Sphere glittered and sparkled. The people laughing and rolling at the far edge of the pool seemed to her more beautiful than anything she had seen in years. The motion of their rocking, the increasing waves they sent outward in the Sauce, the slow, teasing rhythm of their dance seemed to her perfect and irreplaceable. Everything glistened with newness and danger.

And then it dimmed, dimmed, and went out.

She raised her right hand in the gloom, and the cobalt blue of her smallest finger jutted beyond the smooth gold of the back of her hand. On its artificial surface, the Sauce did not bead; there alone it clung and dangled in long, sticky strands. She remembered the softer flesh and bone that had once been there, and the memory of it dropped her back into the day of its loss.

The young man leaned close to her and smiled. "A woman with all of her digits," he said. His eyes were dark and seemed to glow in the long, narrow face. She gave him a look of utter contempt, but he intrigued her. Still, it didn't do for a girl just come into her fullness to encourage any common Grander who happened up to her in the Great Wideway. It did not discourage him. "Not a Risker, eh?" There was a bit of disdain in his voice and a challenge that aroused her attention. She was not entirely new to challenges, and she was certainly no stranger to pleasure, but she was still very young and the world outside the circle in which she belonged was still alien and exciting to her.

Not that she was forbidden anything, but the Great Wideway, with its throng of Fools Up from Earthside and its hordes of Granders, each working his rickshaw for all it was worth, could be dangerous even for someone of her station. Not that anyone would harm her. Wealth glowed around her like armor. And besides, within easy call there were half a dozen of the LeGrange Police in their shock-proof uniforms, swinging their electric canes like a baleful warning against violence toward the privileged. She was safe from everything she did not do to herself.

The young man leaned conspiratorially close again. "Voorpenny," he said. It was apparently his name.

"Drop a mountain on it," she said. But she shaded the intonation so that it didn't quite mean what it said, and she left off the accompanying slap of the palms that would have made it an obscene invitation to get lost.

He raised an eyebrow. "Spicy little thing," he said. It was either an invitation, admiration, or pure, unbridled lust, but like everything on the Grand Sphere, it was probably all three, and neither. He let a beat go by before he added, "For somebody who's never taken a Risk." His air of superiority ruffled her. She knew more about pleasure already than he could guess at, but there was just enough truth in what he said to make it sting. She gave him an icy stare. "Never know what it's like to be One with the Ring," he said.

She gave a derisive laugh. "Poorpenny the Profit," she said.

"Voorpenny," he corrected. "And you don't have to be the Prophet to be One with the Ring."

She'd been warned about Riskers, religious fanatics always trying to make themselves One with the great halo of ions that focused over Iron Mountain like a cloud. There was no mysticism in the Ring for her, though; her grandfather had built it. Back forty years, when the halves of the Grand Sphere had been joined, there was a problem. The halves would not quite fit together, and the solar wind roared through the crack, making life inside nearly impossible until some way could be found to seal it. Her grandfather had had the answer for it. "Drop a mountain on it." Corporation liked that kind of thinking and gave the go-ahead and the promise of a huge chunk of prize space inside the Sphere if it worked. The four Original Speculators set to work.

Nickel smelted from moonrock by the mobile furnaces of Catchcage was poured layer after layer into the crack until *it was sealed, and on the inside, where the sealing metal flowed and spread, a single continuous mountain range was formed around the Sphere's internal equator. Life inside the Sphere became possible. There was only one slight hitch. The stream of ions that had blown through the crack set up changes inside the Iron Mountain itself, and the whole circular range served as a focus for it. A huge halo of glowing ions formed perpetually above the top of the mountains, a visible ring, shrinking and growing in size and brightness with every change in the intensity in the solar wind. Because no one knew what the effects of living in an electrically charged field of that magnitude would be, space on Iron Mountain was the cheapest space in the Sphere. Riskers, those who lived on Iron Mountain and felt that stream of ions rise through them to the Ring every day, grew noticeably different from all the other inhabitants of the Grand Sphere. Their children had a delicate beauty unmatched anywhere in the race. Because they were shaped and transformed by that flow of ions, they worshipped the Ring as a manifestation of the deity and strove always to be at One with its changing patterns.*

Still, being Granders, they were naturally compulsive gamblers and their chief measure of being at One with the Ring was their ability to predict its density, backed naturally by a sizable bet. Because they were not wealthy, the greatest measure of their bet was the Risk of their beauty.

The young man who stood smiling at her did not have the delicate features that made the Riskchild the most beautiful of all human beings, and he certainly did not have that portion of their anatomy which was most beautiful of all, their long, exquisite hands. Because, if there was a bet to be made, there was always a Grander to take it, and there were machines almost everywhere in the Sphere that would put up a sizable piece of credit against a finger or a thumb. A woman who had made her bet and survived it, who had been One with the Ring, was a woman with all of her digits. When Voorpenny had called her that initially, he had meant not only that she was beautiful, but that she was spiritually superior as well. It would have been a simple, honest observation if she were a Riskchild. As it was, it was merely a compliment, or a piece of bait.

"You haven't lived till you've bet the digit," he said. There was a smile on his face that said she was something special. "Never done it, have you?" he said.

"I'm not a Fool," she said. It meant she was not from Earthside and susceptible to some fast-talking Grander's rickshaw.

"Never know what you've missed." It was another Grander pun. He meant that even if she lost, she wouldn't feel it. Just a simple, almost painless slice of a laser and the finger would come back out of the machine neatly amputated and completely cauterized. But he also meant she'd never know what it was like to feel the thrill of everything hanging in the balance.

But she was not buying it. He took another tack. "I feel sorry for you Pack," he said. "What's a bet to you? You could lose half what you got and never live long enough to spend the rest of it." There was a touch of envy in his voice and a bit of bitterness. But there was genuine pity as well, and a superiority at having taken real risks that she would never know about, and survived them. He started to turn away from her. "What do you lot know anyway, bit of grab and tickle, slick and slide. That's naught."

It stung her to hear the focus of her life and the life of her friends and class talked about so contemptuously. "It's more than you'll ever feel," she said.

He gave her a cocky grin. "Oh, I can feel it as well as the rest," he said, "but you can't feel what I've felt." There was a truth to it that made her envious without knowing why. "Not till you bet the digit anyway." The treacherous thing about it was that it didn't even sound like something he said every day.

If she had been as sophisticated about Risk as she was about pleasure, she would have known it was the oldest rickshaw in the Sphere. Her grandfather had pulled off the Big Rickshaw, but for every one of the Speculators who founded the fortunes that the Pleasure Crew spent, there were ten thousand little Specs who worked some subtle edge in providing service or equipment for Corporation, who took the same physical risks but came away with a piece of Corporation only big enough to live off from one day to another. Voorpenny's people had come up at the same time as Eleganza's grandfather, and they had been working their little rickshaw ever since. The betting was part of it.

There was hardly a place on the Great Wideway you could look in any direction without seeing one of the little gray machines where a bet could be made. All you had to do was punch up your credit and pick your number, and the machine would calculate the density of the Ring to six decimal places, and if your number matched the first three, or five, or nine, depending on your bet, you won. Only if you didn't have the credit, or were a fanatic Risker, did you put one of your fingers into the ten small holes at the bottom of the little gray box.

The classic rickshaw was to get somebody to bet the digit with you. The Grander working that rickshaw would even let the Fool pick the number, and they would each put their finger into the slot. The rickshaw was that only the Fool really put his finger in, while the Grander punched up a two-segment bet on the Fool's side without putting his finger in at all. If they won, they split the money. If they lost, the Fool was usually too stunned to realize that he was the only one minus a digit. More often than not, the Grander had already lost a digit and simply pulled off the lifelike artificial segment and stuck the stump in. It was safe enough; nobody really looked closely at anybody's hands unless they were looking at a Riskchild.

But Eleganza had been only warned that everybody on the Great Wideway was working their rickshaw; nobody told her how. Voorpenny taught her.

"Why should I?" she said. "I can't win anything I don't already have."

He snorted his disdain. "It's not what you win," he said.

"It's what you Risk." He waved her away. *"You don't want to know."*

She pouted. Nobody had ever treated her like that before. She struck back from her only position of strength. *"I know things you'll never get to know,"* she said.

He laughed. *"Games,"* he said. *"Kiddiegames."*

She tried to look scornful. *"Not when I play them,"* she said. It was almost convincing.

"Go back Upside to your slicks and slides," he said. *"There's a hundred on the Way can play them better than you anyhow, and any Fool Up from Earthside can have it for five credits."*

She smacked her palms together. *"Drop a mountain on it."* It was what her grandfather had said to Spencer LeGrange, but the palms made it the universal obscenity. She almost turned to go. It would have been better if she had. But she didn't. *"What do you know anyway? You're too short for your pleasure."* It was a Grander saying, and he could take it any way he liked—that he was too young, too small, too weak, too cowardly, too foolish, too poor, or just plain impotent.

He snorted. *"Yeah? Well, I'd do something with you none of your Upside playmates would. I'd bet the digit with you."* He paused. *"And you'd never forget it."*

It was perfectly laid bait. A two-digit bet paid six times what a one-digit bet did. But she was still scornful. *"You just want a two-digit bet for a one-digit risk."*

"Drop a mountain on it!" he said, and it didn't take a slap of the palms to make it an obscenity. He turned away and kept walking. There was a quality in his voice that sounded like genuine hurt, but he was gone in the crowd before she could stop him. She looked at the little gray box and wondered, but she didn't have the courage to try it herself. So she kept walking on the Wideway.

It was a long walk later before she saw him again, and he didn't see her. She watched him for a while before she finally went up to him. He didn't smile when he saw her.

"Why would you then?" she said, as if he had just made the offer.

He shrugged and looked sheepish, as if there was some feeling for her he was embarrassed to admit to. "I don't know," he said.

But she knew, or thought she did. She smiled and ran her finger along the inside of his wrist. "Well, we could play some kiddiegames anyway."

He laughed. There were a lot of places to take your pleasure along the Great Wideway. They took a Stand-up. She had credit for much better, but he paid. He was better than she expected for somebody who didn't make pleasure a way of life, and later, on the Wideway again, she told him so.

He smiled a little sadly. "Yeah," he said, "you're better than I'll ever have again. But I'm just a face in the crowd." It made her feel something she had never felt before that he wanted to be something more. "I coulda shown you something none of those Upside slicks would ever show you." His voice was wistful, as if an opportunity had gone by that would never come again. Then his face brightened. He stopped beside a betting box and put his littlest finger into the smallest hole. "Punch in your ID," he said. He took her hand with his right hand. It meant the bet would go into her account. She looked at him for a reason. "For the Risk," he said. He squeezed her hand. "Even secondhand, you might feel some of it."

She punched up her ID. He looked up at the Ring. "Pick it," he said. "But first you have to feel the Ring." She concentrated hard and he laughed. "You can't try," he said, "you just have to do it."

She let herself go, looking up at the shimmering halo that hung above them. For a moment it shone with a radiance she had never seen before, a glow that made everything on the Wideway shine with dazzling perfection. She punched in four digits, the first four that came to her. There was a short moment before the light on the machine went from yellow to cobalt blue. The numbers matched!

There were ten thousand more credits in her account. She felt the thrill of it run through her. He laughed. "Now you're an honorary Risker," he said. He smiled and started to turn away. It was more than anyone had ever done for her, more than anyone she knew would do. She touched his arm. "Let's do it together," she said.

The hole felt cold at first, and when she punched in her ID number, he put his little finger in the hole on his side as well. His right hand clutched her left like the body of a lover. The hole gripped her finger and the realization that she couldn't take it back out shot through her. She looked up at the Ring. It seemed to blaze, and she could hear it like a high, clear note more beautiful than anything she had ever imagined. Everything around her lit up and she could feel something rushing through her. In that instant between the moment she punched in the numbers and the instant the machine measured and compared, she looked around her as if it were her last moment in the world. She had never seen anything so beautiful as the Way. The colors were dazzling. Every face she could see was haloed in beauty. Everything seemed more magnificent than it had ever been in her life and more magnificent than it would ever be again. She looked at Voorpenny and smiled; he leaned over and kissed her. It was a long, deep kiss that thrilled her more than anything she had ever experienced. The machine measured. The note rang in her mind, a high beautiful trill beyond hearing, the sound of the Ring. The machine matched. She hardly felt the pain; it was just a twinge.

She didn't even realize it was gone until she took it out. He took his finger out before hers. It was a mistake on his part. The false top of it dropped from his palm. She watched it fall, all the colors draining out of the world. He hadn't even bet. She felt her hand withdraw, and when she looked, the irreversible loss of it struck her. It was simply gone. The first two segments had vanished, and there was a black, greasy glaze across the top of what was left that would heal in time. It was gone all the way to the second knuckle, but it was more the betrayal than the horror that stunned her. The emptiness in the pit of her stomach. The terrible feeling of being a Fool. The irreparable loss. Gone. It was simply and irreversibly gone. Darkness closed over her like death.

Darkness closed over her like death.

Chapter Five

Eleganza came out of her darkness with a cry and a shudder. The Glow was gone. The soft, dazzling light had become a glare. The sweet and spicy taste of the Sauce in her mouth had become bitter and nauseating. She felt cold and afraid. Those whose pleasure was ending or whose dalliance was all but at an end anyway struggled toward her across the surface of the Sauce. Their motions seemed grotesque and ungainly. Their bodies gross and loathsome. Where the rutting continued, near the far edge of the pool, waves of disgust rolled out toward her. Odors she had never noticed before clogged her nose. A thickness, a muddiness to the Sauce made it feel greasy and rancid to her touch.

She had floated to the side of the pool during her darkness, and those who jumped in close to her to comfort her made explosions in the Sauce that splashed her with thick, dull liquid that stuck to her and stuck her to herself. The beads that had delighted her seemed to have reconnected into long, sticky bands that held her fast, made her immobile, caught her up in a web of her own making.

The hands that reached out to soothe her, that meant to caress her into an excitement she could lose herself in, seemed awkward and hostile. Touches she would usually have responded to without reservation made her skin crawl, and probings that were meant to arouse her into a frenzy of forgetful passion seemed brutal and invasive. Faces full of laughter seemed hideously deformed and the teeth which had given her so much, the lips which had coaxed so much from her, the eyes that had met her hungers and responded, seemed sharp and bloody and deadly. She felt as if they were each clutching her to tear off a piece of her flesh, drooling with the desire to rend and devour her.

Her arms and legs felt trapped, held down by sticky ropes of Sauce. She thrashed in their grip, lashed out at them. Their laughter seemed terrifying and their merriment horrible. Their motions were so slow and ugly, and everything seemed fogged and smeared and smudged. The air was so thick and hard to breathe, and her muscles seemed cramped and tightly knotted.

She screamed, and it went out at her friends like sharp teeth, and she could see in the eyes of those she had touched with envy a secret delight in her agony. She screamed again, and there was a general clamor for the Count. Angry and worried cries demanded that he appear; angry denunciations of his absence echoed from everywhere. She felt panic. The Count was not around. Only moments before, the fact was of insignificance. Now it was the most important thing in the world. Horror crawled over her. Time crawled and crawled. Bodies bubbled up out of the pool around her to go and search for him.

The Sauce clung to them and dropped back in globs, splattering her with disgust. Her head lolled, and she could see the strands of her hair matted with it. It webbed between the fingers of the hand she raised partly from her side. When hands reached out to soothe her, it hung from them in long, foul strands and slapped against her. It rubbed between their consoling fingers and her skin like a greasy cream, forming a buffer that insulated her from their concern and consolation. Drops of it splashed against her cheek and stuck there. Little ropes of it clung like vines from the edge of her nose to the corners of her mouth.

When they ran along the pool, she could hear the squish and splat of their footsteps. Everything was so slow, so agonizingly slow and lifeless. Even their voices flattened into a monotone, and she could not distinguish what they were saying. Hands meant to hold up her head, hold up her back, hold up her legs, seemed only to cling to her to drag her under, and now and then what was meant as a playful probe meant to coax her back to herself seemed like a malicious penetration meant to humiliate and hurt her.

But the most awful thing was that it went on and on and on. All the color drained away; the faces that looked helplessly down into hers, that chattered and jabbered to one another were all gray and cold and waxy as death. And when she screamed, the sound went out of her in silent waves of despair, and she could not even hear herself and did not know if any sound was even coming out of her except that it set them all milling around her, wringing their hands and bickering and bumping into one another like grotesque creatures out of stories and legends.

And then she felt numb, and then she felt nothing at all, and then the darkness came up over her again and there was nothing she could do to stop it. She felt it fall across her like the shadow of death. Her eyes rolled up and just before it closed over her, she realized that it was the shadow of the Count.

The great bulk of his white pleasuresuit loomed above her, leaning out over the edge of the pool. When he squatted down, she watched his bearded face loom over her, round and sad eyed. Even upside down it seemed the only thing still right-side up in her world. The dark eyes looked deeply into hers, and the huge round face wagged slowly from side to side. For a moment she was afraid he would turn away, telling her he had warned and warned her, and leave her to her fate, and the awfulness of her condition sharpened and even nothingness seemed a welcome alternative. But then he hunched himself up and took something from the collar of his pleasuresuit and leaned down and pressed his middle finger against her forehead between and above her eyebrows, and she began to relax.

The light did not begin to glimmer again, but the shabbiness of things began to fade, and the color began to come back slowly, if not brightly. The Count's voice stopped sounding like a low rumbling and formed into words. The light came back into things; though it did not have the brightness of the Glow, still it was not worse than the most ordinary of moments.

The Count continued to press his fingertip to her forehead. "It will pass," he said soothingly. There was a comforting solidity to his voice, a reassuring certainty, as if he had performed such miracles before and would again. "There now, feel it going . . . going. Everything is getting lighter . . . lighter . . . lighter, brighter and brighter."

The voice seemed to her a comfort beyond words, resurrecting her from the darkness. The world got lighter and lighter, and although its glisten and shine did not return, still it was not that horrible gray. "That's it . . . that's it." The voice was soothing, encouraging, strong, and confident. It built her strength, and her fear grew smaller and smaller. "Everything's fine. Everything's peaceful. Relax. Relax." The voice soothed her.

Her breathing got stronger and she could feel it. She was rising out of the shadow. His voice dissolved the Sauce all around her back into its smooth, liquid texture. The faces of her friends grew less distorted, their laughter less threatening. Things were going to be all right. The Count's face peered down into hers; his smile comforted her, reassured her. "It's all past now," he said, and she felt that it was past. "Nothing to worry about. Everything's fine." The pressure of the finger lightened.

She felt her head able to rise from the Sauce whose tendrils no longer twisted into those of her hair to hold her fast to the surface like some spider-wrapped fly. The voice soothed her and relaxed her. She could even look back on the horror without falling into it again. But she knew it would never entirely go away. She could look down into it like a long, funneling hole, all the way back to other times when it touched her, other times when in the joyous leap into the Risk she had tumbled into its depths.

Count Aerowaffen lifted his fingertip from her forehead. The white dot of the Tickler still clung to it. "You're all right," he said.

Her voice was shaky; the words came out like a croak. "More," she said.

The Count shook his head. "You know how it works," he said. "Anytime you do it could be one time too many." He'd said it to her before. It had never made a difference. His voice was blunt. "You're going around the corner. The next time it could be permanent. You want to feel like that all the time?"

She thought of the horror, but all she could fix her mind on was the ecstasy that had preceded it. She longed for that bliss; she wanted to wipe the horror out of her mind. Every fiber of her body ached for that ecstasy again. "Another," she said.

The face looked down into hers again and shook ruefully from side to side. His voice was firm and final. "No more."

But she did not see the Count's face. In his dark eyes she saw only Voorpenny's. In his round, bearded face, she saw the long, narrow face that had looked into hers a decade before. All around her the world had its color again, but compared to the shine it had had, it was worth nothing. She wanted only that ecstasy. Her words were still sticky. "Drop a mountain on it!" she said.

The Count stood slowly and left. It didn't matter, she told herself. He wasn't the only one with DeeBee. She knew where she could get more, and she knew exactly what information she would use to buy it.

Chapter Six

UWalk Wenn glanced at Roger Count Aerowaffen across the longseat. They had said little since they left Eleganza's Garden except that the Wheel was weighted and there was nothing to do but wait until the thrashing of the Fool gave it some momentum. What they had waited for so long was in motion, but Aerowaffen seemed vaguely dissatisfied with what had happened, and Wenn did not press him for the source of his silence.

Nor did Aerowaffen offer it. Although the necessity for giving DeeBee to Eleganza was indisputable, he was not happy to do it. Her addiction was neccssary for the Revolution, and there was certainly no reason for him to feel sorry for the Pleasure Crew's determination to destroy themselves with pleasure, but Eleganza's face, when the terrors twisted its beauty, kept coming back to him, and he struggled with the necessity for it.

It had not been a pretty sight, and he had not expected to see it so soon. He had expected perhaps a dozen trips to the gardens before her need would grow sufficiently to make free access to DeeBee something she and the others would even support a Revolution to acquire. He had the Grander certainty that everyone had the right to live their own death, but the feeling of guilt he had for abetting it, even for a good cause, furrowed his forehead. He simply hadn't been prepared for it to happen so suddenly, he told himself, but the feeling still remained.

Wenn asked him nothing. He merely worked the wheel and sang a snatch of rickshaw song. "Everybody dance hee own way downside." He sang it over softly, rocking the wheel rhythmically with each note until Aerowaffen had to move with the rhythm as well. The words were not much comfort. It was true that he was not forcing the addiction on her, although for the good of the Revolution, he would have done so if it was necessary. Eleganza was choosing her addiction herself, but he still felt the pain of helping her do it.

Gradually, the rhythm of the rickshaw softened his mood. It was what Wenn intended. "Body dance hee mind," he would have said if Aerowaffen had mentioned the gradual elevation of his mood. It was a fundamental truth of Wenn's philosophy that the physical motion of the body, the succession of postures, the rhythm of physical change determined attitude, mood, and understanding. Everything he taught about both dancing rickshaw and electric-cane defense was based on it. The ride was long, and on the downhill Aerowaffen closed his eyes and stopped breathing.

Wenn noticed only that the huge weight opposite him no longer anticipated his subtle movements, but sat as impassively as an equal mass of stone. It did not matter much on the smooth, or downhill, side of the mountain. The weight of the huge man added momentum enough without his help in shifting the balance. It was easy for Wenn to nudge him slightly off balance with a sudden side-to-side of the rickshaw and then catch him from falling over with another side-to-side in the other direction. At first all he noticed was that Aerowaffen had closed his eyes, and he thought the man had simply gone to sleep. It was not uncommon for anyone coming back from a trip to Eleganza's Garden to slip into blissful exhaustion, and he had no doubt that

Aerowaffen had done more than a single man's share of the pleasuring.

Wenn let him sleep, his weight was easy to manipulate from the longseat, and there was more than enough energy from his weight alone to make the smooth side of the mountain fly by. There was no longer any hurry. The mission was over for one day. Wenn watched the long, declining straightaway. The momentum would carry them down the side of Iron Mountain with ease. The middle of the Great Wideway was thronged with pedestrians except for a relatively narrow lane left open for rickshaw traffic, but even the chance that some Fool might blunder into it unexpectedly did not bother UWalk Wenn.

When the rickshaw had careened almost to the bottom of the mountain, he began to slow its momentum ever so slightly for the passage through the traffic of the Great Wideway. A series of slight shifts in balance stored momentum in the flywheel for use when they were beyond the most crowded areas.

He did not notice until they were almost to the bottom of the hill that the huge man on the longseat with him was not breathing, and only in retrospect did he realize that Aerowaffen had not breathed the whole way down the smooth side of the mountain. The Count's bulk did not move, except passively as Wenn shook it into one position or another with the sway of the rickshaw. Even when they passed into the boiling congestion of the Great Wideway, the noise of the crowd doing the nighttime business of the Grand Sphere did not make him stir.

The rickshaw whizzed along, indifferent to the crowd. Wenn leaned toward him, shifting his weight gingerly above the rim of the flywheel, and looked more closely. The Count's chest was no longer rising or falling, and when he held the shiny side of his medallion under the man's nose, there was no breath. A flash of concern crossed his mind. Aerowaffen was crucial to the Revolution. His connection to the Pleasure Crew was irreplaceable. Wenn touched the tip of his finger to the inside of Aerowaffen's wrist. There was no pulse. A thin, vague smile seemed to suddenly play about Aerowaffen's lips. But the breathing did not start again, and Wenn was about to pull the rickshaw over when some Fool from Earthside stumbled out of the crowd immediately in front of one of the forks, inches from being impaled.

Wenn threw himself against the back of the rickshaw and the forks shot skyward, just grazing the man. He jerked to the side as well; the whole maneuver lasted no more than a fraction of a second, but the point of the left fork rose abruptly into the air and swung aside, throwing the rickshaw suddenly up on one wheel. The Fool pulled back as the wheel passed over his toes, still raised in the air. Its rim touched down again only a foot or two beyond him, and the rickshaw continued on as if nothing had happened. Only when it was passing smoothly along again did Roger Count Aerowaffen open one eye.

His breathing was still only barely perceptible. He let it build slowly, like a bear coming out of hibernation. They were a good half mile beyond the Fool, who stood still cursing at them and shaking his fist to cover up his stupidity, when Aerowaffen finally spoke. His voice was deep and slow, as if he were only partially out of a state of suspended animation. He raised an eyebrow. "Done the smooth, are we?"

Wenn smiled at the pun. "Did it take your breath away?" he said.

It was Aerowaffen's turn to smile. "You've never been to Catchcage, then?"

Wenn shook his head. He knew the rites of passage every child went through to come of age on Catchcage, but like most people in the League, he had never seen it done, nor had he seen the daily exercises that built up such a capacity almost from infancy. It was the first time he had seen anyone who could do it, and it was astounding in a Grander. It was generally believed that if the practice was not started almost in the womb itself, it could not really be mastered. But Count Aerowaffen was amazingly adept at it. "Let the mind dance the body," the Count said. He seemed to be quoting someone, a master perhaps.

Wenn's disciples said just the opposite, "Let the body dance the mind." It was the premise underlying both rickshaw dancing and electric-cane defense. But Wenn was not adamant about it. That his own philosophy worked for him was enough; he had no desire that everyone should adopt it. "There are many rickshaws," he said. It might have meant there are an infinite number of tricks, or it might have meant he recognized the Catchcage Discipline as simply one more way of becoming whole. But tolerant as he might be of other ways, he was not about to adopt them.

Aerowaffen smiled and looked around at the lights of the Wideway that were beginning to flash by again as the rickshaw picked up speed. He took a deep breath and savored it. A dozen aromas mingled in it, and he seemed to single each one out and appreciate it separately—the musky wisps of Godsbreath that filtered out of pipes in the hands of Fools from Earthside exhilarated as much by doing openly what was forbidden on Earth as by the power of the drug itself, the muskiness of Stand-ups and Layers still pungent from near continual use by the growing crowds that bustled along on either side of them, the twisting blends of sweet perfume and pungent "phero," the sex-attractant perfume of Grander women and men out to lure some Fool into a profitable tryst or to cloud the brain in the midst of some more commercial transaction, the aromas of cooking liquids and open food laid out on trays in the Temporaries along the side of the Way. He seemed delighted at each one. "You have to die to come alive," he said.

It was a Catchcage saying, but Wenn understood it. Aerowaffen's resurrection out of the small death he had put himself into had apparently only whetted his appetite for sensation. It would have been a very profitable technique to teach the Pleasure Crew if any of them had had the patience to learn it. But the Discipline took years, and few who were not raised to it from childhood succeeded at it, even with great effort.

It was what made Aerowaffen the insatiable center of every Pleasure Crew gathering. When there was pleasure to be exchanged, it was what sharpened his appetites and made him able to keep up with the Pleasure Crew without the use of DeeBee himself. It was what gave him the zest for new experience that made him even more indispensable to them, and it was what made him able to understand the insatiable need for sensation that drove them.

Aerowaffen stretched luxuriously. It was a very feline stretch, but it did not make Wenn have to scramble to counterbalance it. Instead, it seemed to draw a smooth acceleration of energy out of the flywheel, and before they were two hundred yards beyond the last fringe of crowd on the Great Wideway, they were rolling along at almost as fast a clip as they had coming down Iron Mountain.

Off the narrow was a short space where the curb had been worn away, and the rickshaw flew up it without diminishing speed. It shot up the ramp beside Wenn's quarters and onto the wide common behind it. There were thirty or more rickshaws lined up along an unmarked boundary of the soft green lawn where almost twice as many people moved to their own rhythms through the motions of electric-cane defense. The novices wore brightly colored insulation suits, while the more experienced wore only insulated pads along their arms, or a thin flexible glove. The adepts wore only the clothes they danced their rickshaws in, a varied collection of shorts and loose shirts and clear, tough slippers that covered only the soles and a little of the sides of their feet. Some did not even wear that much. Only the members of the Fist practicing on the field wore full uniforms.

Where Aerowaffen saw a great kaleidoscope of styles, Wenn saw nuances that identified to him not merely the occupations and types of training of each caner but their individual temperaments as well. But even Aerowaffen could tell the Pleasure Crew from the Fist. Their movements were equally ferocious, but the Police movements were stiffer, less resilient, while the insatiable pursuit of stronger sensation passed through everything the Pleasure

Crew did. Two of them even wore pleasuresuits, as if they intended to record the zapping discharge of the cane to play back later. He wondered if it was simply fanatical love of sensation or the fact that the Pleasure Crew wore their pleasuresuits almost constantly and were likely to be wearing them when they fought for real. Although the suits were hardly restrictive, the instrumentation that recorded and played back the wearer's sensations made them several layers thicker and bulkier than simple formalsuits.

The heavily insulated suits of the Fist were bulkier still, and the necessity of learning electric-cane defense wearing them was obvious. No doubt the Police fought equally stiffly, even out of them. It was only one of their vulnerabilities. Wenn trained only the elite of the Police, mostly those who trained others, and he took only those he approved of, even from that select group, but the followers of UWalk Wenn were more than a match for even the best of them. No member of the Fist studied under UWalk Wenn without developing fatal flaws, flaws any of Wenn's better students could exploit. Their own aggressiveness always undid them when it faced the more passive style of true adherents to electric-cane defense.

Electric cane, as taught by UWalk Wenn, was entirely defensive. Whoever attacked was likely to be defeated. Wenn did not teach attack as part of his training, except to the Fist; it formed the basis of the weaknesses he programmed into their style. Their attacks worked well enough against Obees and Fools Up from Earthside, and even on Granders trained in some equally violent style, but what worked against other aggression was all but useless when it came across the receptive style of UWalk Wenn's pupils. It was easy to tell which they were. They wore no insulation, and their motions had a serene fluidity that seemed a tranquil background music to the motions of the field.

The motions and colors seemed to please Aerowaffen enormously. His little death seemed to have given him a desire for exercise as well, and he jumped easily down from the longseat, snapped off his cape, and tossed it back up beside Wenn. He twirled his cane and started off toward the field. Wenn made no move to stop him. It was a good cover. Many came from other habitats throughout the League to study under Wenn, and pupils of his pupils often stayed for brief or extended study. Many of them lived temporarily in the second tier of modules, whose continuous roof formed the floor of the grassy common on which they trained.

Even the Fist housed a small squad in the rooms Wenn provided. It was a perfect cover for keeping Aerowaffen close for a few days, if the Fist were at all suspicious. He watched Aerowaffen with interest. Certainly he moved well on the rickshaw, and Wenn was intrigued to know if the big man could cane as well as he could sing rickshaw. The Count walked directly toward another member of the Pleasure Crew. Wenn's interest quickened. If anyone other than his best pupils could put Aerowaffen's skill to the test, it was Vor Van Vast.

The man was tall and wiry, but he did not seem half as big as Aerowaffen. In electric cane as in rickshaw dancing, it should have been an advantage. He wore a black pleasuresuit that accentuated the stiff white crown of hair that bristled from his head. Wenn had accepted him for training at the request of a former pupil, but the man was a surprisingly apt student for a member of the Pleasure Crew. Unlike most of the others, he had a remarkable amount of discipline, but there was a sinister motivation behind it, a kind of malevolence Wenn did not trust. Van Vast had no desire to understand the defensive maneuvers of Wenn's style and said so from the first. He wanted, he declared arrogantly, only to sharpen his own style against the best of Wenn's "passives." Despite his arrogance, Wenn agreed to teach him as part of the Police contingent.

It was a symbiotic relationship. Wenn's style of electric-cane defense required an attacker. His pupils were allowed only to defend. Without men like Van Vast, his students would have to spend some part of their practice time developing the flaws that came with attacking. Generally, he welcomed men like Van Vast. Like the Fist and even the

Obees, with their own relentless aggressiveness, he provided an excellent contrast for Wenn's pupils to work against.

The field was generally filled with the best caners in the Sphere. Theoretically, the common belonged to the modules above it, whose glass fronts opened on to it like a front lawn, and Wenn had no legal right to bar anyone from practicing there. Nevertheless, those who became obnoxious could usually be discouraged by a few bouts with the master. Those who came only to bully usually left after a few humiliations or a particularly painful stinging, but Van Vast always seemed to restrain himself sufficiently to keep from provoking Wenn to combat, and he was always contemptuously courteous to his victims.

He had a natural aptitude for aggression, and its strengths filled his style with weaknesses. Like the Fist, he was interested only in the attack. Even overmatched against the best of Wenn's pupils, he attacked relentlessly, and no amount of stings could teach him otherwise. He worked out continually against Wenn's pupils or whoever else came to the common. Mostly, he fought with other Granders and the Fist, who liked his ferocious style. He always insisted on fighting with canes turned to the higher levels, and the Fist admired that kind of bravado. Although they managed to sting him occasionally, they respected his attacks and not a few of them had lain quivering from the sting of his cane. What troubled Wenn most about him was that he seemed to enjoy the pain of his adversaries more than any other part of caning.

He was sparring with a Police Blue when Aerowaffen approached him. It was a quick bout in the rough-and-tumble style of the Fist, full of lunges and kicks and blows with the empty hand. The Blue got close enough to him to catch him with the butt of his cane once and raised a small welt along Van Vast's cheek, but Van Vast beat him back with an overwhelming flurry of strikes and lunges and ended the attack by hitting him with an upsweeping palm to the chin that snapped his head back, and jabbing the prongs of his cane into the center of the Blue's throat just above the protective collar. The Blue went down like the dead and lay twitching on the grass.

Two Police Reds laughed heartily and shook their heads. A Bronze finally came over and helped the young rookie to his feet. He glared at Van Vast but said nothing. Van Vast smiled at him smugly and cocked his head as if waiting for a challenge from the officer, but the Bronze had fought him before and was not about to try to chastise him and risk the same humiliation as the recruit. Van Vast touched the tip of his cane to his forehead in mock salute as the Blue was helped away. He gave a snort of disdain and turned away, looking for another victim. Aerowaffen was there waiting for him.

Wenn jumped down from the longseat and moved quickly toward them. Even at a distance he could see that they obviously knew and disliked each other. Aerowaffen's greeting was civil enough. He gave a nod of his head. "Vor," he said.

Van Vast's smile was more of a sneer. "The Panda." His voice was rich with disdain. "Come looking for something to amuse the Crew?" He did not wait for Aerowaffen to answer. "Save yourself. None of them have the appetite for it."

"They had appetite enough when I left them," he said.

Vor did not smile. "They always have an appetite for play." He snorted as if their pleasures were beneath his contempt.

"You were missed," Aerowaffen said. He did not say who had missed him, but it was clear Aerowaffen had not. Vor scowled as if there was no one worth being missed by. Aerowaffen persisted. "Eleganza missed you."

Van Vast's cold, dark eyes flashed. "Did you come to cane or babble?"

Aerowaffen smiled. "I came for the pleasure," he said. It was a common greeting among members of the Pleasure Crew, and it had a half dozen meanings, most of which were enough to infuriate Van Vast.

Vor looked at him with contempt. "You *do* cane?" Almost

everyone in the Sphere carried a cane, but not a tenth could really use one.

"With pleasure," Aerowaffen said. He cupped the intensity collar. "Six?" he said. The setting was enough to cause the spasm the Blue had just hobbled away with. A higher setting could cause several hours' worth of pain, but Vor fought always on the higher levels, exhilarated by the risk.

Vor twisted the collar of his cane sharply. "Nine," he said. The setting could mean hours of crippling pain and a burn that would last a week if both prongs touched the skin. It suited Aerowaffen perfectly.

It was Vor's Playday, and Eleganza wanted a Chase. Aerowaffen arranged it as he did everything. He had done it before. There was nothing to worry about, and yet he was uneasy. Had it been anyone other than Vor, he would not have given it a second thought. Certainly there was no real danger. The Chaseling he had selected was an elegant Riskchild, more than a match for the Pleasurers, even if they were able to run without stumbling. She sat idly by the pool, waiting for the fun to begin.

He suspected she was about ten, but it was difficult to tell; even adult Riskers were so delicate that they looked childlike even in old age, and it was almost impossible to tell the age of the young ones. They all had a kind of unblemished innocence that made them look like children when they were well above the age where it mattered. This one had long white hair and blue-white eyes. She looked a little bored, but she watched with rapt attention as the Pleasure Crew drew for goblets.

Eleganza held the tray and turned it so that the goblet matching the color each had drawn was close enough to reach. No one knew what was in them. It might be anything, which of course was part of the game. Some of the drinks felt like nothing at all until the running began, and then they might make everything seem upside down, or turn the runner's legs to rubber, or switch the gravity every other step from zero to Earthside Max. There wasn't much chance any of them would catch the Riskchild in any case.

There were three terraces of shrubbery and hedge, pools and fountains and trees to hide in, and Riskers had that extra sense that kept them always running down the right turn of the maze where nobody could follow. The Riskchild caught his eye and cocked her head as if asking him when it would begin. He only smiled. There were a half dozen still to draw and drink. She looked up at the Ring that hung in the half-light like a giant halo. The habitat's mirrors still had a good fifteen degrees to rotate yet, and it was only beginning to shade from dusk into the dimness that passed for night in the Grand Sphere, but the Ring still blazed against the twilight.

The Riskchild stared up at it as if every time she saw it, it was for the first time. Aerowaffen wondered what it must be like to feel that same awe every time. It contrasted sharply with the decadence all around her. Her contentment seemed almost an accusation of the Pleasure Crew's frenzied search for something out of the ordinary, something new in sensation.

The Riskchild could sit there looking up for hours, blissfully unaware of everything around her. The Pleasure Crew could not do it for ten minutes without an agonizing restlessness pulling them away. It was not something even Aerowaffen could successfully explain to them. Peace was something none of them had ever known; all they knew of serenity was the nameless longing made by its absence.

When he looked back at them, everyone had a goblet, and they all raised them, laughing, and drank. On some the effects were immediate. One or two suddenly sat down where they were, giggling and looking around with the amazed and bewildered expression of those who know where they ought to be but can't for the life of them recognize where they are. Next to the tranquility of the Riskchild, they looked ridiculous. Others who were still waiting for the effects of their goblets laughed and pointed. Those who could still stand shook their heads. Aerowaffen stifled a chuckle. They were all children after all, even Eleganza; spoiled perhaps, but not malicious.

The Riskchild looked suddenly down from the Ring and stood up. She did not need Aerowaffen's nod to tell her to be off. A great shout pursued her along the side of the pool and past the turn of the first hedge. It was followed by a ritual chant that undoubtedly had some ancestor in children's games on Earth but whose meaning had been long forgotten. A few of those standing ready to begin pursuit chanted a syllable or two behind the others without seeming to realize it, and from time to time a general laughter would spread through the group, making them lose their place and begin again. About halfway through it again, they gave up and poured past him along the poolside, laughing and shouting.

Aerowaffen waited patiently to fish the stragglers out of the Sauce before they drowned themselves. By the time he had retrieved the two who had been knocked in by the press of the crowd and the other three who had wandered into it on their hands and knees trying to find out why the ground was so different there, the cry of the pack had thinned out and dispersed. From different directions, startled laughter and cries of jovial despair floated back as the effects of the goblets began in earnest. Aerowaffen listened for voices with the sharp edge of panic in them, ones that needed to be retrieved and brought back to the twisted familiarity of the fountain and the pool. A few of those he would calm and reprogram and perhaps send out again into the twilight.

There were none for a while, and he listened lazily to the cries of pursuit or discovery. Every once in a while, an excited cry would come floating back from the lowest terrace as if one of the Crew had spotted the Chaseling, but Aerowaffen knew sight was all they were likely to catch of her. With all of their wits about them, she would have led the best of them a merry chase; as it was, she was a phantom to them, a shadow of light passing like a comet just along the periphery of their vision. From the terrace below, he could hear someone trying to thrash their way *out of the hedges and failing miserably, and he listened for the telltale groans of frustration that would tell him if they needed to be retrieved. But the thrashing stopped, and he knew that either they had freed themselves or had settled into the bush to enjoy their dilemma.*

He walked to the edge of the hedge and looked down on to the terraces that could be seen from the upper pool. Dark shapes staggered or careened through the semidarkness, laughing and stumbling. Some were in pairs and in threes; few were alone except those whose disability had left them immobile somewhere, trying to find out which way the Sphere was rotating or why gravity seemed to keep reversing itself every few minutes. Somewhere out of sight around the curve of the second terrace, a voice kept starting and restarting the Starting Chant, trying to get it right. The voice seemed perfectly delighted with its failure, but it tried over and over again nevertheless. Aerowaffen shook his head. They were so easily amused. None of them seemed to need retrieving, but it was early yet, and the game had minutes, perhaps hours, to run.

Even if someone, through sheer dumb luck, stumbled on to the Chaseling and managed to hold her and return with her to the fountain, the game would not be over until all of the Pleasure Crew had found their way back without help or had been retrieved. It might take Aerowaffen half an hour to round up the strays, usually longer, if one of them had crawled under something or wedged themselves so far into the hedging they could not be seen in passing. The Overgobbed, those who were too confused to find their way back without help, were as likely as not to start exploring each other. It was like most Pleasure Crew games; even when someone won, nobody really lost.

Even the Chaseling, if caught, came out of it all with a pile of presents and gifts from the Chasers, and if she eluded them all for the duration, she might have anything she wanted as well from the mound of gifts Eleganza had left near the gameclock before the Chase began. Every once in a while he could hear the Riskchild's laughter echoing back and up from some indeterminate location, followed from time to time by a shout of enthusiastic good humor. It sounded like the ringing of chimes or small silver bells jangled at random.

Once a shriek of delight told him someone was at least close enough to touch the Chaseling, but the disappointed groans told him of her immediate escape. For a long while there were only intermittent cries and shouts, like people trying to locate each other in the dark. He watched two Overgobbed Pleasurers on opposite sides of a hedge on the first terrace shouting back and forth for five minutes before giving up trying to locate each other. The Count enjoyed watching them enjoy themselves. He found them a source of constant amusement, and like any Grander, it delighted him equally that they provided him as much amusement as he provided them, except that they had to pay him, in one way or another, while they provided him entertainment for free. He liked the irony of that the most.

From down on the next level, he heard the complaining of someone who had been left alone and couldn't begin to find the way back. Aerowaffen shook his head and started around the hedge to look. Before he turned the corner, he gave one look back to see if the ones he had rescued earlier were still content to lie where they were and had not gone staggering toward the pool. In all likelihood, they would right themselves before they drowned anyway, but he did not want them falling in and panicking while he was gone. One bad experience was likely to cast a pall over the whole crowd, and he had seen panic spread among them until it took him a full night's work just to distract them enough to calm them down.

But the Overgobbed seemed perfectly content to lie side by side trying to figure out where they were and why. Only as he started to turn the corner of the hedge did he see Vor. He did not like what he saw, the dark malevolent eyes, the look of disdain that passed over the face when he looked at the Overgobbed, the cruel curl of the lip. Vor stood leaning against the gameclock, resting his elbow on it. His hands were cupped around the goblet. When he was sure Aerowaffen was looking directly at him, he raised the cup in salute and poured it out on the ground. His smile was arrogant and malicious. He was gone beyond the far end of the hedge before Aerowaffen could react. No laughter echoed back up to mark where he had gone.

Aerowaffen frowned. Certainly the odds were still in the Riskchild's favor, but it made him uneasy. If it had been anyone else but Vor hunting her without a handicap, he would not have thought twice about it, but he did not like Vor, not because he held the others in contempt, not even because he held Aerowaffen in contempt, but because there was a hint of cruelty to everything he did, and he did not want to see it leave its mark on the Riskchild he had brought. It was true, less than savory things were sometimes done to children around other pools and fountains where the Pleasure Crews gathered, but none of that was Aerowaffen's doing, and even Eleganza's Crew as a whole deplored it. Certainly none of them would knowingly harm a child, but there was no telling what twisted, impulsive action Vor was capable of.

He turned the corner of the hedge and hurried down the path. His own chances of finding the Riskchild were not much greater than Vor's. In the closing twilight she had all the advantages. There were more places for a person of her size to hide than there was time to search, and she had the Risker sensitivity to what people were going to do next. He had no doubt that, about to be cornered, she would simply look up at the Ring and then dart in the one direction where escape was certain. Still, he felt uneasy as he went down the slope to the next terrace. He met the Riskchild coming up. She stopped as soon as she saw him, poised to flee, but she seemed to know who he was before she could see him clearly, and she continued up the slope.

"Having a laugh?" he said.

She smiled and looked back down toward the shadows chasing each other and figments of their brains across the terraces below. "Like Fools on the Wideway," she laughed.

Aerowaffen smiled at its meaning. There was no greater sport for a Grander than a shipload of Fools Up from Earth turned loose for their first time on the Wideway.

Below them, a group of dim shadows chased illusions in the half-light. "Watch the white-haired man," he warned.

"The young Spencer," she said. It was a perfect description. To a Grander, anyone with steely white hair was a Spencer, after the white-haired monarch of Corporation, Spencer LeGrange. It fit Vor more than perfectly. He had not only the hair but the malevolence, the ruthlessness, and the cruelty. For all anyone knew, it was more than that. Vor was Eleganza's partbrother, a relationship that existed only among the Pleasure Crew, where paternity was often ambiguous. All it meant was that there was some possibility that they shared a biological parent along the way. Not that it mattered, except as a point of conversation. The Pleasure Crew was already too inbred to worry much about the genetic relationship of pleasure mates. Still, the Riskchild could not have known that the common partparent they were rumored to share was Spencer LeGrange. She seemed to know it anyway. Riskers always did. "He hasn't a smile," she said.

"But he does have teeth." The Riskchild nodded agreement as if Aerowaffen was only confirming something she had suspected from the first, that Vor hadn't drunk his goblet. She smiled and unjoined the ends of the thin, transparent tube she wore around her waist like a belt.

She winked. "He can't bite what he can't see," she said. Aerowaffen had only an inkling of what she meant, but he felt more at ease about her safety. She was gone up the slope and around the hedge before he could say anything else.

On the third terrace he could see a flash of Vor's white hair moving relentlessly along. Indignant cries for assistance turned him away from it and down the path. When he got back to poolside with another of the Overgobbed, the Riskchild was nowhere around. He looked at the dial of the gameclock and watched the green unwind into white. He

*had to go back down all the way to the third terrace to
retrieve another one before the time ran out and the sound
of a gong rang out over the gardens. There were two or
three more that had to be helped back, but by the time he
got the last of them poolside, they were all there, including
Eleganza. She looked radiant, and her laughter was as
high and melodious as a Riskchild's. He felt a bit of relief
that the Chase was over.*

*Even Vor was back, and Eleganza hung on him, teasing
him with long strokes of her hand. Vor looked both pleased
and embarrassed. She enjoyed teasing him, making him
angry and then mollifying him. It was a game between
them, but Vor did not seem to find it as amusing as she did
at the moment. He glared at Aerowaffen. The Count stood
by the side of the pool. The surface of the Sauce was
rippling color where the fountain splashed out strings of it,
and even along the side it flashed a rainbow in the bright
light of poolside. The thin, clear tube was almost invisible
along the side wall of the pool. The Riskchild at the other
end was completely invisible below the surface. Aerowaffen
smiled to himself.*

*Eleganza turned and smiled at him. "A wonderful
Chase," she said to him, as if he had choreographed everyone's movements himself for their maximal pleasure.*

*Vor only scowled. "Call her out," he said. His tone was
imperious, as if Aerowaffen had no choice but to obey
instantly. Aerowaffen turned away from the pool toward
the hedge; the Pleasure Crew flocked toward it to look over
and see where she came from and how close they had been
to her without knowing it. It was one of their favorite parts
of the game. They strained to see over the hedge and down
into the lower terraces, each one offering a guess about
where she would suddenly appear from.*

*There was a short peal of tinkling laughter from behind
them, but it was cut off too abruptly for anyone but Aerowaffen to notice. He turned abruptly. Vor knelt by the side
of the pool, facing away from them. One hand reached
down into the Sauce, holding the Riskchild's head down,*

while the other pinched the top of the tube. Aerowaffen pushed through the crowd and ran toward poolside. The crowd ran with him, and he let them push him forward so that he plowed into Vor, knocking him face forward into the Sauce.

The Riskchild came up sputtering at the edge of the pool as soon as Vor's hand slipped off her head. She coughed out Sauce in gobs, and Aerowaffen had no doubt Vor would have held her under long enough to drown. It made him wish he had hit Vor harder. The Riskchild was not crying, but she was close to tears, and each gagging cough seemed to bring her closer. She looked up to the Ring for solace.

Aerowaffen reached down and lifted her easily to the side of the pool. Vor had righted himself and swam a few short strokes toward the laughing crowd. His eyes blazed, and he pulled himself up out of the pool and took a menacing step toward Aerowaffen. The Count seemed not to notice him and patted the Riskchild on the back, trying to help her clear her throat. But inside him a rage boiled toward the surface. It was all he could do not to turn and knock Vor back into the pool and rip off his arm as he went sailing in. But too much depended on his entrée with the Pleasure Crew, and he knew that even if the Child had drowned, he would not have killed Vor, no matter how much he might have wanted to. There was too much at stake.

Vor took a second step toward Aerowaffen before Eleganza flung herself onto him and announced to the crowd that she had a very special present for him in honor of his Playday. Vor glared at Aerowaffen, but Eleganza coaxed his face away with a pout and a promise. She ran to the side of the gameclock and brought back a bubble and handed it to Vor.

At first it looked like she was handing him a ball for some other sort of game, but when he held it, she pricked it and it dissolved to reveal a long platinum cane. Its entire shaft was covered with a sharply detailed etching of everyone in their set of the Pleasure Crew, all gathered around the pool, laughing and enjoying themselves. Even Aerowaf-

fen was on it, rising from the Sauce like some creature out of Earthside legend.

Vor saw only the duplication of Eleganza, her taut body hanging lovingly on the arm of an exact duplicate of himself. It was exquisitely etched, easily the most beautiful electric cane any of them had ever seen. Vor smiled his appreciation. Aerowaffen helped the Riskchild to sit down; she turned and hung her head over the pool.

Vor hefted the cane in his hand and turned the power collar to maximum. He looked at Aerowaffen and turned it back as far as burn. Aerowaffen took a half step back from the Riskchild and waited for the lunge. But it did not come.

Instead, Vor snapped his arm to the side and the points came into contact with the smooth white flesh of the Riskchild's thigh. She shrieked and jerked away. There were two little black burn points on her thigh that would never come out. On anyone else they would have been no more than a blemish, but on the flawless skin of the Riskchild, they were a permanently disfiguring blotch.

Aerowaffen's hand clamped on Vor's wrist before he could draw back the cane or move it to touch again. He squeezed until Vor's hand opened and dropped the cane to the ground. Even then he did not let go. Eleganza commanded him to stop. His mission hung in the balance. He weighed what a quick upward jerk of his hand would do to the structure of the bones in Vor's arm. He consoled himself with what he might do, what he would do, someday, when the Rickshaw of the Revolution was at full speed. It was enough to let him release Vor's wrist. Eleganza glared at Vor and moved to comfort the Riskchild. Vor glowered at Aerowaffen. "Pick it up," he said, jerking his chin toward the cane.

Aerowaffen glanced down at it. "Is it mine, then?" he said.

Vor looked as if only Eleganza kept him from picking it up himself and burning Aerowaffen in a way he would never forget. "One end of it is," he said. He looked at the points, but there was no need to underline his threat.

Aerowaffen smiled. "Give it to me when you can, then,"
he said.

Aerowaffen looked up at the Ring. It blazed fiercely.
"Cane for cane?" he said. Wenn frowned at the wager. His
own pupils were forbidden to wager on the outcome of
electric-cane defense, and it disappointed him that Aerowaffen would do so. Still, it was a Fool's bet. Van Vast's
cane was a finer instrument, much more expensive, its long
platinum handle covered with an elaborately etched picture.
Aerowaffen's cane was thinner than most, almost a magi-
cian's wand, long and black and tapering. It was well
crafted and balanced, but clearly less expensive than Vor's.

Wenn smiled to himself at the subtlety of Aerowaffen's
approach. Wenn did not approve of the bet, but he admired
the way Aerowaffen had increased the pressure on Van Vast.
It was a double advantage; it would make him even more
aggressive and intensify the flaws in his style, and it would
make him sweat. The more sweat, the more conductivity to
the skin and the greater the shock.

It was one of the disadvantages to Aerowaffen's size that
a bigger man tended to sweat more, and the sweating made
him more vulnerable. Wenn smiled with a Grander's appreciation of the way Aerowaffen had evened up the odds. Most
of the combatants on the field had fought and lost to Van
Vast at one time or another, and they stopped their practice
to watch. Aerowaffen did not give Vor time to answer. He
raised a palm as if Van Vast had already declined. "No, no,
you're right. It's a gift. It wouldn't be right." His tone was
mocking.

Vor seemed about to strike for a second. "Drop a mountain on it," he said. He didn't need the gesture to make it
obscene.

Aerowaffen shrugged as if he had only been being polite.
He stepped back and spread his hands. "Whenever you're
ready, Voracious." The nickname was one only Eleganza
called him, and the Count knew it would infuriate him
enough to attack. The words were followed immediately by

a vicious lunge. It was exactly what Aerowaffen had anticipated. He whacked the cane aside and spun away from it,
turning his back toward it as it passed. The lunge carried
Vor past him as well and as he went, Aerowaffen helped him
along with an elbow to the back of his head. It knocked Van
Vast facedown in the grass, exposing him to an easy touch.

The tips of Aerowaffen's cane poised an inch or so above
the exposed Achilles tendon of Vor's leg, and then lifted
away without the sting that would have knotted Vor's calf
for days. Wenn approved of the way Aerowaffen had parried
the strike and spun out of its way, but he disliked the rest of
it. The elbow had been something Aerowaffen could only
have picked up in Hardcore. The Fist smiled appreciatively
at it. Only the Bronze scowled. It didn't look good for
anyone who had dispatched one of his men to go down that
easily. He had felt Van Vast's sting more than once himself,
and the times he had managed to return the tingle had been
hard fought and difficult. It was a personal embarrassment
to see someone who had bested him more than once handled
so roughly.

Vor rolled over quickly, with the prongs of his cane
pointing up to catch Aerowaffen coming in, but the big man
stood well back out of reach, waiting patiently for his
adversary to get up. Van Vast rolled over backward and
came up facing the Count. There was a little trickle of blood
from the corner of his nose where he had hit his face on the
grass. Aerowaffen looked at him apologetically, as if he had
committed a foul, although there were no rules to electric-
cane defense. Even for sport, the cane was used just as it was
in a fight, with any other method of self-defense that came
to hand.

Van Vast's second lunge was parried even more easily. It
went directly for the heart sensor of Aerowaffen's
pleasuresuit. At the minimum a touch would have meant a
complete rewiring of the suit's sensors. But Aerowaffen
jammed his cane straight down, and the tip of it wedged
between the prongs of Van Vast's. The stiffness of his arm
allowed him to slide himself backward without seeming to

move his feet, with the result that the cane at full extension was more than an arm's length from touching any part of him. "Too short," he said. It was another Grander pun, a shortened form of the Grander idiom for impotence of any kind, "A man too short for his pleasure." It implied both his impotence in the fight and at the fountainside. It was a perfect response to increase Vor's rage, and put him further out of control.

Aerowaffen made a sudden sharp circle with his cane, and Van Vast's weapon shot out to the side. It made Vor stumble, giving Aerowaffen another perfect opening, but again Aerowaffen let a chance for an easy touch go by. The Fist raised their eyebrows in surprise. Obviously, Aerowaffen did not merely want to beat Vor, he wanted to humiliate him. Wenn scowled. It was a double mistake. It was a mistake for Aerowaffen to call attention to himself like that. His face would not escape remark by the Fist wherever he went, and their business was too important to jeopardize it that way, no matter what personal animosity there was between them.

It was a mistake as well to give Vor too many chances. Instead of lunging, Vor walked closer until they were only a half a lunge apart. His next attack was a series of unrelenting slashes meant to beat the larger man backward. Aerowaffen parried them all, but their sheer ferocity took his momentum away, and the last one cut downward toward Aerowaffen's face with such force that he had to hold the cane with two hands to stop it and throw it back.

Van Vast rebounded instantly and caught him with a stiff kick to the stomach that knocked him stumbling backward. He followed it with a lunge that Aerowaffen barely managed to roll aside from. He moved with great agility for his size, but Van Vast's quickness and will were formidable weapons, and Aerowaffen did not come back to his feet as easily as Vor had. Van Vast lunged again just as he stood. Aerowaffen's cane circled inside and swept the strike outward past his left arm. As he blocked, he stepped in toward Vor and struck him with the heel of his hand in the forehead.

It was a Police maneuver, and Wenn's frown deepened at the murmurs of appreciation from the Fist. Vor staggered backward, and Aerowaffen went on the offensive. He drove Van Vast back with a series of crossing strikes that Vor barely managed to deflect. Aerowaffen circled to his right to avoid a counterthrust, and the men stood facing each other for a moment. Van Vast was sweating heavily, but Aerowaffen had only a light film across his forehead.

They stood facing each other for a long moment before Van Vast made his final lunge. Van Vast struck Aerowaffen's unprotected wrist, and the Count landed an overhand right. The canes touched their targets simultaneously. At that charge level, the location of the strike should not have mattered. The Count caught Vor with both prongs under the ear. There was a sharp crackle and Van Vast seemed to fly to the side.

There was a simultaneous flash as his cane touched Aerowaffen's wrist, but the Count only rocked back a bit. He seemed a little blank for a moment, then he steadied himself and bent down to pick up the cane that had fallen from Van Vast's hand. Wenn moved to help Van Vast to his feet, but it was several minutes before he regained consciousness, and when he did his face was rigid with pain. A man in a red pleasuresuit came forward and half carried him to a rickshaw. Wenn turned and scowled at Aerowaffen. There was a nasty burn under Vor's right ear that would not fade from his skin for months, and not for years from his memory.

Wenn turned and lifted Aerowaffen's hand to examine the sting. There was an equally ugly burn on the inside of his wrist, but the skin was surprisingly dry. It was probably what had reduced the discharge and kept Aerowaffen from being knocked out along with Vor. He frowned. It was one more remarkable thing that would stick in the mind of the Fist. The habitat's mirrors were turning away for the windows, and dusk was beginning to fall. Wenn nodded and Aerowaffen followed him toward his quarters. The entire Fist watched them go.

Chapter Seven

Wenn led the Count to the lightshaft in the middle of his quarters and nodded him down the steep, winding staircase. He was about to follow him down when he saw a new rickshaw roll up onto the apron at the far end of the common. He motioned Aerowaffen out of sight and turned back to the field. The man in the rickshaw waited for his approach. Wenn walked the length of the field slowly; the Fist had noticed the arrival, and their fighting had quickened and become more fierce. It was not often that their commander made an appearance to watch them train. Wenn knew the visit was not to watch the caning.

He nodded to Pock and stepped closer to the rickshaw, but he did not climb up into the longseat as Pock gestured he should, and Pock did not come down. The conversation was not loud, and it was brief. "Roger Count Aerowaffen," Pock said.

Wenn nodded. "He rides in my rickshaw." Pock had no idea that Wenn meant the Great Rickshaw of the Revolution. He took it to mean only that Aerowaffen rode literally in Wenn's rickshaw and that he was caught in the coils of one of Wenn's many intrigues as well.

"Then so must we," Pock said. He knew Wenn would understand that he wanted reports of Aerowaffen's whereabouts.

Wenn smiled. "Corporation always rides in the rickshaw of UWalk Wenn." Pock considered only the literal truth of it; what plots the rickshaw man might have in motion did not bear thinking about.

"We have a mountain for you," Pock said. It meant both a problem and a mountainous reward. Wenn said nothing and Pock went on. "Find the Universal Tickler." Wenn laughed. It was either a joke or an insult; only Fools Up from Earthside went looking for the mythical Universal Tickler.

He treated it as a joke. "Tell me what it looks like."

Pock's face was perfectly serious, but he did not look as if he really believed it existed. "A white dot."

Wenn still smiled as if it were a joke. "Where should I look?"

Pock scowled. "Try your rickshaw." There was no need to mention the need for secrecy.

Wenn's face remained impassive, but a smile of understanding flashed across his mind. If Pock was seriously looking for it, someone of importance must believe it existed. He wondered if more than he knew had been taken from Stefan Standard at Eleganza's. If the Universal Tickler had been perfected and Aerowaffen had it, the possibilities for the Revolution were endless, and a lot of things suddenly made sense. Aerowaffen had said he would weight the Wheel of the Revolution with pleasure.

But an even greater number of things didn't make sense. If they believed Aerowaffen actually *had* anything as dangerous as the Universal Tickler, they could have picked him up easily. Why did they simply want him watched? It might have been that they only knew Aerowaffen and the Tickler were connected, not that he actually had it. But there was a more sinister answer, and Wenn did not like it. If Aerowaffen was working for Corporation, Wenn must be intended only to keep an eye on him to make sure he wasn't working some rickshaw of his own.

When he returned to the lightshaft, he found Aerowaffen waiting patiently for him. He shook his head when Aerowaffen began to talk and pressed his palm against the entry plate. When the glass panel slid aside, Aerowaffen followed him silently down a long, narrow corridor to the first room of the module. Its glass wall gave a view of the terrace formed by the roofs of the bottom layer of the hill and the roadway winding out of the narrow toward the Great Wideway. Wenn waved a hand across it and the view disappeared in a swirl of colored fog. He turned and led Aerowaffen into the interior room.

His quarters were made up of seven modules, the forward one and an oblong block behind it two rooms deep and three across. The small hill, of which the rooms made up roughly two percent, was five layers high and ten modules deep in the bottom layer. The two modules behind Wenn's quarters formed storage space for the whole complex and part of the central network of passageways that honeycombed the hill for quick travel. It was a useful arrangement, one that allowed the population of the Grand Sphere to be much larger than it would otherwise have been without crowding, and similar hills covered most of the two quadrants of Downside that CORPQ and the agricultural fields did not.

On either side Wenn owned at least half a tier straight through, and if the modules of his followers were included, almost the entire hill offered sanctuary or escape. Three of the single-room units in the front row were being rented from Wenn by a contingent of the Fist, there for extended training and electronic surveillance. It did not matter to Wenn; most who could sing rickshaw could talk openly in front of the Fist without fear of being entirely understood. So much of rickshaw song was taken for granted, so much depended on context and on things not mentioned or never mentioned that it was all but impossible to follow, and a look or a gesture could negate everything that was being said. The surveillance was almost a formality anyway. The Fist seldom got anything of value out of it. It was one of the reasons Wenn had no fear of letting the Fist contingent within the complex. He took a Grander's delight in charging them for the futile opportunity.

Infiltration would have been far more effective, but those who were properly trained were too rigid for undercover work, and those who were flexible enough to do it were never fully trusted by the rest and were treated as outcasts. Few within the ranks wanted to volunteer for it, and for most of the Fist it was the equivalent of a death sentence or banishment. In any case, all kinds of information was available from the Granders themselves, for a price, and people who supplied it were left relatively free of interference. An agent was necessary only for the most dangerous and secret assignments. Certainly Aerowaffen's position would qualify, and there were those small flashes of LeGrange brutality to his cane work that Wenn found disturbing.

Still, he motioned Aerowaffen to follow him into the center room. If Aerowaffen really was an agent, he was already in on far greater secrets than could be found there. The room seemed empty, but there were marks of a half dozen Aireclines on the rugging, and it was clear the room could become a dormitory if necessary. Wenn cleared one of the inner walls and exposed a bank of screens. Most showed empty rooms, or the flurry of activity on the caning field, but two had people in them Aerowaffen could recognize as Wenn's students, and several showed the rooms of the Fist's contingent.

In one of them, a small group of Bronze and Reds were shaking their heads and talking. In another a Blue was monitoring what was going on in Wenn's quarters. His words came up along the bottom of the screen in a line of white print. Aerowaffen smiled. The Blue was reporting that Wenn and a larger man were in the middle of Wenn's quarters. Wenn pressed a handpanel and the room filled with the sound of surf. He had never been Earthside, but like many Granders, he shared a human longing for a sea he had never seen. Like almost everything else Granders did, it had another purpose: to obscure the sound in the room. There was an announcement on the screen to the effect that

Wenn had turned on his sea sounds again, and the Blue gave a shrug and slumped back on his Airecline.

Wenn nodded Aerowaffen to one of the Aireclines, and the Count waved his hand above the floor to make sure it was active. The movement made him clench his fist and frown with pain. Wenn looked at the black burn and shook his head.

"You're in Pock's ear," he said.

Aerowaffen smiled ruefully. "Better than his hand." It could have meant that it was better to be under Pock's observation than in his custody, but Wenn could not ignore the accusation that might underlie it. Either of them might be working for Pock. It was a dangerous thing to trust a Grander. Still, it would not be the first time the Rickshaw of the Revolution had broken a wheel on someone's greed and perfidy.

But it had crashed more often on mutual suspicion, and Wenn confronted it head-on. "Are we in Pock's hand, then?"

Aerowaffen shrugged. "What did he want?"

Wenn looked him directly in the eye. "You."

Aerowaffen nodded. The eyes did not evade his. "Why?"

"For pleasure."

Aerowaffen did not blink. "His or mine?" he joked.

"Everybody's." Wenn took the risk. "He wanted the Universal Tickler."

Aerowaffen's face dropped. "He asked for it?"

Wenn nodded. "He wants it found. He wants you watched."

There was a great deal of satisfaction in Aerowaffen's smile. Too much to suit Wenn. "Then he doesn't want you to kill me."

Wenn waited for an explanation. When it didn't come, he said, "Maybe others should."

Aerowaffen's laugh shook the room. "Indeed, they should, Master Wenn. And they will."

Wenn frowned, unsure whether Aerowaffen had understood him. "Others close at hand," he said.

The thought seemed to fill Aerowaffen with a secret mirth. "The Great Rickshaw cannot roll without my death," he laughed. He seemed to find it enormously funny. When he finally stopped laughing, he looked solemnly at Wenn. "And yours, my friend, and yours." The thought made him start laughing all over again. Wenn was not sure he understood, but he was sure Aerowaffen was telling him the truth.

Chapter Eight

The wait was shorter, but Pock was no less angry. Earthside gravity was an annoyance at any time, but twice in as many days, it was an ordeal. He was sure Standard had called him back just to aggravate him. It was the kind of erratic behavior he would expect from a DeeBee. What he saw when he entered Standard's office only confirmed his suspicions.

Standard lay stretched out on the Airecline with the same glazed look on his face he had had when Pock had seen him last. If it were not for the fact that Standard was wearing a pleasuresuit instead of the green formalsuit he had had on two days before, Pock would have wondered if he had even moved. The same skinner was even playing on its thighscreens, except that the sensations were more than visually real to Standard this time. The suit was stimulating all of the nerves the original experience had stimulated, and Standard rocked slightly in the throes of a previous delight. Pock only glanced at the picture of Eleganza on the thighscreens. Her head twisted and shook, and her hair flew back and forth across her face until it seemed about to wipe the white dot from her forehead. The image faded and another started to take its place when Standard reluctantly put it on hold.

Pock frowned. The thought of Standard carrying on a private debauch in his office day after day just didn't seem to make sense, not with Old Spence's eyes poised to open on him at any time, and yet Standard kept sliding off into the Glow, just as he had during the first visit. Each trip Down, Pock seemed to find more worrisome inconsistencies Earthside than in the Grand Sphere, and he did not like it.

Standard struggled to remember his purpose. Pock looked at him with contempt. "No bigger Fool than one too short for his pleasures," he thought. When Standard finally spoke, it was as if he thought their previous conversation was still going on. "This Wenn," he said, "exactly what work has he done for us?"

The question seemed innocuous. Pock was not sure whether it was a trap or just another example of Standard's dwindling memory. Standard knew as much about it as he did, but he answered with a vagueness that would have made a native Grander proud. "Runs rickshaw for Execs up to CORPQ, bodyguards all Upper Level personnel arriving from Earthside, gathers intelligence." It was a true enough report, but not entirely accurate. The only certainty was that whatever Wenn did for Corporation, it represented only the tip of what he was really doing.

Standard seemed dissatisfied and impatient. His mind seemed to be clearing, but his next question was far too blunt. "Has he ever flashed anyone for you?"

It made Pock raise an eyebrow. "He's no assassin."

Standard seemed surprised. There was no reason he should have been. "It's not an assassination," he said indignantly. "It's an execution. Trial held, sentence passed, Corporate warrant signed and dated."

Standard seemed to think it made a difference. Pock doubted that the Corporation's warrants would mean a thing to Wenn. "He's not an executioner," he said. "Besides, if there are warrants on this man, he's the Fist's business.

We'll take care of him ourselves." Wenn was the last person he would send; P. C. Softer was the first.

Standard smiled with mock politeness. His tone was sharp. "If we wanted it done *officially,* I wouldn't have asked about Wenn."

The situation was getting less to Pock's liking by the sentence. A fugitive who had to be killed on the quiet did not sound right. Certainly the Grand Sphere could hide a hundred cutthroats, and undoubtedly did, and there might even be a dozen men and women in Hardcore who had flashed an official or two in their time, but one important enough for Old Spence to want him *quietly* killed was more than unusual. He knew Standard had used the "we" intentionally, to make it perfectly clear to him that it was Old Spence and not Standard who wanted the man killed, but that did not mean it was really so.

It wasn't like Old Spence to worry about influential people. There wasn't anybody more influential than Spencer LeGrange. Officially or unofficially, the LeGrange Corporation controlled most of the planet and all of the habitats. It owned the power satellites, and without the satellites there wouldn't be any Earthside economy and probably not much else. There was no reason for Spencer LeGrange to worry about *anybody's* influence. There was nobody, on the planet or off, that Old Spence couldn't have had erased without unbearable repercussions. That he would worry about appearances in the death of a convicted felon was more than unlikely. If it was true, Pock had good reason to worry. The fact that the victim was in the Grand Sphere made it even more dangerous for him. The skin in the grasp of the gold fist started to throb.

Standard was drifting again. Pock could see it in his eyes. His hand moved to the thighscreen, almost touched it, then glided away from it again like the ghost of itself. When it settled, he was clear again. "Wenn . . ."

"Wenn won't flash him." He didn't wait for Standard's objection. "But I have someone who will." He did not mention that the Blue he had in mind was an Ear. He knew

from experience that nobody trusted a man who went undercover in the Sphere.

Standard took the contradiction in stride. "Very well," he
said. "Will Wenn deliver Aerowaffen to us?"

Pock's scowl seemed to loosen the fist's grip a little. "Not
if he knows what for."

Standard gave him a long look down his nose. "Have you
taken to letting your squeals in on everything you do?"

Pock flushed. Standard never tired of insinuating that he
was losing his hold on the Grand Sphere, that he had gone
native, that he was too embroiled in the plots and intrigues
of the Sphere himself to be trustworthy. It was the attempt
more than the likelihood of its success that annoyed Pock.
He was reasonably sure Old Spence took his part against
Standard's insinuations, if only to keep the enmity going.
Old Spence encouraged squabbling among his subordinates.
Internal enmities kept them from ganging up against him,
and kept any one of them from becoming too powerful.
There was a cost, of course, in efficiency, but all in all it
showed the prudence Pock had come to expect from Old
Spence. The old man might be devious, ruthless, cruel, and
despicable, but he was always prudent.

When and if Pock fell from power, it would take more
than Standard's jealousy to do it. It would take some colos-
sal blunder of his own, some crucial failure, and he was not
a man who was used to failure. He had not risen his fist to
gold by making mistakes, and he had not survived ten years
in the Grand Sphere untangling plots within plots within
plots to fall on the innuendos of some office flunky. Besides,
what he could not say directly to Old Spence in his defense,
he was sure the old man would get for himself when he
reviewed the tape of the meeting. "Wenn's no average
squeal," he said.

Standard dismissed the idea that anyone who was not an
Exec could be anything but ordinary, however quick he
might be with a cane. "He gathers intelligence, doesn't he?"

Pock ignored the question and asked one of his own.
"Why Wenn?"

Standard hesitated. "Aerowaffen will be in touch with him." Pock said nothing about knowing as much already, and he knew better than to ask Standard how *he* knew. It would have been useless anyway; Standard was drifting out again. His smile was broadening without reason, and his voice rose slowly up out of the lingering fog of his pleasure. "Burn him," he said languorously, "and keep the Corporation out of it."

Pock scowled. He'd accomplished the execution of Corporation Executives with less secrecy. It didn't make sense that somebody as insignificant as Aerowaffen would warrant such precautions. The whole thing sounded more like a grandiose plot on Standard's part, the kind of fatuous overreaching that came from brainfry, like using the Fist to accomplish some personal vendetta.

There was no way he was going to go out on that limb without authorization. Old Spence might have most of the power, but there were others who had plenty and not a few of them were part of the Pleasure Crew Standard was such a favorite of. They would be glad to help set Pock up to look like he had killed Aerowaffen for some private motive, like covering up his own plot against Spencer LeGrange. He had no idea what Standard's plan was, but he was sure there was one. "Not without an order," he said.

Standard gave an exasperated sigh. "You *have* an order."

Pock shook his head. "Not from you, Slick. I want to hear it from Old Spence himself."

The room suddenly crackled with the voice of Spencer LeGrange. "Do it," was all the voice said.

Pock had no doubt who it was. The hairs on the back of his neck began to rise. He felt suddenly like a Fool on his first visit to the Sphere who realizes he is neck deep in some Grander conspiracy he can't even begin to understand. It made him want to get somewhere he could figure it all out as quickly as possible. "Is there anything else?" he said.

Standard nodded smugly. "Yes. Get rid of Wenn as well." Pock offered no argument. He stood at attention, waiting to be dismissed, but Standard seemed already to have forgotten about him. His fingers had pressed the pleasuresuit into action. Pock caught a glimpse of the thighscreens before he turned to go. On both, Eleganza worked and worked; sweat made the white dot on her forehead glisten. Standard groaned and gyrated.

All the way to the shuttleport, something about what he had seen annoyed him, but he could not get a grip on what it was. All he had was a vague feeling that he was missing the significance of some detail that would make everything fall into place. It was not until he was halfway back to the Sphere that he realized that the skinner was not of Standard's trip to the Sphere. It was new! Just before the shuttle docked at the Big Door, a second realization struck him. The images of Eleganza on each thighscreen had been different. It meant that part of the skinner had been made from a third pleasuresuit. There must have been a third person, someone who took part in the whole thing and whose sensations were being fed into Standard's pleasuresuit along with his own and Eleganza's. Pock knew it could only have been Spencer LeGrange himself.

Chapter Nine

Wenn left Aerowaffen in the inner room and answered the door cautiously. The Blue who stood in front of it was not someone he had seen before, but it was not suspicious. The contingent for training was always being changed, and there was a steady stream of Blues passing through the monitoring room. Still, there was something odd about the recruit, although he could not place what it was at first. He unsealed the door and stood in the opening, waiting for the Blue to say what he wanted.

"Master Wenn?" the recruit asked. Wenn nodded. "I've come to help you with your rickshaw." The statement made no sense. There were times when his rickshaw blocked some other rickshaw from moving in or out of the practice field, but several of his students were entitled to move it without asking for permission, and one of the Fist would not have helped him move it in any case. What was even more odd, there was a tone in the young man's voice a Grander would have used if he was saying something he thought could be overheard by the Fist. Even his posture said there was a deeper and more important meaning. But Wenn could not begin to guess what it was.

He eyed the recruit suspiciously. The Blue was young, with a ruddy complexion and blue eyes that had a mischievous glint to them. They gave his smile an ambiguous quality, as if he were in on some sort of enormous joke that the rest of the world had yet to catch on to. It still did not strike Wenn immediately that the greatest oddity was the fact that the Blue was smiling at all; he was too intrigued with the Blue's hair. It was a very vivid orange, so vivid that he would have suspected that it was not natural except that it would have been a court-martial offense for a Blue to color his hair, especially a color as striking as that.

There were not many redheads among the Fist, although they were common in Catchcage and not unknown in other habitats, especially Hardcore, where the Fist did most of its recruiting. But the Blue did not have the scars and calluses of a young Corehard, and he was certainly far too young to be an Obee. Nor did he seem to have the undertone of belligerence someone raised in Hardcore would have. There was a possibility that he was from Earthside, more than half of the Fist were, but green as he looked, he did not seem to be a young Fool suckered Up from Earthside with the promise of glory and adventure in the orbiting habitats. Wherever he was from, there was obviously more to him than the baby-face novice he seemed.

"Does the Fist think I'm so old I need help?" he said.

The recruit grinned. "It's a very big rickshaw," he said. It was true that Wenn's rickshaw was somewhat bigger than the others, but he doubted that that was what the Blue meant. If he were talking to Pock instead of the Blue, Wenn would have taken it to mean that the Fist was onto some large scheme of his and wanted a percentage of its proceeds, but the Blue was not high enough to be working that kind of rickshaw on his own, and the only other rickshaw he could have meant was the Great Rickshaw of Revolution.

"Who sends me this help and comfort?"

The recruit seemed to be laughing at his private joke again. "Nohfro Pock," he said.

"And why does Nohfro Pock think I need help dancing

my rickshaw?" He wondered if the answer was what amused the young man so much.

"You have a very big passenger."

Wenn's face remained expressionless, but it would have showed a worried scowl if he had let it. If Pock was moving against Aerowaffen already, everything was in danger. There was no allowing the Count to be taken into custody, but getting him out without exposing the Revolution was going to be difficult at best. And yet it did not seem likely that Pock would send a mere Blue, however much of a veteran he might be, to take in someone like Aerowaffen.

"I have many passengers for my rickshaw," Wenn said.

The Blue seemed suddenly older and a lot more worldly. "Aerowaffen," he said. It was what Wenn had feared. "Take me to him."

Wenn stepped back from the doorway to allow the Blue to come in. There was no denying him, and whatever had to be done with him was better done inside than within plain view of half of Downside. He walked toward the inner door and stopped. A sudden worry washed over him. What if Pock had sent the Blue to kill Aerowaffen? There was no letting the Blue inside the inner room with its secrets in any case. He stopped at the door. "I'll get him." He expected an argument, but the Blue only nodded, and Wenn stepped inside the inner room. He looked around the room and smiled; the monitors were concealed. Aerowaffen had taken care of it almost as soon as he had gone to answer the door. The Count cocked his head. Wenn nodded toward the closed panel. "A Blue. Pock sent him to see you."

"What's he look like?"

It was an unusual question. "Young, bright orange hair."

Aerowaffen smiled. "Bring him in."

"He could be here to kill you," Wenn warned.

Aerowaffen laughed. "He is. He is."

Wenn drew his cane and Aerowaffen's laughter doubled. He was still chuckling as he stepped to the panel and cut off the energy. The Blue stepped immediately through the opening. Aerowaffen closed and clouded it again. He raised a palm to stop Wenn's attack and put a hand on the Blue's shoulder. "This is Push," he said, as if it explained everything. Wenn looked at him blankly. "He dances rickshaw in Catchcage." There were no rickshaws in Catchcage except the Revolution. He turned to Push. "What have you brought?"

Push smiled. "A plan and a weapon." He took a small device from his uniform and placed it on the floor; a transparent image of the Grand Sphere about a yard across suddenly floated before them. In a moment it folded open where the Iron Mountain divided it into halves; the yellow band of the Great Wideway cut each hemisphere in two. The blue of the Crossway cut the halves into quadrants.

Push pointed to where the Wideway crossed Iron Mountain. "Obviously," he said, "we have to control the highest ground, and the most important ground is the heights between CORPQ and Lesser CORPQ. The Wideway across Upside is the safest way to try to reinforce the Little Door once it's taken. And when Gun Sub Runn takes the Annex, the Fist'll have no choice but to try to retake it, and the shortest way is over the mountain."

Wenn raised an eyebrow. Things were organized so that each of them knew and could betray as few others as possible, but it did not seem likely that the Rickshaw King would be involved. Push went on before he could raise an objection.

"They'll think it's just another riot and come right up the Wideway." He pointed to a spot a few hundred yards down from the crest of the hill on the CORPQ side. "We'll need most of your caners here," he said to Wenn. "There's a lot of gullies and crevices there to conceal them."

Wenn nodded. The advantage would clearly be with his students, even though they would be greatly outnumbered. The Fist would be winded from the long run uphill, and they would have to fight the grade as well as Wenn's superior caners. The element of surprise would work in their favor as well.

Push drew a line across the Wideway. "Five rickshaws

ought to make a big enough barricade. Could you make it look like an accident?"

Wenn nodded. At least five rickshaws were usually stationed at the gate of CORPQ for the benefit of Execs and such Police as needed quick transportation somewhere. Pock's first response would be to send as many as he could up the grade by rickshaw. If he didn't sacrifice speed, he could send a maximum of six men per rickshaw. Thirty of the Fist would make a dent in any mob until the sight of a hundred more coming down the hill could put it to flight.

"Once the main force starts up the mountain, we'll need another ten rickshaws to show up at CORPQ." Wenn nodded that it could be done. "Pock'll load them up with reinforcements, ten, maybe twelve to a rickshaw. That'll give us a good excuse to take them up the Offshoots to get up momentum." It was obvious what would happen to them once out of sight of the main roadway. "We keep ferrying them in there and ambushing them until they catch on. We'll need the rest of your caners here." He pointed to the narrow, curving branches that stuck out a third and two-thirds of the way up each side of the Wideway. "Except for the ones dancing rickshaw. They're the real key." He smiled. "Next to the Count, of course."

He drew his finger along the Great Wideway across Downside. The entire lower half of the Sphere was filled with the habitation hills of Downside. "The mobs here will make it impossible for them to get to the Little Door to relieve the garrison there, and we can eliminate half the Downside Crossway for the same reason. That leaves them only one way out of CORPQ." His finger traced a red line from the gate near Pock's quarters, out between the orchards and the Inner Fields to where the Downside Crossway started up Iron Mountain. On the other side of the Crossway, the red line continued through the Outer Fields to the Police compound at the Little Door.

Aerowaffen saw the strategic mistake immediately. "If he's got any sense, he'll send the whole force up the mountain. If he splits them and sends half to the Little Door, he won't have the numbers to take the mountain *or* the Little Door." Without the advantage of troops already inside, the Little Door would be almost as difficult to retake as CORPQ would be, even *without* contending with the mass of reinforcements available from across the Wideway. With the sheer numbers available from there, the attempt to come to the aid of the Little Door would be foolhardy.

"Pock's a long time Up," Wenn said. No native Grander would make so simple a mistake, and Pock had been matching wits with Granders for longer than either side wanted to think about.

Push nodded. "So, we have to hold the Orchard Notch." There was no doubt the cut in the ridge of Iron Mountain where the Crossway passed into Upside was crucial. A look at the Upside Sphere showed why it was going to be hard to do. At the noon mark of the Sphere, where the Crossway came over the mountain, there was very little population. At three o'clock on the circle, across the Wideway from the Annex, the large spread of freestanding modules that made up Dah Beel's Village stretched almost the whole way from the mountain to the Upside Window. But between it and the curve of the mountains at the top, there was only the thinly populated pyramid of Eliot Dah Beel.

From the window out to the mountain at nine o'clock, the freestanding bachelor and family units of Tinker's Stretch crowded against the other side of the Wideway, but on the same side of the Wideway as Dah Beel's, there was nothing but Van Vast's Peak and the gardens of Eleganza. "The question," Push said, "is what we're going to hold it *with*?"

Aerowaffen's answer was less than optimistic. "The Pleasure Crew."

Push frowned. "Maybe we can reinforce them by rickshaw from Tinker's, or at least hold Upper Crossway Bridge." All four bridges were narrower than the roadways and could be held easier, but the Fist would have downhill momentum. It would even be possible for them to bypass the bridge by going around the curve of the Upper Window, although it would mean they would have to fight their way through the three curved habitation mounds of Little Dah Beel. Still, if they did, it was only a short stretch of Wideway before they could turn off onto the Annex Narrow and make their way up it to Lesser CORPQ. The best solution was to keep the ridgeline of Iron Mountain. But it would be a lot easier said than done.

The young Blue turned his attention to Wenn. "How long can your caners hold the Little Door?"

Wenn pondered it. Even at its maximum, the force under Yung Gun Runn would be outnumbered ten to one. He was sure they could take the Little Door. The entryway from the docking trees outside the Sphere was large, but the inspection area everything passed through was a bottleneck and could be sealed at either end. His caners were more than a match for an equal number of the Fist, and even outnumbered two to one, they would more than hold their own, but the garrison outside the Little Door in the compound numbered close to two hundred and they were some of the best fighters in the Sphere. "Alone," he said, "not very long."

Push nodded. "Then we'll see to it that they're not alone." There were certainly enough people in the quadrant to mount a sizable attack on the compound and keep the Fist busy on two fronts, but the compound was well fortified, and Push seemed to have something else in mind. He did not say what, but his smile hinted at some private joke again.

He turned to Aerowaffen. "That leaves everything up to you," he said. His smile broadened. He reached inside his uniform and pulled out a small bundle from under his arm. His grin widened as he peeled the layers of duracloth apart. What they revealed made Wenn's mouth drop open. Nestled in the folds of the cloth was something to which every Grander reacted with fear and rage. Push unwrapped the gun and handed it to Aerowaffen. The Count hefted it with glee. The black polish of the metal gleamed with a sinister glory. Push turned and unclouded the panel. "See you on the Wideway," he said. A moment later he was gone.

Chapter Ten

UWalk Wenn watched with distaste as Aerowaffen laid the handgun onto a piece of suit fiber and covered it with another. The Count pressed the edges of the cloth together until they formed a seal and then fitted the package against his formalsuit under his arm until it stuck. The weapon could not be easily drawn, but it would be even more difficult to discover. A gun was the last thing a Grander would think to look for.

The inhabitants of the LeGrange League had an abhorrence of guns found nowhere on Earth. The history of firearms in the League was short and bloody. They had been obviously too dangerous when the habitats were being built and the only place to live was the cluster of dormitory and cargo containers that became known as Hardcore. A stray bullet could puncture a wall, and more than one in the same area might cause an immediately fatal decompression.

It was true a bullet might travel a good deal farther in the Big and Little Wheels, or even in Henson's Tube, without hitting anything major, but every habitat had windows, and a bullet could cause the same damage as a small meteorite if it hit the glass at full velocity. The fact that such a hole would take days to empty even half the atmosphere of a habitat made no difference. It was an almost universally believed myth that an unlucky shot could fracture an entire window, emptying the atmosphere in minutes and killing everyone in the habitat.

The astronomical odds against such an accident were even greater in the Grand Sphere, but despite a three-mile diameter, the bullet from a high-powered rifle was not without danger. Earthside, the strongest rifle would have lost its killing power within half that distance, but from the moment a bullet began to rise across the diameter, it was subject to a lessening gravity that could be felt even going from the bottom of one of the habitation hills to the top. A bullet would not lose the velocity it would on Earth as it passed upward toward the ball of zero gravity inside the Ring.

Beyond the ball, the growing pull of gravity would only increase its momentum. The idea of being killed from above by a bullet meant for someone miles away around the Sphere was a Grander nightmare, and a hatred of firearms was one of the few things all members of the League had in common.

That hatred had always been greatest in Hardcore, where the first fatal shots in the League were fired. It had occurred just after the completion of the Grand Sphere, when the Corporation announced that the Bonus due to Obees who had survived twenty years' laying up structure was to be paid, not in space in the Grand Sphere, as the Obees had always believed, but with the space they already occupied in Hardcore. The riot that ensued was relatively brief, but more than fifty Obees were killed and almost twice as many of the Fist.

On the second day of rioting, the head of the Fist fired three pistol shots into a crowd of Obees. A Silver fired another shot from a second handgun. The bullets killed two Obee men and wounded one woman, and a ricochet killed a child who was watching the fighting from some girders near the top of Main Bay. No part of the LeGrange commander was recovered, and of the Silver, only a shoe, with a foot still in it, remained when the mob finally dispersed. The shoe and the foot were sent by return shuttle to Spencer LeGrange, and although there was some lengthy discussion about the necessity for upholding the absolute rights of Corporation in the Sphere, it was finally agreed that the use of such weapons was not worth the considerable cost of putting down rebellions every time they were displayed.

Nevertheless, Spencer LeGrange negotiated a settlement with Hardcore that was mostly to Corporation's advantage. The Obees agreed to submit their claims against the Corporation to the courts Earthside, a process even the Obees knew would take decades and probably result in defeat unless Spencer LeGrange died in the meantime. In return, the Corporation would remove all firearms from Hardcore and never issue them to the Police contingent there again. However, when it was announced that all firearms were being removed from Hardcore, no mention was made of the rest of the League. The omission passed unnoticed because everyone simply assumed that if Hardcore could be kept from insurrection without guns, the rest of the League would never have to worry about them again.

That assumption was wrong, and less than a decade later a gun was fired on the Great Wideway. To the astonishment of Corporation, the results were even quicker and bloodier than they had been in Hardcore. Ironically, the gun was not fired in anger but by a careless Blue who was apparently under the influence of one of the numerous drugs for which the Grand Sphere was famous. A number of conspicuously large handguns had been issued by Pock's predecessor, a Gold named Swyn. (He pronounced it "swin," but outside of the Fist it was universally pronounced "swine.") They had been worn as a show of force in the face of mounting resistance to a tax imposed on all business done on the Great Wideway.

The gun was fired from the upper end of the Wideway in Downside, and although the trajectory of the bullet was not straight up, it struck and killed a member of the Pleasure

Crew in a rickshaw halfway down CORPQ Hill. The inebriated Blue did not get to fire a second shot into the air. He vanished without remains under the mob on the Great Wideway. If his victim had been an ordinary Grander, the results would have been the same for the Blue, but things would have been a lot easier for Corporation.

The victim could not have been worse for Corporation if he had been selected by the Revolution. Elgin Dah Beel had been a student of Wenn's, and Wenn remembered him well as one of his most likeable, if not one of his best, pupils. He was also one of the best liked members of the Pleasure Crew, which, to the great surprise of everyone, took a very active part in the storming of CORPQ by the rioters. Most important was that Elgin Dah Beel was the favorite son of Eliot Dah Beel, the toughest of the Original Speculators and one of the most powerful men in the League. Dah Beel was a self-made man who had worked his way up from assignment boss to controlling the Original Builders who had worked off their passage laying up structure and become independent contractors. Even the Obees considered him one of them, and he was as powerful in Hardcore as he was in the Sphere. If there was a man in the League who was a match for Spencer LeGrange, it was Eliot Dah Beel.

Corporation had no choice but to negotiate. Spencer LeGrange apologized personally, but it was hardly enough. Even the voluntary declaration that no firearms would ever be used again anywhere in the League was insufficient. Reparations had to be made as well, both economic and political. The details would never be announced, but they were widely known. Nothing was to be said about the heavy damage done to the facade of CORPQ when the Granders stormed it. No reprisals were to be made against those who rioted, even though there were shreds of uniform and pieces of Police equipment hanging in half of the busiest stalls on the Great Wideway, and the murder of the Blue who had fired the shot was to be treated as merely a justifiable homicide by persons unknown.

A Silver named Nohfro Pock had opposed the issuing of

firearms from the beginning, and although he was distrusted Earthside for being too much like a Grander himself, he was sufficiently disliked in the Sphere to be promoted to Gold and made commander of the garrison. Most important, control of the Little Door, the smaller of the two space-docking facilities in the Sphere, was to be turned over to Eliot Dah Beel.

It amounted to the right to smuggle duty-free goods into the Sphere, and it cost the Corporation a sizable amount in lost revenue, but not nearly as much as it would profit the Speculators. Even the Pleasure Crew would be mollified by it since it meant free passage of much of the contraband of pleasure into and out of the Sphere. But there had been important details still to be argued out when Eliot Dah Beel and the new commander of the Fist rode through the Sphere in UWalk Wenn's rickshaw.

Wenn shifted his weight slightly back along the forks, but Pock's scowl sent him back out to the tips. It didn't matter; he could hear well enough from there, even though both men kept their voices conspiratorially low. The rick-shaw had already covered much of the Wideway, and there was only the curve of Upside still above them and a short crosstravel through Downside before they would be back at CORPQ. The trip was a public parade, an indication that negotiations had borne fruit, that the incident was closed and the relationship with Corporation reestablished.

Dah Beel's voice was stern. "You will remove the guards from the Little Door today." Control of the docking facili-ties was as good as a license for piracy, and although Corporation had agreed to it, the Fist did not like it. Pock was taking over a diminished realm, one that would be as difficult to secure as a house with one door guarded by criminals.

He saw it as an enormous strategic mistake, but he had no choice but to agree. "As soon as you have suitable replacements," he said.

Dah Beel nodded. "And there will be no interference in

trade." It was more a command than a question. Pock accepted it silently. His bargaining position was not strong. Although the attack on CORPQ had been repulsed without its prize, Commander Swyn, it had demonstrated the vulnerability of the building, and the Fist needed time to reinforce the garrison and build more formidable defenses. It was the closest the Grand Sphere had come to a real uprising and, although the independence of the colony was never mentioned, a costly and prolonged state of siege was entirely possible, and the Fist as well as the Corporation knew it.

Both Dah Beel and Pock waved or nodded to the crowd that lined the Wideway. There was a mixture of boos and cheers wherever the rickshaw went, but there seemed a general air of relief that the fighting was at an end. Unlike Obees, Granders generally preferred negotiations, since they seldom lost a settlement and inevitably came away with far more by cleverness and the threat of force than Hardcore had ever been able to get from the Corporation by force alone. Dah Beel smiled and waved to the crowd. He spoke through his smile. "And the done commander?"

Pock shrugged as if he did not understand the question. But he understood only too well that Dah Beel meant the commander was both finished on the Grand Sphere and as good as dead. "Returned to Earth," he said, as if the answer were obvious.

Dah Beel shook his head. "Not enough."

Pock scowled. He saw a precedent forming that he did not like, but he was aware that agreements had been made that he could know nothing about. The danger made him sweat. Dah Beel and the Specs wanted Swyn killed, but there were no guarantees that Old Spence had agreed to it. If Pock carried out the execution, he would get the kind of cooperation he would need from the Speculators to establish his new position; if he didn't, there was always the possibility that Dah Beel would inform Old Spence that the new commander was no better than the last and still another might be appointed.

It was risky business any way he looked at it. Conspiring to kill another Gold was something that could get him killed from within his own ranks if it was ever discovered. Still, he had been on the Grand Sphere long enough to have more than a little Grander in him, and he said, "Done." It meant both "agreed" and "dead." Dah Beel's smile broadened, but Pock raised a finger. "On one condition."

Dah Beel's smile faded a little, but there was a hint of amusement in it, as if he liked the fact that Pock had responded like a Grander and not simply acquiesced as any ordinary Exec would have done. He waited for Pock's condition. "No Obees on the Little Door."

Dah Beel considered it. It was a strategic advantage for the Fist. Obees were the best fighters in the League, and it would be harder to recapture the door from Obees, if push came to shove, than almost anyone else. It meant that the Fist could retake the door in any emergency. Dah Beel shrugged noncommittally. "Granders, then," he said.

Pock nodded agreement. It was a better deal than he could have hoped for. Granders on the Little Door would inevitably be running their own rickshaw as well and could be easily corrupted, and in any case, they would form a far less formidable obstacle to retaking the door than Obees would. Still, like any Grander, Pock went for an additional concession. "By accident," he said.

The old Speculator would have preferred an unambiguous death for Swyn, one the populace as a whole could see as vengeance for the death of one of their kind, but he was willing to compromise. His mouth was set in a firm line. "A suitable accident," he said finally. Pock nodded and Dah Beel took a small bag of jewelry from a sideslip in his formalsuit and pressed it into Pock's hands. "See that these are found on him."

Pock smiled. All that was needed was a painful and reasonably accidental looking death. With the jewels on him, the done commander would look like he had been smuggling the best of his bribes back to Earth in anticipation of deserting Corporation and fleeing into one of Earth-

side's teeming population corridors. If Pock were ever confronted by Spencer LeGrange, he could always claim that he had known about the attempt and had killed Swyn to save Corporation the embarrassment. He slipped the small sack into his uniform, and the ride continued in silence.

The trip through Downside was as quick as Wenn could make it. Although Upside might be satisfied a solution had been worked out, there was still a raging anger Downside that made Pock an obvious target. Just beyond the second bridge of the Downside Window, a chunk of metal came hurtling out of the crowd. Pock and Dah Beel ducked, and Wenn threw the rickshaw quickly up on one wheel. The chunk bounced harmlessly off the side of the rickshaw, and Wenn set it back down on two wheels without even losing momentum. Pock twisted on the longseat and tried to catch sight of whoever had thrown it. Dah Beel looked only at Wenn, but he said nothing about what he was thinking until Pock had dismounted at CORPQ and they had crossed the mountain into Upside again.

Wenn was still out on the forks. There was nothing to hear, and Dah Beel was no Fool from Earthside who could be intimidated into a larger tip. Halfway down the mountain, the Spec leaned forward and spoke to him. "Does it tire you to run rickshaw, Master Wenn?"

Wenn nodded. "Yes," he said. "But not to dance it."

Dah Beel smiled. "I have a longseat for you, if you'd like to ride?" Wenn took the words as simply the offer of a place on the longseat, and he made the leap up from the forks in a single, fluid motion. Dah Beel became more direct. "I have another seat at the Little Door," he said. "A man like you could dance all his rickshaws from there and never have to run them up to speed again."

It was a generous offer, but not an entirely altruistic one. Dah Beel needed someone relatively trustworthy to guard the smaller entrance to the habitat, and behind the implied willingness to overlook whatever personal dealings Wenn might conduct as guardian of the Little Door, there was an assumption of reasonable honesty in collecting its revenues and a reasonable dishonesty in checking on what the Specu-lators brought through the gate. It was a very tempting offer for Wenn.

For the Revolution, control of the Little Door would mean free access to the Sphere for any agent it wanted, and the ability to seal off any hope of reinforcements from outside the Sphere when the real battle for the Grand Sphere finally erupted. But it needed the information Wenn gathered even more. There were too many Execs whose care the Corporation would trust only to Wenn himself for him to abandon his running rickshaw, even for the power of the Little Door. "A man should dance his own rickshaw," he said finally.

Dah Beel frowned. He had not expected any Grander to turn such an offer down. He tried another tack. "You have many students of the cane." Wenn nodded. Dah Beel hesitated. "My own son"—his voice broke very slightly—"studied under you for a brief time."

Wenn remembered the young man. He had been enthusiastic, but he had had a better feel for the meaning behind the Defense than for the technique. Still, he had shown promise before the lure of the pleasure fountains had drawn him away from the hard labor of the rickshaw. Wenn had seen a vague longing in Elgin Dah Beel for the serenity that came with electric-cane defense, and he had expected that eventually, when the fire of pleasure had burned out in him, the young man would return for further study. The bullet had put an end to any hope of that.

Wenn felt a greater sorrow for it than the Old Spec could know. He knew that the Revolution had lured the Blue into drawing and firing the gun. But it had never been meant to actually hit anyone. If the Blue had simply fired straight up, no one would have been hurt. But some passing Fool from Earthside had grabbed the Blue's wrist and bent it away, hitting the young Dah Beel. "I remember him," Wenn said. His voice was heavy with sorrow. "He would have filled the longseat when he finished playing."

There was a weary sadness in Dah Beel's voice. "Of all

my sons, I thought he would be the one that would make a Spec." The Old Spec was quiet for a long time. "*He had a friend,*" he said finally, "*among your students.*"

Wenn nodded. "*Yung Gun Runn.*"

Dah Beel nodded. "*He dances rickshaw for you.*" It was both a question and an answer.

The young man was one of Wenn's favorites, although Wenn showed no favoritism, except to work those he liked best a little harder. Wenn nodded. "*He dances my own rickshaw,*" he said.

"*Can you spare him and a dozen others to sit your longseat at the Little Door?*" It was the perfect solution, and it was not as sentimental an offer as it seemed. If anyone among Wenn's followers would remember his son's death, it would be Yung Gun Runn, and Dah Beel was sure he could depend not only on the young man's loyalty but on his ferocity if the door ever needed to be defended against the Fist. There was only one group that it would be harder to take the door from than Obees, and that was the students of UWalk Wenn. Pock had obviously never thought of them when he had accepted Granders to guard the door. He had been sure Dah Beel would staff it with people from the Pleasure Crew or with ordinary Granders from his own staff. He would be furious when he found Wenn's hand-picked caners guarding it.

The thought of it made UWalk Wenn smile. "*Done,*" he said.

Aerowaffen's voice brought him back from Dah Beel's Mountain. "Are you ready?" When Aerowaffen lifted his arm to throw his cape around his shoulder, the bulge of the gun was visible, but when his arms returned to his sides, it was gone. The knowledge that it was there at all troubled Wenn. Aerowaffen saw the frown. "Can you see it, then?" he said.

Wenn shook his head. "Only in the mind."

Aerowaffen laughed and headed toward the door. "The best place to use it," he said.

Chapter Eleven

The rickshaw went past the Police compound outside the Little Door and up the side of Iron Mountain. Wenn worked it easily. Most of the traffic from the Little Door was going the other way, down the Great Wideway into Downside and toward CORPQ. He stopped the rickshaw at the top of Iron Mountain, and they looked out over the whole of Upside. At the center the Upside Window gleamed through the cross formed by the overlap of the Upside Crossway and the Lesser Wideway.

In each quadrant, at varying distances between the window and the mountain that ringed the hemisphere, one of the Peaks of the Speculators rose in banked or terraced splendor. The largest, Van Vast's Peak, dominated the swirl of erratic curves to their left. On the far side of it, Eleganza's Garden blossomed with promise, both the easiest and the hardest of their obstacles. Away from it to their right, the spiky points of Tinker's Tor rose in the sunlight. On its outer side blue grottoes and narrow, twisting blue lakelets caught the sun. The Pleasuer Crew of Tinker's Quadrant was already busily at play.

On a diagonal across the window, dominating the far

upper left quadrant, the squared terraces of Dah Beel's Mountain gleamed with a mechanical brightness. Most of the water there was in moats and canals, with only an occasional fountain. The gardens that had once flourished with Elgin's friends from the Pleasure Crew were now subdued; only his sister's smaller crowd lolled by the fountains. His brothers and his former friends were dispersed to other fountains on Tinker's Tor or at Eleganza's.

Below it, the freestanding modules of Dah Beel City crowded against the Wideway, a short walk for workers from the Annex of CORPQ just across the roadway, a short, steep ride over the mountain from the main complex. Except for its strategic location at the base of the farthest rim of the mountain, it was difficult to imagine it as a potential battlefield. Yet in less than a day, it would be either a historical landmark for the newly freed colonists or just a bloody stretch of roadway nobody wanted to think about.

Just to the right of the Wideway, at the Upside base of CORPQ Hill, a concentric spiral of glass and terraces formed the Annex, or Lesser CORPQ, the Corporation's main point of control in Upside. Between it and the Crossway, the quadrant was dominated by their destination, the Halls of the Rickshaw King. It was in some ways both the most lavish and the most forbidding of the four peaks. The bottom two tiers, inhabited mostly by the friends and relatives of Gun Sub Runn, the Rickshaw King, were separated from the main rise by a sharp decline.

It was a fortress of sorts. The lower tier formed a wall over which four slender and easily controlled bridges carried traffic from the Wideway and the Crossway, and from a road directly to Lesser CORPQ. All of the Speculators had their own private guards, but the Halls of the Rickshaw King were best prepared to fend off an assault. Or launch one. Of all the peaks, it was the most strategic and the least likely to join the Revolution. Aerowaffen nodded toward it, and the rickshaw started down the mountain.

It hit the main straightaway at a good speed and flew by the narrow that branched off toward Tinker's Tor. Traffic on

Tinker's Narrow was light, and Wenn expected it would be even lighter when they made their way back across it toward Eleganza's. The bridge over the first curve of the Upside Window passed beneath the wheels, then the circular island where the wideways crossed. Just beyond the second bridge, they turned right onto the narrow that led to the Halls of the Rickshaw King. The sharp upright planes of the peak flashed like the edges of twelve upraised swords. Aerowaffen wondered whose heart they would be pointed at when the meeting was over.

They leaned forward to feed the momentum into the wheel as the rickshaw shot down the short decline between the first and second tiers of the mountain. The energy carried them across the narrow bridge and well up the first stage of the incline onto the second tier. On either side of them, water poured in small waterfalls between the living quarters and ran down into a wide, fast-moving stream that circled the raised tier. The clear planes of glass that fronted the modules in Downside were stained with color everywhere in Upside, but those of the Rickshaw King were the most beautifully decorated.

A few slid aside and heads peeked out at them as they passed along the terrace and began the long ascent to the top of the man-made mountain. Wenn smiled and waved to relatives he recognized, and several children playing beside one of the waterfalls sang some rickshaw song at him as he passed. The energy they had stored in the wheel in the long ride down from Iron Mountain carried them up the second stage of the incline, along the second terrace, and up to the third, but they were forced to maneuver it with considerable skill to make it up the last two stages, and the rickshaw came to a rolling halt before two of the huge glass planes that jutted out to form the first of the twelve points of the peak.

A door opened at the base of the nearest pane even before they stopped, and several family members in the red-and-gold cloth of Gun Sub Runn's clan welcomed them and ushered them inside. The sun that poured through the glass of the peak focused on the center of the grand hall, where it seemed to form a glowing ball of light even brighter than outside. The group moved steadily toward it across a floor that danced with shifting color. Wenn had walked across that hall many times before, but it never ceased to amaze him.

He looked up at the huge sheets of colored glass that seemed to dangle in midair above them. Big as they were, the sheets seemed to turn in a shifting breeze, constantly changing the pattern of color they cast on the floor of the hall. At any other time it would have been a delight, but neither UWalk Wenn nor Roger Count Aerowaffen could appreciate it.

Midway to the glowing center of the hall, Gun Sub Runn's eldest son greeted them, bowing to Wenn as his master and embracing him as longtime friend and honored guest of his father. He bowed courteously to Aerowaffen, and the Count nodded ceremoniously. Neither kinship nor friendship would determine Gun Sub Runn's decision, and both UWalk Wenn and the Count knew it.

They followed their host toward the dozen men scattered on Aireclines at the center of the hall. The halo of light that surrounded them made them seem more than human, but both Aerowaffen and Wenn knew them too well to be deceived by it. Still, they were as close to deities as the Grand Sphere had to offer, and they could not have had much more power over the fate of the Revolution if they had really had the supernatural powers that seemed to surround them. Everything depended on what the Original Speculators did, and what they did depended on Aerowaffen.

Of the hundred or so Speculators who occupied most of the space Upside, only a dozen were considered the Original Specs, and of that dozen, only four families were of real importance. Although the others would eventually vote on what course the whole of Upside would take, all but a few would follow the lead of one or the other of the four Original Speculators whose peaks dominated the four quadrants of Upside.

Viktor Van Vast, Eliot Dah Beel, Gun Sub Runn, and Tinker Manwalker had all made their fortunes very early in the development of the Grand Sphere, a long time before. All four had gouged their power out of the flesh of Corporation in their youth, when Risk was still the salt of life. But they had grown older, more sedate. None of them had any great love for Spencer LeGrange, but they all had a lot to lose, and, although they were still Granders, they were not as inclined to gamble as they had been in their prime.

Viktor Van Vast had earned his peak from the creation of the circular mountain range that had sealed the hemispheres of the Grand Sphere and made it livable. He was scarcely a decade the junior of Old Spence, but despite his wealth, he lacked the secrets of Corporation's genetic engineers that kept Old Spence on the last frontiers of youth. Age and ill health had left marks on his face and body, even though they had spared his mind. The passage of time that had barely touched Old Spence had thinned Viktor Van Vast and wasted the muscular frame that had once attracted Eleganza's mother. He looked gaunt and old and seemed perpetually bent over, even lying back on the Airecline.

Eliot Dah Beel was even older, but he had maintained almost as much of his physical power as Old Spence, though without the use of the restorative surgery and hormone washes that kept Old Spence young beyond his years. He was a short, thick man with heavy eyebrows and a broken nose. His eyebrows and knuckles carried the scars that came from dealing with physical people and handling life-or-death disagreements, but the scar that showed the most was the invisible scar of his son's death.

Tinker Manwalker was half a decade younger than the others, but only the graying of her hair and the web of fine lines in the coffee-colored skin of her face gave any indication that she had been in the Grand Sphere almost as long. Widowed early, when the husband she had come up with perished laying up structure on Henson's Tube, she had made her fortune reversing one of Old Spence's most insidious schemes. To insure that the colonies would always be dependent on Corporation, all equipment came up from Earthside with built-in defects, mostly in parts which could easily be shipped back Earthside for reprogramming or repair.

Even before the death of her husband, Tinker Manwalker ran a little shop that diagnosed and repaired equipment too necessary to lie idle for months while parts went Earthside. Because it was illegal for colonists to repair their own equipment, her prices were only a little shy of exorbitant, but her business flourished. She channeled the profits back into the business and within a few years had a chain of underground Fixer shops throughout the League. Eventually, even Corporation was forced to recognize her right to perform "temporary repairs," although even the parts her shops fixed had to be sent back Earthside once replacements parts were available.

Of the four, the small black woman was the only one Aerowaffen could count on for support. Her contribution to the Revolution had been as great as it was unknown. Her discovery that all equipment sent to the League was being intentionally sabotaged Earthside and the loss of her husband in an accident caused by a defective tool, had turned her early toward the struggle against Corporation. Her skill in deprogramming defects formed the basis for the League's economic counterattack against the Corporation. Whenever one of her shops corrected a defect programmed into a piece of equipment, they added their own programs that would cause flaws in the repair machinery Earthside.

As often as not, this equipment was also connected to the central production computer in each plant, and her counter-programs created weakness and equipment failures in production unrelated to equipment to be used in the habitats. It was the kind of counterattack only a Grander would have thought of, and for Corporation it represented only an inexplicable increase in product failures that seemed part of a long and continuing decline in the quality of almost everything produced on Earth. In addition, the "temporarily" repaired parts were sent back to Earth with different flaws than had been programmed into them, thus tying up the repair facilities and creating a backlog that eventually forced Corporation to grant Tinker her right to repair equipment within the League. It was a rickshaw every Grander would have been proud of had they known about it. Of the four, she was the only one that still seemed to burn with the fire of youth.

Gun Sub Runn was another who had made his fortune correcting the flaws created by Corporation. He had designed and built the centrifugal rickshaws that UWalk Wenn danced. Originally, the main form of transportation outside of Hardcore had been a fleet of two-to-four-passenger robotcars, but their continual breakdowns and the fact that their progress could be monitored from CORPQ made them highly unpopular. When CORPQ shut them off entirely during a disagreement with the League, the rickshaws took their place, and no one went back to using them. Corporation made a brief attempt to enforce their use, but sabotage and their own defects caused so much havoc that eventually even Corporation turned to the centrifugal rickshaw.

However, most of Gun Sub Runn's wealth came from the production of centrifugal rickshaws for sale in the increasingly impoverished parts of Earth, and his ties to Corporation were stronger than any of the other Original Speculators. It was no accident that his peak had a road running directly to a part of CORPQ.

There was little need for introductions. They all knew Aerowaffen and he knew them. To most, he was little more than someone who kept the children amused so that they did not interfere with the business of their elders until they came of age. They did not disdain what he did for a living, but they were not greatly impressed with it. He served a necessary function in a convenient arrangement. The pursuit of pleasure occupied their offspring and kept them from the usual intrigues and sibling rivalries family dynasties were prone to.

But ultimately, they expected the best of the next generation to put away their amusements and devote themselves to the continuation of the family fortunes. Each had at least one or two children they expected to take their place manipulating the power they had won in the League. If the pursuit of pleasure kept the rest busy all of their lives, all the better. They knew the tendency for empires to fall through the squabbles of the second generation.

A master of distraction like Aerowaffen was enormously useful to that end, but, unlike UWalk Wenn, he was not someone who trained the best and the brightest to take their positions of power within the elite, and they treated him accordingly. It was doubtful that on their own they would have assembled to hear anything he had to say, but Tinker had insisted, and the encouragement of UWalk Wenn had brought both Dah Beel and Gun Sub Runn. The presence of the others had brought Viktor Van Vast. Of the four, only Tinker had any inkling of what it was all about.

Gun Sub Runn motioned them to Aireclines, but Aerowaffen preferred to stand. He did not seem the flamboyant, jovial bear they had often seen around their fountains entertaining the younger generation. He looked at them like equals, and they were not prepared for the tinge of disdain they saw in his eyes. Nor were they prepared for the candor of his speech.

"All of you took what you have from Corporation. You took the Risk," he said. "You were young then. Now you are not." What he said was true, but the tone of it disconcerted them. It implied that they had lost something along the way. "Now you hope time will carry Old Spence away, leaving room for your sons and daughters. You think death will give his empire to your children, because Old Spence has none." He shook his head. "Do you think Spencer LeGrange has forgotten his defeats at your hands? Do you think he doesn't know to the grain what you've cost him and what the interest on it comes to?"

Viktor Van Vast gave a loud sigh of exasperation. "Are we here to be amused with stories, Panda?"

Aerowaffen liked the father almost as little as the son.

"Does it amuse you that Old Spence plans the ruin of your heirs?"

Van Vast looked skeptical. "How?"

"With pleasure."

Van Vast laughed aloud. "Certainly. But what with?"

Aerowaffen reached into the neckband of his formalsuit and held up a finger toward the Old Spec. There was a white dot on its tip. "With this."

Van Vast gave him a look of amused contempt. "With your finger?"

"With the Universal Tickler." Everyone but UWalk Wenn and Tinker burst out laughing.

Van Vast's laughter stopped first. "Do you take us for Fools?" Aerowaffen closed the gap between them in two strides and pressed the dot into the middle of Van Vast's forehead. It was so outrageous a move no one even attempted to stop him. He pulled it back again in a second, but Viktor Van Vast's eyes were already glazed. He turned to the others. "This is one of dozens already built by Corporation for the sole purpose of addicting the Pleasure Crew. How long do you think they'll run the League with the only source of their addiction in the hands of Corporation?"

He looked back to Van Vast for an answer, but the old man seemed lost in a dreamy fog. "No Fool like an old Fool," he thought. He looked at the others. The great ball of light was dotted with worried faces.

Gun Sub Runn spoke softly; his voice was unconcerned in the way only a man with a great many heirs could be. "And how do you propose to stop this? Young people will always pursue their pleasure."

"Have I ever said they shouldn't?" he asked. "The question is whether they'll pursue it into the hands of Spencer LeGrange, whether they'll become the slaves of Corporation, or free citizens of the Grand Sphere."

The Rickshaw King leaned forward with interest. He seemed already to have an inkling of Aerowaffen's solution. "So," he said, "the Great Rickshaw is rolling again as it did when I was young." Aerowaffen nodded. Gun Sub Runn gave him a wistful look. "A beautiful dream," he said. "But still a dream."

Aerowaffen shook his head. "It will not be stopped this time. You have only two choices. Ride it, or be run down by it."

The Rickshaw King smiled. "And how will it run us down?"

"Through the Little Door." There was no doubt of the importance of the Little Door. In the relatively short time Granders had controlled the Little Door, it had become an integral part of the Sphere's economy. The loss of it would destroy more fortunes than one, and Gun Sub Runn's would be one of them. What he made trafficking in contraband through the door was almost as much as he made from the Earthside royalties on his rickshaws. The loss of it would mean economic ruin.

"I've seen this rickshaw run before," the Rickshaw King said. "It never makes the top of Iron Mountain."

Aerowaffen did not argue the point. "Will the Fist wait until it does to retake the door?" Gun Sub Runn pondered the point for a moment. He could see what Aerowaffen was saying. Whether the Revolution failed or not, the Fist would use the fighting as an excuse to retake the door. "And when they take it, will they ever give it back?"

Gun Sub Runn smiled. "It will not be easily taken," he said, "by either side."

Aerowaffen shook his head in exasperation. "And who do you think holds it now?"

The Rickshaw King's answer was quick. "My second son."

Aerowaffen nodded. "And the caners of UWalk Wenn."

Gun Sub Runn conceded the point. "Then the Fist will never take it."

Aerowaffen shook his head sadly. He reached under his arm and pulled the package free. He unsealed one end like a pouch. "They will with this." He drew the gun, turned, and fired. It sounded like the end of the world. A sheet of red glass fifty feet in the air burst into fragments that showered down onto the floor.

The group recoiled in horror. The gun was not as big as the guns that had started the last insurrection, but it was big enough. No one in the hall looked at it without fear and loathing. Eliot Dah Beel sat upright on his Airecline as Aerowaffen held it up. His face was white with rage. "Where did you get that?!" he shouted.

"From CORPQ Annex. And there are fifty more still there waiting to be used." He let the magnitude of Spencer LeGrange's betrayal sink in before he added, "And there are a hundred in CORPQ itself." He looked directly at Gun Sub Runn. "A dozen of these will be at the Little Door ten minutes after the fighting starts." He did not need to point out that Yung Gun Runn and the others would not surrender the door no matter what the opposition. He let the implications sink in for a moment before he added, "Unless you take the Annex."

All eyes turned to Gun Sub Runn, but even with a favorite son in the balance, he could not be rushed. He considered whether or not it could be done and decided it could. He certainly had the military strength to do it. Half the population of his mountain had been trained by Wenn or one of his best graduates. And they would have almost unchallenged passage along the road that linked the Halls of the Rickshaw King to the Annex. At least fifty of his people had clearance to penetrate almost every part of the compound's security, and they could disable enough of it to allow the rest of his force to enter. Once the guns had been taken, most of the rest of his forces could be moved up to the top of Iron Mountain to stop reinforcements coming uphill from CORPQ.

There was only one problem. The force from Fist headquarters would be armed. Even fighting uphill against overwhelming odds, they would eventually take the ridge and from there retake the Annex. He looked to Aerowaffen for a solution. "What about the guns at CORPQ?"

His answer came from Tinker Manwalker. "Leave them to us."

Gun Sub Runn raised an eyebrow. "But how will you get inside?"

Tinker smiled. "We've been inside for twenty years."

Runn hesitated. Even in his youth his risks had been calculated, if not always prudent. Snap judgments disturbed him. There were still so many things to be considered. Even if the whole of the Sphere could be taken, there was no guarantee that it could be held. Still, it would be a better negotiating position than living in a Sphere where firearms were commonplace and all in the hands of the Fist.

He was still trying to decide when Dah Beel came storming forward. "I can get men inside the Annex if you won't," he said. He turned to Aerowaffen. "I'll take them myself. Where are the guns?"

The Rickshaw King shook his head at Dah Beel's impatience. "We'll both go," he said.

Aerowaffen smiled. "Good, then maybe you'll both come back." He held the gun out to Dah Beel. "You may need it."

Dah Beel shook his head. "When do we go?"

"Immediately. Once you're inside, signal Tinker and she'll tell you when to begin the attack."

Dah Beel raised an eyebrow and looked at the Rickshaw King. Gun Sub Runn nodded. "Done," they said in unison.

Chapter Twelve

The downslope out of Gun Sub Runn's mountain had given them adequate momentum, and the rickshaw cruised down the Lower Narrow and out onto the Crossway. They turned right toward the bridge and on the far side of it they turned left onto the Wideway. But before they started over the second bridge, Aerowaffen motioned for Wenn to pull over. When he did, Aerowaffen jumped down and walked over to one of the booths. He took the package of cloth from under his arm and handed it to a man. It disappeared under the counter immediately.

Aerowaffen climbed back up onto the longseat and smiled. "No more need for noise," he said. Wenn looked at him as if he had expected the Count to take the gun out again and fire it for the Pleasure Crew. Aerowaffen answered the unasked question. "*Need*'s a better weapon," he said.

Wenn shrugged. "Or belief," he said.

It was far truer than Wenn imagined, and when Aerowaffen smiled, he looked exactly like Push. He seemed a man with a knowledge that made everything ironic, someone playing a grand joke on people who would thank him for it eventually. It was what the Pleasure Crew paid him for, what he was good at—being the puppeteer, manipulating all the seeming catastrophes, the sudden dangers and miraculous escapes, being the only man in the entertainment who knows what's real and what's illusion. It seemed to be what he was born for.

It struck Wenn suddenly where he had seen that look before, and the realization made him laugh. It was the smile of the Skyshockers, the traveling lunatic saints who performed the news and other entertainments all over the League, and it was the inevitable result of their belief that everything, ultimately, was an illusion. Aerowaffen's breathing trick should have told him; only Catchers could do it, and the Skyshockers were all from Catchcage.

It all fell into place. Push was from Catchcage. The Revolution was from Catchcage. Who else but the Skyshockers could have organized and played a game for twenty years for one grand finale of a night. Who else but the Skyshockers, always in costume, always in disguise, would have created a Revolution that depended so much on nobody being what they seemed. Who but such game lovers could have thought of infiltrating the Corporation from top to bottom; who else would be crazy enough to try it and charismatic enough to carry it off?

Aerowaffen's bit of drama at the Rickshaw King's had had the mark of the Skyshockers all over it. Wenn had never asked who was behind it all; it was enough for him that people he knew and respected had devoted their lives to the Revolution, enough that he believed in its necessity. He had always been content with following the rightness of the motion; who played the music for it mattered little. Life was a rickshaw, and the dancing had taught him that when the motion was right, it was its own reward. It was all he knew or needed to know.

He had thought very little about who ultimately ran the Revolution, and it did not matter greatly to him that for the first time he was sure who it was. The realization was nothing more than a cause for delighted laughter. It was a wonderful joke; the most important event in the history of the League, probably the most important event in the history of the Corporation, something that would change forever the lives of eleven million people in the League and four billion more Earthside, and it was all being planned, organized, and carried out by crazy people.

There was no doubt that the Skyshockers were crazy, by anybody's definition. To the inhabitants of the League, they were lovably lunatic; to Corporation and Fools, they were amusing or pathetic, but to everyone, they were certifiably crazy. And for good reason. All of the Skyshockers had earned their madness at an early age. It was the way of coming of age in Catchcage.

Once a year all the co-parents and tri-parents went off to a public meeting, and the kids went up to the Catchway where the kidneycars came in. The kidneycars were big, kidney-shaped ore pods the gravitational accelerator on the moon lobbed moonrock up to Catchcage in for smelting and processing. Every year at least one of the kids whose brothers and sisters helped them climb into those airtight pods for a trip around the Circuit failed to come back. And yet almost everybody in Catchcage risked it.

How they came through it determined what they would become for the rest of their lives. Scrambling out of those ore shells on the moon, inches ahead of the rotary blades that scoured the returning pods free of debris, gave all Catchers an aura of power that never left them, no matter what they became afterward. Some never got out of the ore pods in time, and others, that accident or foolishness brought too close to the blades or deprived of air long enough, became Skyshocked.

They had a special place in the League. People said they had been "handled by God," and everywhere they went they were treated with a special kind of tenderness and respect. The worst of them were looked up to as oracles of a sort, and people believed that their random babblings contained infallible predictions about the future. And when their craziness took a creative form, as it almost always did, they were the best form of entertainment in the League. Small bands of Skyshockers traveled everywhere from Henson's Tube to the Grand Sphere, providing entertainment the way people wanted it, without the censorship of the LeGrange Amusement and News Network. They were a kind of living gossip column acting out the news and foretelling the future.

It delighted Wenn that their predictions were self-fulfilling prophecies, that they *made* the future they pretended to predict, and it made him laugh to think that some people had insisted that the Skyshockers were the eyes and ears of the LeGrange Police. The laughter rolled out of him, and he fed it into the flywheel. Aerowaffen cocked his head and waited to be told the joke, but Wenn had no intention of telling him. There was a moment when his laughter slowed enough for him to speak, but he didn't. It was Aerowaffen's turn to laugh without knowing why, and the thought of it made him laugh even harder.

Aerowaffen gave up waiting for an explanation. He had his own reasons for laughter—the exhilaration of the night, his own secret knowledge, and the Skyshocker certainty that everything was all a wonderful joke that would come out right in the end. Their laughter weighted the wheel like downmountain momentum, and the rickshaw roared up the Wideway.

They were still laughing when the rickshaw flew into the turn for Van Vast's Lower Narrow, and they were almost on top of the roadblock before they saw it. It took a couple of quick lunges from side to side to keep the rickshaw from crashing into it, and they were lucky to keep it from tipping over as it bounced off the roadway and up the curved bank alongside it.

They were less lucky about where it came to rest. There was a sudden gully just above the top of the bank, and the left wheel of the rickshaw sank into it up to the hub. They struggled to milk enough momentum back out of the flywheel to free it, but they had used up everything they had as counterfriction to bring the rickshaw to a stop. Finally, there was nothing to do but get out and lift the wheel out of its rut. But it was wedged in tight between two rocks, and even with Aerowaffen's enormous strength, the job took almost half an hour. They were well behind Aerowaffen's timetable before they were out on the Wideway again.

A sign on the roadblock directed them to the Upper Narrow, but it gave no explanation. Halfway up the second narrow they understood why. Just ahead of them, Vor Van Vast stood in front of a makeshift barricade with half a dozen Obees dressed in the livery of the Van Vasts.

The ground on either side was level enough, and it would have been easy for Wenn to go around them. But a look from Aerowaffen told him to stop, and he went down between the forks. He stopped the rickshaw just short of them, and three of the Obees stepped forward.

One tried to take hold of the left fork, but Wenn let him reach and then dropped the points to the ground, making the Obee miss his handhold and stumble forward over the fork. Wenn let the points spring back up to level, and the bar of the forks caught the Obee in the ribs. It made him look like a Fool, and he lunged at Wenn across the near fork with his cane.

Wenn stepped aside and let it pass him to full extension, then he caught the wrist from above and ducked under the fork with it. He stood up again immediately on the other side of the fork and instead of pulling the Obee completely over it, he simply levered the back of the man's elbow against the fork until he dropped the cane. It clattered to the ground, and Wenn looked at Aerowaffen with a sigh that seemed to say that Obees would never learn the futility of attacking.

He bent to retrieve the cane without letting go of the wrist. The Obee went up on his toes to take the pressure off his elbow, but he was in no position to struggle. Another Obee would already have given it the quick snap that would have left it bending the wrong way, but Wenn seemed content merely to disarm and immobilize him, and the Obee seemed content to let things as they stood. The others who had stepped forward to secure the rickshaw were not.

The first came at Wenn from behind as he bent over, intending to club him with his cane, but Wenn merely swept the fallen cane up and back without looking and caught him coming in. The points stuck him in the armpit of the upraised arm, and the force of the charge knocked him flying over backward, as if he had been hit by a moving rickshaw.

The cane was apparently set on one of the highest levels, and Wenn looked as if he found that equally foolish. The third Obee had been outside the right-hand fork and started to duck under it, but as he did, Aerowaffen leaned sharply forward and the fork came down on the man's head like a long-handled club. It released the pressure on the first Obee's elbow, but Wenn dropped to a squat, yanking the arm down with him. When the forks sprang back up again, they hit him under the armpit and Wenn gave a sharp tug on the wrist, pulling the Obee completely over it and tossing him flat on his back next to the one Aerowaffen had just knocked facedown.

The Obee was about to come up off his back when Wenn stuck the points of the cane in his face and convinced him to lie still. Three others started to come forward, but Vor put out his hand and held them back. Aerowaffen looked as if he had been served only half a dessert. "A short pleasure," he said. He meant both brief and impotent, and Vor knew it, but it did not seem to enrage him.

"Better than a long pain," he said. He seemed surprisingly pleased with the situation.

Aerowaffen taunted him again. "Better not to promise than not deliver." He expected Vor to draw his cane and make good the threat, but Vor only laughed.

He walked toward the rickshaw until he stood hardly a yard from Aerowaffen, but he made no attempt to draw his cane. "Then let me deliver," he said. Aerowaffen waited for a lunge, but none came. "A message." He had a smug look on his face, as if he had an attack Aerowaffen could not hope to counter. "From Eleganza."

Aerowaffen waited for the message, but Vor only

extended a finger toward him. On the tip of it was a blue dot. He took a half step closer so Aerowaffen could not miss it, but the Count already knew what it was and what it meant. Eleganza had found her own source of DeeBee. Vor reached up and pressed the dot off onto the edge of the longseat. "Take it," he said. "She has pounds of them." He watched Aerowaffen's face with immense satisfaction. There was no question that Vor was not exaggerating, and there was only one place Eleganza could have gotten Corporation DeeBee in that quantity and only one piece of information she could have gotten it with.

Aerowaffen made no attempt to hide its impact. There was nothing in the news that was not disastrous. The least important was that she had confirmed the existence of the Universal Tickler to Spencer LeGrange. The next least that she had betrayed Aerowaffen to him. Except for what it meant on a personal level, the betrayal did not matter; if Pock had not acted on her information yet, he would never get the chance to. But on a personal level, it mattered more than Aerowaffen cared to admit. He did not permit himself to think about what access to that much DeeBee would do to Eleganza.

Vor turned and walked away. He delivered the last blow over his shoulder. "You're not to come back," he said, "until you've learned to appreciate her properly." There was no doubt it was a quote from Eleganza herself.

It only underlined what Aerowaffen already knew. There would be no opportunity to rouse the Pleasure Crew to the defense of the Orchard Notch. There was nothing left he could lure them up the hill with, and no opportunity even to make it a game they could not resist. Vor motioned to the remaining Obees to help the others up. The fight was over, and there was no further use for the canes. The Obee scowled at Wenn, but the rickshaw dancer only handed him his cane and ducked back between the forks. There was nothing left to do but turn the rickshaw around and go.

Chapter Thirteen

Pock stood before the forty-foot hologram of Stefan Standard without the intimidation he always felt standing before the head of Spencer LeGrange. He had no doubt that Standard had chosen to communicate with him on the big holo only to impress him. It was a futile gesture. He was an expert on that kind of intimidation himself, and except with Old Spence, it had no effect on him. The enlargement of Old Spence seemed an even truer representation of his power; with Standard, it seemed only to enlarge his defects.

The strain lines in Standard's face seemed like scars. He looked like a man who needed something very badly and was forcing himself to hold together until he got it. Pock did not have to guess what it was. Spencer LeGrange was obviously withholding the DeeBee Standard had become addicted to. Whatever reasons he had had for indulging his Exec, they apparently no longer suited his purpose. It put a sharp edge of irritation in Standard's voice that had nothing to do with what he had to say. "A shipment is coming to you on today's shuttle," he said. "You're to unload it yourself and bring it directly to your office."

Pock restrained his anger at being treated like a common laborer. "What kind of shipment?"

"Three cases," was all that Standard offered.

"Cases of what?"

Standard looked as if he believed they were being overheard. "You'll see when you get them," he said. Pock frowned. "And do not, *under any circumstances,* mention them in any communication with Earthside."

Pock was indignant. "Are you telling me you think *my* communication is compromised?" It was nothing less than an accusation of incompetence. He waited for Standard to explain it; when he didn't, Pock reversed the accusation. "Or yours?"

Standard answered neither question. "You are *not* to mention them in any communication with Earthside."

"Is this more of your paranoia, Standard?" he sneered. "Don't tell me now the rebels have invented the Perfect Ear."

Standard's voice was arrogantly cold. "Spencer Le-Grange is aware of your failure to take this matter seriously," he said. "I would think you'd learned from your last visit to take orders."

Pock shuffled uncomfortably. It was possible that Old Spence was monitoring everything they said. It was a precarious position. If Old Spence was behind Standard's orders, it would be dangerous to question them, but Standard was not above using powers he did not really have. To take Standard at face value put Pock in real jeopardy. A false order could make him do something he would never do on his own, and once the blunder was made, it would be almost impossible to justify it to Old Spence.

And there would be no tape to back him up. Standard was sending everything code & scramble on the silent priority. It was almost as inviolate as the things said in private with Spencer LeGrange. The code always made Pock uncomfortable; it was for giving orders that could be later denied, and Old Spence used it often. The best he could hope to prove was that Standard had used the code to send an unauthorized message. But there was no way to be sure Old Spence hadn't authorized the communication. It was even possible that Standard had authorization to use the coding but was filling it in with disinformation that he knew would never be recorded. If Pock recorded it, he would leave himself open to accusations of treason.

The safest thing to do was to make the conversation as short as possible. "They'll be unloaded," he said. He waited for Standard to add something else; he was not disappointed.

"We're beginning to wonder about your loyalty, Pock." He made it sound as if he and Old Spence talked of nothing else. "Unless it's just that you're losing control up there." Either accusation would be equally fatal if true. But what bothered him most was that Standard would even make the accusation. It did not make sense. If there were serious questions about his loyalty, they certainly would not warn him about their suspicions. And Standard would be the last person to warn him for his own good. He wondered if it was Standard's way of making sure he did not question anything about the shipment. He had a cold dread of what the cases would contain.

Whatever it was, he would not have long to wait; the shuttle was almost due. Undoubtedly, Standard had timed his call precisely for that reason. He could feel the gold fist tightening in his forehead.

"You'll be given directions for the use of what's in the cases at a later date." He did not wait for Pock's response. The huge figure simply disappeared.

There was nothing more to do but get the cases. He left the hexagonal building that housed the Fist and walked across to the Great Well of the Big Door. He passed the curved pool and made his way between the cluster of fountains and circular pools where the Execs from CORPQ Main and their families spent their leisure hours and went down into the circular opening. Although the Big Door was actually farther up the wall of the Sphere than the Hexagon, he seemed to be going down into a dark hole. It felt like going down into a grave.

He saw the trap the moment he stepped into the shuttle. The cases were larger than he expected, more like boxes with handles, and they were specially sealed. They were surprisingly heavy, and it was a long walk back to Hexagon and his office. If he carried them himself, he would have to take them one at a time and to do that, he would have to leave two of them behind him unguarded. If he used his own men to carry them, Standard would claim he had exposed them to tampering, or at least compromised their presence.

The solution came to him more easily than he expected. He simply ordered the officers who brought them to carry two cases while he carried the third. If they were trustworthy enough for Corporation to send the cases up with, they were trustworthy enough to carry them to the Hexagon. The officers obeyed without question, and after a long, silent walk the cases were deposited safely in Pock's office. Only then did he thumbprint the voucher the Silver presented to him. He did not open the cases until they were gone. When he did, he groaned. The cases were filled with handguns.

The holopad in his office glowed, and a life-size figure of Standard suddenly appeared before him. He spoke without preliminary. "Have you secured the shipment?"

Pock felt as if the fist had the whole of his head in its tightening grip. The cases were filled with his potential destruction. He could not believe that Old Spence had authorized their shipment, and yet he doubted that even Standard would take such an action on his own. "They're here," he said. "All three."

"Good. Don't let them out of your sight for a second."

Pock raised an eyebrow. "You expect me to stay with them day and night?"

Standard acted as if it was nothing unusual. "Until this is over, yes."

Pock was incredulous. "I have work here!"

Standard shrugged. "You don't seem to be doing it very well or you'd know how long you can expect to guard them."

"What are you talking about?!" Pock's voice rattled with fear and rage. Information was being kept from him, crucial information he could not find out on his own. It gave him a feeling of helplessness. He knew the danger of not knowing enough. The cases made him aware of the danger of knowing too much.

Standard shook his head at Pock's ineptitude. "You don't seem to know very much about your situation for someone in the middle of it." His voice was full of mockery.

"How long?" Pock demanded.

"Until they're used." The figure disappeared.

The mere presence of guns in the Sphere was a terrible mistake. If they were discovered, it would be bad enough, but the thought of using them was insane. He had seen what had happened the last time guns were brought to the Sphere, and he had no desire to be the third commander to perish because of them. And yet the only way he could communicate with Old Spence directly was through the larger holo chamber, which meant leaving the guns alone. He carried them one by one into the chamber next to his and set the controls for Silent Norecord. Standard appeared in gigantic arrogance before him.

"I want to talk to Spencer LeGrange," he demanded.

Standard shook his head. "This continual refusal to carry out your orders is being noted, Pock."

Pock was adamant. "You worry about your own orders, I'll worry about mine. Now put me through." He looked as if he were about to grab the figure by the throat and snap its head off, but Standard was a long way beyond arm's reach and he knew it.

"You know your orders. There's to be no communication about this matter."

"I have only your word for that."

"It's all you'll get."

"It's not all you'll get if you don't get me Old Spence."

Standard was unperturbed. "Don't think that threat will go unreported," he warned.

"I'll give you another threat. If you don't get these guns out of here on the next shuttle, I'll ..."

He did not get to complete his threat. Standard disappeared and in his place was the gigantic face of Spencer LeGrange. It was livid. "You Fool! You were told not to communicate about that shipment. Do you think I give orders to have them ignored by the likes of you?!" The voice boomed out over him like gunshots. Old Spence did not wait for an answer to his question. "When Executive Standard gives you an order, *I* give you an order. Do you think he'd take an action like this on his own?"

Pock weighed an answer and decided he had nothing left to lose. "Yessir."

Old Spence's voice was incredulous. "What in the world would make you think a thing like that? Have you gone native up there?!" It was the old accusation; Nohfro Pock was a Grander at heart, he'd been away from Earth too long, too many years in the Sphere had warped his mind, he thought like a Grander instead of an Exec. The same distrust he had met as an undercover Blue. All the old innuendos, the slights, the suggestions that he was less than loyal because he thought of everything in terms of the Grand Sphere had kept him from being rotated to a better position Earthside time after time. Finally it was out in the open. The only reason he was still there at all was because he could do the job better than anybody else, and Old Spence knew it.

He felt like yelling, but he kept the rage out of his voice. The sending of guns to the Sphere was stupid beyond belief as far as he was concerned, and he was sure Spencer LeGrange would not have done it without Standard's provocation. Undoubtedly, when they were still under the influence of Eleganza's visit, Standard had put the idea in his head and had fed it continually since.

"They're the only thing that could unify the League," he said. He was careful not to mention the guns directly. If he made his point strongly enough, there was a chance he would survive the confrontation, but there was no sense in giving Spencer LeGrange an excuse not to listen. "You don't have to be a Grander to know what those cases are going to cause here!"

"They won't *cause* anything; they'll stop it."

"Sir, you know what happened the last two times—"

"I don't need anybody to give me a history lesson. Corporation is not going to be intimidated. *I* am not going to be intimidated. It's time the League learned who owns those habitats!"

Pock could see that the argument was lost, but he tried anyway. "Sir, if we show those weapons—"

The old man's voice thundered over him again. "I don't want them *shown*, you idiot! I want them *used*!"

"But—"

"There *are* no buts. I didn't build those habitats to turn them over to a bunch of misfits! Corporation owns them. *I* own them! I'll blow the damned things out of the sky before I'll let that riffraff have them. There's going to be an end to this opposition to Corporation once and for all." The face seemed to lean menacingly toward him. "And if you can't do it, say so, and I'll get somebody who *can*!" The huge face waited a moment for an answer and then disappeared.

Pock was too stunned to answer. The guns were the ultimate intimidation; he couldn't imagine what could have made Old Spence mad enough to use them. Something must have happened that Pock did not know about, and he had a terrible suspicion that if he didn't find out what is was soon, it was going to be the end of him. There was one man in the Fist who might know.

Chapter Fourteen

It was several hours before Pock could make contact and more than an hour more before two Blues came through the cloud of his wall and half shoved, half threw their prisoner toward him. The young man jerked his shoulder as if to free it from the grip that no longer held him and straightened. He was dressed in Low Style, a ragged-looking skinsuit under a set of vagues, the legs of which were ragged and frayed at their hand-cut ends, a shirt of vague, the shifting color of the cheapest kind of duracloth, a larger than necessary cape, and a ridiculously large hat decorated with odds and ends and a long green feather. He was tolerably well dressed for a Skyshocker.

He looked back over his shoulder at the Blues and gave them an impish grin, as if they were his prisoners and didn't know it yet. Other than the perfect blue of his eyes, the smile was his most striking feature and it infuriated the guards, but they did not move to hit him as they would have if he had given them the same look on the other side of Pock's wall. They were entitled to rough him up on the way in, but once they passed into Pock's presence, any abuse was entirely up to him and required an order, unless he did it himself. They looked as if they hoped he would leave the interrogation's persuasive points up to them, but Pock merely raised a fist of dismissal. The Blues returned the salute and left.

The Skyshocker turned and mimicked them as they went out; they ignored it. When the wall had clouded closed behind them, he turned to Pock and came to attention. Pock glared at the hat, and the Skyshocker swept it off, revealing a tuft of bright orange hair. Pock grimaced at the hair. It was necessary for undercover agents to look authentic, and no one would expect hair like that to belong to a member of the Fist, but it annoyed him without his being sure why.

It was no wonder the Fist did not trust its own once they crossed over the line into disguise. Still, he had as much trust for the Bronze before him as he had for anyone in the Sphere, probably more. He felt a sympathy for him. He had been undercover himself for a year when he first came Up, and he knew the isolation that came with it. He knew how it dogged a man's career as well; the better a member of the Fist was at it, the more he was distrusted, and the Bronze before him was *very* good at it.

The Skyshocker came to attention. "Bronze P. C. Softer reporting, *sir*." It was rigidly correct procedure, and yet it always seemed to Pock to carry just the slightest edge of mockery. Even at attention the mysterious Skyshocker smile never seemed to leave the young man's face. It wasn't safe to trust a man who could never get completely out of character, and yet he knew himself that it was what made an undercover good. He was aware that a good deal of the Obee he had posed as when he first came Up still remained in his own personality, and he recognized the same fanatical identification with the disguise in his best Ear.

The rigorous attention to protocol reminded him of his own early attempts to overcome the distrust that went with being an Ear. It was always doomed to failure. Even Softer's fist of salute—palm-butt forward, the knuckles perfectly aligned with the shoulder—seemed about to be slammed down on the other palm in the classic Grander obscenity. He thought of how he must have looked to his own superiors at that age, the desperate attempt to seem proper and professional whenever there was a chance to get out of character. He could see why none of them had completely trusted him either. The memory of those days never failed to make him uneasy, and he knew it made him vulnerable to placing too much confidence in Softer.

He was more comfortable when Softer was completely the Skyshocker. "Rest it," he said. "I have enough starch-asses around me." Softer slipped back into character, and Pock nodded him to an Airecline. "Take an air."

The young Bronze threw himself on the Airecline as if he were going off duty. Pock winced. It was a typical Skyshocker gesture, flinging himself where the invisible column of air should be and trusting that it would take his weight. A Fist would have touched the surface subtly with his fingers to make sure the air was on, or put just the tip of his boot over the outline on the carpet to make sure. But a Skyshocker would simply have flung himself down, as Softer did, trusting that invisibility was no bar to reality, and that every illusion is real after all and everything real simply an illusion.

Pock came directly to the point. "What's going Earthside?"

Softer shook his head. "Old Spence's biting everything that moves."

It confirmed what Pock suspected. "Why?"

Softer shrugged. "Tends to piss him off when people try to kill him."

Pock raised an eyebrow. "Who?"

"His Perscom." There were people closer to Spencer LeGrange than his personal communications engineer, but few had easier access to him. The great forty-foot head did not materialize in CORPQ of itself; every aspect of it was carefully manipulated by a team of engineers. Each of them handled only a part of the transmission to make sure they didn't overhear it, but someone was required to put it all together, and the Perscom was it. He may not have had much authority, but in some ways his clearance was as high as Pock's. It explained both Old Spence's outrage and his paranoia about communications.

Softer shook his head as if marveling at the audacity. "Right in his office," he said. "Bullet even grazed his head." He drew his finger along his left temple. Pock remembered seeing a faint reddish line on the holo, but he had been too stunned to really notice it. It made him glad he wasn't Chief of Security Earthside. It explained why the old man had sent the guns and why he intended to use them. He gave a small sigh of relief. Old Spence must have been on the holo only hours after the attempt; there was a good chance he would calm down the longer things went on.

The very fact that he had left Pock in charge instead of immediately relieving him of command showed that, mad as he was, Old Spence was not totally out of control. Pock had no illusions; the old man would certainly not forget what had happened, but his position was relatively safe for the moment. When the crisis was over, he would have to deal with a crisis of his own, but Old Spence was not likely to turn his command over to some Fool fresh Up from Earthside while he thought a revolution was imminent. Whatever Pock's flaws, he knew the Sphere, and even if Standard was right that he was slipping, he would still be better able to handle things than someone fresh into the command. Old Spence might have replaced him with his Silver, Ah Bir, but even Standard would have to admit Bir did not have Pock's ability.

Softer glanced at the cases but said nothing. Pock turned his attention away with a question. "What's turning in the Sphere?"

Softer shook his head. "Earthside's right."

Pock scowled. "Full-scale insurrection?" He still found it hard to believe.

Softer laughed. "The Great Rickshaw," he said. "Starting in Hardcore."

Pock knew the date without asking. Standard had hinted at it; he was right that Pock should have guessed. "Dah

Beel's Day?" he said. It was hardly a question, but Softer nodded affirmation. The annual celebration of the death of Elgin Dah Beel, killed by the stray bullet of a raw recruit just up from Earthside. The symbolism of it was perfect. It was as close to an Independence Day as the League had because it marked the final removal of firearms from the Sphere. If the League had a day when its consciousness turned to independence, it was Dah Beel's Day. "And here?" he asked.

"Next day, if Hardcore falls. The Sphere isn't going to jump into it until it tests the Ring." Pock agreed. Granders weren't going to place their bet until they saw how things were flowing, whatever sympathy they might have for Hardcore. Still, if Hardcore was even holding its own twenty-four hours after the fighting started, the Sphere was more likely to accept the odds and join it than any place else in the League. It left him three days to stop it. He had a good idea where to begin. If Old Spence's Perscom had been corrupted, it gave a lot more credence to the idea that there was a Universal Tickler.

"Have you found the Tickler yet?"

Softer shook his head. "But I've found Aerowaffen."

Pock nodded. "With Wenn," he said. The Bronze confirmed it with a nod. He seemed a little disappointed that the information was not new. Pock weighed his options. If he waited, Aerowaffen might lead them to the Tickler. On the other hand, he might disappear on Dah Beel's Day and come back to haunt them. Whatever was planned for the Grand Sphere, Aerowaffen had some significant part in it. The best thing to do was eliminate him as ordered. "I want him flashed," he said. "And Wenn as well. Quietly."

Softer rose from the Airecline. "A rickshaw accident would be good," he said. The Skyshocker's enigmatic smile had returned in full force, and for an instant Pock felt as if there might be another meaning to the words he wasn't getting, but the feeling passed. Still, he wondered how long it would be before the Bronze would be wearing the gold fist of League commander. He was glad the young man was not any nearer in line for it, but in a decade or so, he was going to be a real danger. He made a mental note to keep a stricter eye on him. Pock smiled. "And not a trace of the Fist," he said.

Softer put his hat back on with a flourish. The disconcerting smile persisted. He made a fist, then opened his hand. The fist vanished. It was exactly the kind of gesture a Skyshocker would have made.

Chapter Fifteen

The rickshaw rolled out of the High Narrow. The upper part of the Wideway was relatively empty, and they crossed it easily. The downhill slope from Van Vast's had given them ample momentum, and it carried them quickly up the main narrow toward Tinker's Tor. As they went up the rise of its first plateau, Wenn let some of the momentum drain from the wheel in expectation of stopping, but Aerowaffen shifted and fed momentum back into it. "No time," he said.

Wenn moved out onto the forks to build the speed back up as quickly as possible. The sudden change of plans disturbed him, but he said nothing. He did not see what alternative there was to persuading the pleasurers of Tinker's Tor to replace Eleganza's crew at the Orchard Notch. Certainly it could not be left unguarded. With CORPQ Hill and the Little Door taken, it was the only route the Fist could use to move their forces through the Sphere.

Aerowaffen answered the question he did not ask. "They'd never make it through the mob on the Wideway in time." The answer made no sense. The Wideway was filling as it always did at that time of day, but the crowd was certainly not a barrier. Wenn looked over his shoulder for an explanation, but all he got was a Skyshocker smile. It was all the explanation he got out of Aerowaffen, even when he returned to the longseat.

When they neared the end of Tinker's Upper, Aerowaffen nodded toward the mountain. "Tinker's Notch," he said. The destination made no sense either. It was as far from the Little Door, CORPQ, and the Annex as they could get. The loops of the Downside Main might take them to the Off-shoots of CORPQ Hill unnoticed, but if they had no time to stop at Tinker's Tor, they certainly had no time for such a roundabout route to the most important fighting.

The rickshaw careened out of the Tinker's Upper and turned right onto the Crossway. The stored momentum carried them easily up the mountain, but Wenn saved as much as he could for the Downside Main. The downhill would help, but the sharp left at the bottom of the hill would waste a lot of it, and the way the Main hugged the irregular-ities of the mountain's bottom would use up a lot more. As they reached the crest, he waited for Aerowaffen to shift his weight forward and add to the downhill force, but Aerowaf-fen threw all his weight counter to the wheel.

The forks shot up into the air, and it took all of Wenn's skill to keep them from falling completely over backward. He brought the forks down level again, but the rickshaw stood motionless, facing into Downside. He raised an eye-brow at Aerowaffen "Are you crazy?" he said. It was a pointless question to ask a Skyshocker.

Aerowaffen's laugh boomed out over Downside. "Would I be here if I wasn't?"

Wenn was not mollified. "If that's the way you dance rickshaw, only dead men should ride with you."

The Count gave him that knowing smile. "Only dead men do," he said.

Wenn looked out over Downside and the words seemed all too true. The Wideway was filling rapidly, but there were no raging mobs. In forty-five minutes, even without rickshaws, Pock could have troops at the Little Door. He looked back into Upside, where the Wideway ran in a great blue arc overhead; it looked almost deserted compared with Down-side. There was nothing to keep Pock's troops from going the whole length of the Wideway and coming up on the Annex from behind when they couldn't take CORPQ Hill. They could even come along the Main or up the Crossway for all anybody in Downside seemed to care. There did not seem to be an angry person in the whole of the Sphere. Wenn looked at the peaceful bustle of Downside in despair. He had waited a long time to see it all come to nothing. He pointed toward the Wideway. "Where are the mobs?" he demanded.

Aerowaffen handed him three soft packets of Earthside plastic, each a little smaller than his palm. "They're in here," he said.

Wenn looked at the packets blankly. They bulged with a liquid of some sort, but he could not see into them through the pinkish covering. They were sticky on one side, and they seemed to have something hard inside them, a thin but tough card that bent slightly when he folded the ends of the packet toward each other.

Aerowaffen slapped at his fingers as if he were a child. "Don't play with them; put them on!" He had his own pleasuresuit open and had already pressed three of them in place across the dark mat of hair on his chest. He pressed them again and again with his palm, but each time they seemed to come loose and hang precariously on the ends of the hair. Finally he gave up and pressed the opening of his pleasuresuit together again. "The suit'll hold them," he said.

Wenn looked at him without comprehension, and Aer-owaffen gestured impatiently for him to open his shirt. "Hurry up," he said, as if Wenn were dawdling over some task he had performed dozens of times before. He reached over and unsealed the opening of Wenn's shirt. "Hurry up, I have my own to put on. Just press them against the skin." He pulled Wenn's shirt aside and slapped one on his upper right chest. "You're lucky you don't have a lot of hair," he said. He looked very pleased, as if he himself had arranged for Wenn's chest to be such a secure resting place for the packet.

"Now put one down your sleeve along your upper arm," he said. Wenn moved reluctantly, and Aerowaffen gave an exasperated sigh. "Don't stick them all on your chest either."

Wenn had no intention of putting any more on his chest, or anywhere else. Aerowaffen busied himself trying to stick a dark packet to the back of his head. He pulled his hair aside and tried to get it to stick to the skin at the base of his skull, but he had almost as little luck as he had had with his chest. He pressed it firmly with his fingers and then looked irritably at Wenn, as if he were responsible for the bad adhesion. Wenn reluctantly stuffed one down his sleeve and pressed it firmly into place over his biceps. The adhesive puckered his skin, and he reached down the sleeve to pull it out again, but Aerowaffen stopped him. "Is it falling off?"

Wenn shook his head. "No, but it's sticking my skin together."

"It's supposed to. Now leave it alone." Wenn stretched his arm uncomfortably, and Aerowaffen shook his head in exasperation. "You won't have to worry about it for long. Now put one on your thigh."

Wenn started to stick the third packet where he was told, but Aerowaffen's voice stopped him. "*Under* the cloth," he snapped. "*Under*." Wenn lifted the corner of his shorts and pushed the packet up under them. He pressed it down firmly and Aerowaffen nodded his approval. The Count took a very wide flesh-colored packet and pressed it firmly against his forehead. He rubbed his palm across it until he was sure it was in place and none of the edges were sticking up. "How does it look?" he said.

It was only barely noticeable, even from just across the longseat. Wenn shrugged. "Can you see it?" Aerowaffen demanded. Wenn shook his head. "All right," he said, "then we're ready." He pointed down the Crossway. "Straight across the bridges and on up the other side until you get to Outer Fields Upper." He pointed to the thin roadway almost all the way up the far curve of the hemisphere. Wenn's eyes followed it to the right until it reached the back entrance of the compound at the Little Door. He wondered how long his students and Yung Gun Runn would be able to hold out against the Fist. "Turn in there and stop," Aerowaffen said.

He looked at Wenn steadily for a moment. "You *must* get us there," he said, "no matter what happens. This rickshaw must arrive there with both of us in it. It mustn't stop." He looked out toward the Little Door and then back at Wenn. "Everything depends on that. *Everything*!"

He paused and looked over Downside again as if it were the last time he would ever see it. The Downside Window seemed to blaze with a supernatural light. "Slow it down just a little before the second bridge," he said, "then kick it all out of the wheel. You'll know when."

He offered Wenn his hand, as if they were about to part. "You've got to die to come alive," he said. "Let's weight the wheel." They shifted together and the rickshaw dropped over the edge of the ridge and began to gain momentum down the Crossway. About a third of the way down, Aerowaffen stopped breathing again. Wenn knew it was just the Catcher relaxation technique, but Aerowaffen looked eerily lifeless, and Wenn felt a chill pass over him. But he turned away and worked the forks to increase the momentum.

He stored the rush of the downhill in the wheel and slowed the rickshaw as they approached the first bridge. Aerowaffen's chest started to move again, and Wenn felt a wave of relief without knowing why. The crowd was thick on the bridge, but the rickshaw lane was open, and he fed a little of the momentum back into the rickshaw. The crowd whirled by on either side, a rush of color and sensation. Aerowaffen took a deep breath, as if he were trying to drink it all in, every color, every sensation.

A few of the Pleasure Crew waved to him as they entered the crossroads at the center of the window. The crowd was thickest there, and a half dozen Granders who knew Aerowaffen by sight called to him or waved as the rickshaw rolled by. The rickshaw lane was empty, and Wenn let the momentum take them. The rickshaw jumped ahead, the colorful flash of pleasuresuits and formalsuits mingled with the drab biocloth of Fools Up from Earthside. He caught sight of the Blue at the last instant, and he did not see the gun at all until the Blue raised it.

He knew it was too late even as he did it, but he tried to raise the forks to throw them out of the line of fire. Everything seemed to stop. The forks began to rise with incredible slowness. The gun swung the last few degrees up into position. There was a flash from the barrel and he felt the rickshaw jerk backward with the impact of Aerowaffen's bulk. He turned his head to look, and there was a giant red hole in the middle of Aerowaffen's forehead. There was a little spurt of blood from it and then another before the muffled roar of the shot rolled over them.

The rickshaw moved closer to the Blue as if inch by inch. The second shot flashed from the muzzle, and Wenn saw a splash of blood from Aerowaffen's chest. The dark red stain spread until it was bigger than his hand, and still the firing went on. The forks were rising, but Aerowaffen's weight seemed to suddenly settle, and they came back down again before Wenn could stop them. He could not tear his eyes from the wound in Aerowaffen's forehead. Blood poured out of it, covering Aerowaffen's face. The Count's head lolled back and his mouth was open. His eyes stared widely at the great curve of Upside above them, but it saw nothing. The shots came in flashes, one after another, low, muffled rumblings that seemed out of a bad dream.

Only slowly did he become aware of who was pulling the trigger. The orange flash of the barrel made the connection for him. The gunman's hair was black, but there was no mistaking the smile. It was Push.

The realization seemed to hit him in the chest, and he felt himself kicked back into the longseat. There was an amazing pain in his chest, and he looked down and saw the sticky redness bubbling through his shirt. A great bang jarred everything back into ordinary motion. The rickshaw pulled abreast of Push and he fired once more. The sound of the gun was like the Sphere being ripped apart. Wenn felt a stinging in his upper arm and the lower half seemed to spring violently toward his face. His fingers knotted, and he could not straighten the arm back out. It ached as if he had held it in an awkward position for a very long time.

Horrified faces looked and looked away as the rickshaw passed. There were great shrieks and cries on every side. He looked back over his shoulder and saw one final flash. The back of Aerowaffen's head seemed to burst open and the huge body fell forward, one arm dangling down over the shortseat. Blood poured down the back of the neck. Blood smeared along the back of the shortseat. He saw Push disappear untouched beneath a Skyshocker's cape.

Everywhere there were cries of outrage and despair. Somewhere before the end of the bridge, he heard Aerowaffen's name called and a chorus of denials and refusals to believe it had happened. A woman's wailing died away behind them, and he could hear men crying hot tears of rage and running madly toward the release of revenge. Even before the rickshaw cleared the second bridge, the crowd was already a mob. And by the time it passed the lower narrow, the news of the murder would have covered half of Downside. By the time they reached Outer Fields Upper, it would be all over the Sphere, and it would take every gun in CORPQ to move a contingent of the Fist through even a hundred yards of the Wideway.

He looked down at Aerowaffen. The body had slumped down behind the shortseat entirely, and there was only the red starburst at the back of the head for him to look at. His chest ached and burned, and he wanted to stop and look to Aerowaffen, but he knew his duty lay elsewhere. The momentum was almost gone from the wheel, and he had to shift against the dead weight of Aerowaffen's body. Every motion seemed to increase the pain in his arm and his thigh. Only the rickshaw song allowed him to move at all. He was surprised at how easily the words came out. When he sang, he could no longer feel the pain in his chest except for a vague stinging, and his breathing seemed to come easier with each word. The words rang out over Downside. "Hill he go, round he go, upside down." They fed all the remaining momentum into the wheel. "Rickshaw song he be Grander frown." The rickshaw shot forward.

Chapter Sixteen

Pock waited on the Airecline for word of the "accident." The steel cases were again stacked neatly near his desk, the wallway secured and guarded. He still had three days to wait, and no way of leaving his post, but it didn't matter. The office was comfortable enough, and it would not be the first time he had spent days on end without leaving it. Still, it was a useless task, something more fitting for a Blue than the Commander of the LeGrange Police on the Grand Sphere, and he resented it. The idea that someone could tamper with the shipment within the Hexagon was ludicrous, but Standard had Old Spence's ear, and there was nothing he could do about it at the moment except fume over the cleverness of the trap.

Standard had pinned him to his desk at a time when he ought to be in the field. Even if the uprising were minor, there would be things that required his presence if they were to go flawlessly. Without his direct supervision, there were bound to be slipups, the kind of mistakes Standard would be looking for to use against him with Old Spence. The battle for the Grand Sphere would come, if it came at all, in three days, but his own battle for the Sphere would not begin until the physical battle was over. For him, the real danger would come when things were safely under control again, and Spencer LeGrange could afford to think about replacing him. Simple victory would not be enough. Anything less than perfection was going to provide Standard with opportunities.

Still, his position was far from hopeless. There was no possibility that the revolution was going to succeed. He'd land a full half of the Fist in Hardcore the eve of Dah Beel's Day and squash the uprising the minute it began. It no longer worried him that Old Spence would order the guns used. By the time there was an opportunity for them, he was sure the Old Man would have cooled off sufficiently to see the foolishness of it, and although he would never admit it, he would probably recognize that Pock had been right. That alone would go a long way to countering the charges of incompetence and disloyalty Standard was sure to make.

If the rebellion were put down quickly and harshly enough with ordinary means, Old Spence might even turn on Standard for encouraging the use of the guns. The chances of that kind of success diminished with Pock not actually at the scene, and Standard was certain to check from time to time to see that the guns were still under his watchful eye. It would be foolhardy to give Standard the chance to accuse him of disobeying orders again. Short of an extreme emergency, he was stuck where he was until things started to happen.

The sudden alarm from the holopad in the center of the room brought him quickly upright on the Airecline. It was an emergency signal from inside the Sphere. He touched a command switch on his sleeve, but the three-dimensional image did not form. There was a swirling ball of light and a voice, but it was choked off with static. All he heard clearly was "Annex" and "attack" before the transmission faded altogether. He tapped another control on his sleeve and the Basecom's image appeared in the center of the holopad. He looked worried. "What was that?" Pock demanded.

"Message from the Annex. It's still going on, but I can't

get it on small wave. Something's interfering, probably the Ring." He continued to struggle with his instruments while he talked.

"Get me that message!"

"Sir, the only way I can get it is if they're sending Earthside as well; we could pick up from outside the Sphere without interference from the Ring."

"Don't talk about it, do it!" The Blue struggled with his equipment.

"I've got it, sir."

"Then send it in here!" He waited for the technician to disappear from the holopad and some other figure to take his place, but nothing happened.

"I can only bring it in on the large wave, sir, the big image."

Pock was already on his way to the wallway between his office and the large holopad. "Transmit," he shouted back over his shoulder. The wall unclouded and even before it closed again, the giant figure of Gun Sub Runn had begun to form. The words were clear even before the image. "The Annex is under attack. Can anybody hear me?"

Pock's voice was commanding. "What are you doing in the Annex?"

The figure went on as if he had not heard anything. "Heavy casualties already. We're under attack. Can anybody hear me?"

Pock touched a command control on his sleeve and shouted into it, "Why can't you hear me?"

The Blue's voice was agitated. Pock could not see him, but he was sure the man was still frantically manipulating his equipment. "We can't send direct, sir; there's too much interference. Everything has to go outside the Sphere and be bounced off one of the satellites. There's a delay on every transmission."

Gun Sub Runn's face brightened. "Who is this?"

"This is Pock. What's going on?" The Rickshaw King waited for an answer, then spoke again. "Is this CORPQ or Corporation Earthside?"

Pock shouted at the technician again. "Why can't he hear me?!"

Gun Sub Runn beamed. "Ah, Pock. Finally. The Annex is under attack. It's being overrun. The—"

The voice of the Blue drowned him out. "We're getting his signal directly from his transmission Earthside, so there's no delay. But he's getting your message delayed because of the rerouting."

Gun Sub Runn's image paused, apparently waiting for a reply. Pock sent one. "Where is the Security commander? Why are you the one sending this message?"

The Rickshaw King shook his head in exasperation. "Can you hear me?"

"I can hear you, but my response is being delayed because of the interference. Let me speak to—"

The voice of the image cut him off. "The Security commander is dead. The only Bronze here is out at the first tier trying to keep the mob out, but there's too many of them. The whole Wideway is filled with people, and the narrows. You must send . . . immediately." The image broke up into a huge cloud of swirling photons and then disappeared entirely. When it reappeared, there was only an image, no voice. And then there was no image at all.

Pock's response was immediate. When he spoke his voice was heard throughout CORPQ. "Hold all available rickshaws at the main door. Barracks One, Three, and Five assemble immediately for deployment to Lesser CORPQ. Full insulation gear, canes set for lethal force. Rickshaws to depart in a body immediately upon loading. One squad per rickshaw. Barracks Seven, Eight, and Nine secure the perimeter of the compound. This is no drill. This is no drill."

He pressed the control to have the message repeated in its entirety until the contingent was all under way, and then turned his attention to the Blue in charge of communications. "What happened to the image from the Annex?"

"Disengaged at the source, sir."

"Disengaged how?"

"I don't know, sir. It could be at the communications

center itself or at the transmitter. No messages are coming out either internally or Earthside." The news was not good. The communications room was on the highest tier of the complex at Lesser CORPQ. If the transmission was cut off by the rioters, then the whole complex was overrun. If the transmitter was destroyed, things were not much better, but there might at least be pockets of resistance within the Annex.

In either case, it would just be a matter of routing a mob. There would be no organized defense. The most pressing problem was getting an idea of what they were facing. The Annex was on the far side of the mountain and could not be imaged directly from CORPQ. The best view would come from the Little Door, on the same side of the mountain as CORPQ but directly across the Sphere from the Annex. "Give me an image from the Little Door." He waited for a picture of the Sphere from the cameras at the compound at the Little Door, but nothing appeared. He switched back to the technician again. "Where's that image?"

"I can't contact the Little Door, sir. There's no response."

"More interference?"

"Nosir. Just no response."

Pock scowled. "Keep trying, and give me the chief officer on duty as soon as you can." The thought crossed his mind that it was already under attack, but he did not want to waste forces he might need to send over the mountain on a false alarm at the Little Door. "What kind of image can you give me of the Annex?"

"Only what can be seen from the top of the Hexagon, sir."

Pock cursed to himself as the image appeared. A view of Upside directly overhead curved away before him. The cameras arched and dipped, but no matter how they were directed, he could only see the part of the Wideway nearest the Upside Window and beyond. The farthest tip of Dah Beel's and a small slice of the Halls of the Rickshaw King were as close as he could come to Lesser CORPQ. He directed maximal enlargement of the Wideway. The crowds were thicker than normal, thick enough to be the fringes of a mob that could overrun the Annex. What was worse, the traffic on the Wideway was thickening and seemed to be flowing toward Lesser CORPQ as well. Its movement seemed to be picking up speed, and there was a great frenzy of activity at the Upside Window. What he saw was not a mob, but it certainly seemed to be a mob in the making. He tried for a closer look and the image disappeared altogether.

"What happened?!" he shouted to the Basecom.

"We've lost the image, sir."

"I *know* that! Why?!"

"Malfunction of the equipment, sir!"

"Malfunction! Get it fixed."

"Yessir."

A new voice interrupted. "Sir. This is Bronze C. P. Walker, Officer of the Door. The rickshaws are dispatched. Foot contingents still assembling."

"How many?"

"Five, sir."

"There's supposed to be a minimum of six rickshaws at the door at all times!"

"One was dispatched down the Wideway, sir, to recruit others."

"Good thinking, Walker. Load the others and dispatch them at will. Report when the foot contingent is away."

He cut back to the Basecom again. "What kind of image of the hill can you give me?"

The response was the image itself, an upcurving view of the Wideway from the top of the Executive Building, CORPQ Main, that seemed as large as life. The Wideway rose off to the left; five rickshaws were already a third of the way up and moving at a good speed. They formed a wedge, spread out across the Wideway almost wheel to wheel. The fist on Pock's forehead loosened slightly. Things were finally beginning to move in his favor. With some forces finally in the field, he felt control of the situation coming back into his hands. He was still without a clear picture of the situation, but as soon as the rickshaws got to the top of the hill, he would get a report from the Bronze in charge of the contingent. He watched them go past the halfway mark of the hill with mounting relief. The voice of the Basecom added to his pleasure.

"Sir, the In-Log shows there's a repair crew in the Executive Building headed by Tinker Manwalker. They're on their way to the Hexagon now, sir. They think the equipment problem is in your office. Shall I clear them to come up when they come in?"

"Yes." Pock smiled with satisfaction. Finally, a coincidence that worked in his favor. If the equipment could be fixed, Tinker Manwalker was certainly the person who could do it. With information from the Little Door and the cameras of the Hexagon working again, he would be able to deploy his forces for maximum effect. The rickshaws rolled steadily up the curving hill in front of him. He watched them speeding upward with a sense of mounting confidence. Another third of the hill, and the balance would shift in his favor. He could not believe his eyes when they suddenly crashed.

The center rickshaw seemed to swerve to the left for no reason, hitting the forks of the rickshaw next to it with its wheel and bouncing back to its right. There was a chain reaction of bumping and swerving and suddenly all five rickshaws were tumbling over each other in a huge crash. When they stopped moving, all but one of them were on their sides, and that one careened toward the side of the roadway, bounced over the curb, and disappeared down one of the gullies.

There were bodies all over the roadway, some pinned under the rickshaws, some scattered along the hill like a trail. It was a catastrophe. The wrecked rickshaws clogged the Wideway, making it impassable. The injured were spread over a hundred yards. It would take half the next load up the hill to untangle the pieces and clear the way for a new force of rickshaws. Pock shook his head at the impossibly bad luck. Before he could do anything to change it, the hill disappeared and the figure of Stefan Standard appeared in its place.

Old Spence was apparently still depriving him, and his face was tight with desperation. His pain came out as anger and indignation. "What's going on up there?"

"No time, no time!" Pock shouted. "Clear the holo."

Standard ignored him. "There's no use covering things up, Pock. You can't hide your mistakes indefinitely."

There was nothing to do but waste the precious seconds. "There's a riot in Upside. The Annex is under attack by the mob and the cameras on the Hexagon aren't working, so I can't get an image of the situation. The first six rickshaws up the hill just crashed, and you're tying up valuable time and the only communications channel I have. Now clear the holo!"

He touched his sleeve and shouted to the Basecom, "Clear this Fool and image the hill!" Standard disappeared before he could object.

But instead of the Wideway, Pock found himself looking at the figure of Tinker Manwalker. "You want to see Upside or not?"

"Where are you?"

"Outside the wall to your office. You want us to fix this or don't you?"

"Can you get the cameras on the Hexagon working?"

"Not until you get this wall down," she said.

"It's down, it's down!" he shouted. "How soon?"

The little woman shrugged. "We got a lot of equipment to set up. Five, ten minutes, if we hit it right off. All night if we don't. Never, if I have to stand here talking to you." She had always had the testiness of somebody who knows they're indispensable. There was nothing to do with her at any time but get out of the way and let her work. Her image disappeared before he could answer her, and he knew she was already busy setting up her equipment.

The Wideway curved up and away in front of him again. The next wave of rickshaws was just starting up the hill; the dancers were out on the forks trying to translate the momen-

tum of the little hill in front of CORPQ into enough speed to
get the heavily loaded rickshaws up the grade. It was obviously a losing battle, and he was not surprised when they
peeled off one by one up the Offshoots. The curving side
roads dipped sharply and then rose again in steplike stages
to give rickshaws coming back out of them enough momentum to make it up the Wideway.

The rickshaws were heavily overloaded, and they would
have to climb to the very top of the Offshoots before the
added weight would put enough force into the wheel to carry
the rickshaw at least as far up the Wideway as the next
series of Offshoots. It meant they would have to make two
detours even before they got to the wreckage. He watched
them disappear behind a small ridge as they went into the
first dip, but before they climbed back out, Standard's
image was back. He was fuming.

"How dare you cut me off?!" He didn't wait for an
answer. "What are you doing about the Little Door?"

The question took Pock by surprise. Things were moving
so fast he had had no time to think about contacting the
Little Door. "No contact," he said.

Standard was incredulous. "You mean you don't even
know it's under attack?!"

Pock said nothing. He should have guessed, but there was
no way he could have known. Fighting was almost certainly
inside the structure, which stuck out above the shell of the
Grand Sphere. He doubted there would be anything visible
aboveground even if the Hexagon's cameras had been working. He might have turned the cameras on CORPQ Main
toward the Little Door, but the disaster on the hill had
driven the situation completely out of his mind. It didn't
matter; Standard was going to have a field day second-
guessing him no matter what he did. He hated to give
Standard the satisfaction, but there was nothing to do
except admit he didn't know what was going on, and ask.

Standard didn't wait for his admission. Instead, he
touched one of the medallike rows of buttons on his chest
and his image disappeared. But the hill did not return.

Instead, Pock found himself looking at a badly wounded Red from the Little Door. There were only Bronzes and Reds at the door, and if a Red was reporting, it meant things were at least as bad as they were at the Annex. He could not believe that Yung Gun Runn's handful of caners could have inflicted that much damage so quickly on some of his best troops. The pride of the Fist had been stationed there for the sole purpose of retaking the door in an emergency.

The Red's speech was halting and came between obvious waves of pain. He tried to salute, but it almost cost him his balance. His nose was broken and still bleeding. "Red L. Garcia reporting, sir. The Little Door was seized by the Grander contingent at six-forty GST. All attempts to retake it have failed. The garrison under Yung Gun Runn took control of the Inspection Area and could not be dislodged."

The pain of the failure seemed greater than the pain of his wounds. The formality of his report dwindled. "We tried to retake it, sir. We killed at least half of them and most of the rest were badly wounded. We almost had them driven back out into the cargo bay, but they put up a last-ditch resistance at the entryway." He seemed to marvel at their tenacity. "Most of them could hardly stand; all of them were burned or bleeding." He shook his head in disbelief. "But they wouldn't surrender." His voice cracked. "We lost most of the Bronze in the assault." The pain seemed to overwhelm him again for a moment. "We almost *had* them."

Pock did not want to hear what was coming next. There was a long pause. The Red lowered his eyes. "There were only about ten of them still able to fight, and we forced them out into the cargo bay. But they didn't break, even there. They stayed in a tight bunch and kept us from getting through the door in force." His voice failed him again. He tried to finish the report, failed. Tried again. And failed again. His head twisted, trying to force himself to continue. Finally he pulled himself up rigidly again and found the words. "By the time a full squad fought its way through, the cargo bay was full of Obees, and more were landing at the docks. They retook the Inspection Area. The compound itself is still under control of the Fist, but reinforcements are needed immediately. All efforts to contact CORPQ have failed." The Red disappeared and Standard returned in his place.

"The Little Door must be retaken," he said. "Immediately." He looked as if he would be just as happy if Pock failed to retake it.

"Then stay out of my way, and let me take it!" He did not wait for Standard's objections. His first command went to the only Silver on the base, Ah Bir, his second in command. "Take Barracks Two and Seven and secure the compound at the Little Door." He had no intention of attempting to retake the Little Door before he finished with the Annex. As long as the Fist held the compound, the Obees would be bottled up inside the Little Door. Ah Bir's reinforcements would allow them to drive the Obees back inside, even if they were out into the compound. The area around the barracks, and the cargo storage areas, were all broad, open spaces where the numbers would be on the side of the Fist. Without the close quarters of the Inspection Area, the Obees would be no match for the caners of the Fist.

He gave another command to the Basecom, and Standard disappeared. In his place the hill stretched before Pock again. But the wrecked rickshaws were still solidly jammed across it, and the second flight of rickshaws was nowhere in sight.

He kept the image of the hill but switched to the officer of the door. "Walker, where are the rickshaws?"

"The third flight just left of the door, sir."

"Third!?"

"Yessir. The scout rickshaw returned with seven others, and just after they left, ten more arrived."

"But where is the second flight?"

"I don't know, sir. I've been supervising the loading. All of Barracks Three not in rickshaws has already started up the hill on foot, and Barracks Five is departing at this moment."

Pock watched the third wave of rickshaws break into two separate groups of five; each swung up a different Offshoot. One by one they disappeared from his vision behind an outcropping of stone. None of them came out the other side. The officer of the door's voice returned. "Sir, ten more rickshaws have arrived and are loading now. Barracks Five has disembarked on foot."

Pock waited for the rickshaws to reappear; when they didn't the truth was apparent. "Hold all rickshaws! They're being ambushed in the Offshoots! Send the Fifth up the Offshoots and have it secure the Wideway just above the turnoffs in case they try to come in behind us. Load half the rickshaws with Bronze from the Second and get the rest to Silver Bir at the Orchard Gate."

He rolled the focus of the image up the Wideway. For a moment there was just the downed rickshaws, and then a wave of people came flooding over the hill and filled in behind them. He still believed they were a mob, the overflow of the great crowd attacking Lesser CORPQ. He even hoped they were the mob from the Annex itself, driven out by the rallying forces of the Fist. But his hopes disappeared as a stream of them in the silver-and-black uniforms of Dah Beel's guard filed out from behind their makeshift barricades and set up in battle formation.

They came forward a hundred yards down the Wideway and waited to engage the Fist. As soon as they did, a second group in red and gold streamed out from between the barricades to take their place. Pock knew them instantly as the caners of Gun Sub Runn. All hope that it was just a riot faded. If Gun Sub Runn and Dah Beel were both taking part, it was the revolution Standard and Old Spence had been afraid of. He was afraid to think who else was involved.

He rushed to the wallway and cleared it. His office was empty. He was almost afraid to look at his desk. But the cases were still there. He gave a sigh of relief and rushed back to the holopad. Tinker Manwalker's image was waiting for him superimposed on the hill. For a moment she looked like one of the rebels near the barricades.

"You should take better care of this equipment," she scolded. "Half these camera mounts are rusted; no wonder they wouldn't turn."

"Where are you?" he said.

"Roof. You can see Downside now."

"What about Upside?"

"It's going to take awhile."

"And the Little Door."

"Communication mast's down; you can see it from here."

"What else can you see?"

There was no answer, but the Wideway disappeared and the whole of Downside spread before him in its place. He searched the Wideway for the rickshaws of the Second Barracks hurtling toward the Little Door. What he saw was even worse than the hill. The rickshaws hadn't gotten more than a quarter mile from CORPQ before they were overrun. The whole of Downside seemed to be on the Wideway—half churning toward the Little Door and half surging toward CORPQ itself. He had hoped to outflank the forces on the hill by way of the Crossway, but there was no hope at all of getting through Downside.

The mobs were everywhere, angry, violent throngs raging through the twisting narrows of Downside and flowing out onto the Wideway. The Wideway was packed solidly from CORPQ to the Little Door, and he could see that the compound was already coming under attack. It was a nightmare coming true. What forces remained at the Little Door would be overrun by the mob, and even if they weren't, they could never contain the Obees and fight off the mob at the same time. The compound was as good as lost.

He made his decision quickly. "Ah Bir!" He scanned the Outer Fields Narrow for the rickshaws and found them just about to cross from the Inner to the Outer Fields. The mob seemed to have stopped at the Wideway; the fields had no interest for them; only the physical representations of Corporation at either end of the Wideway attracted them. "Ah Bir! Return immediately." There was no answer, no acknowledgment.

He buzzed the Basecom again. "Get me Manwalker. She's on the roof."

In a second the image of Tinker Manwalker appeared superimposed on the whole of Downside. "What you want now?"

"I can't reach the rickshaw on Outer Fields Narrow."

She turned aside as if talking to someone else on the roof. "That man wants everything." She turned back irritably. "OK, what you want first, Upside or the rickshaw?"

"The rickshaw."

"Done," she said. "You want Downside still?"

He had almost forgotten about the hill. "No, the Wideway!"

The tiny figure disappeared. The hill returned. The first wave of Bronze was just flowing over the solid wedge of Dah Beel's caners. He could not see individuals, but the bronze and silver-and-black figures were inextricably mixed all along the wedge. He watched the battle rage. The silver-and-black held its formation. He could see that the First was not going to crack it. They were winded from the long run uphill; they were fighting against the grade; Dah Beel's caners were as good or better. But the numbers began to shift the tide.

The whole of the First Barracks was finally engaged, and the wedge was beginning to become ragged at its edges. He waited for it to disintegrate. The bronze wave flowed all around the wedge, surrounding it. It seemed about to envelop it when the crescent of red-and-gold figures near the barricade came forward and closed like pincers around the foremost part. What Pock saw on the hill might have been beautiful to someone watching only the colors. The dark black of the mountain, the yellow band of the Wideway, and in the narrow defile formed by the sheer sides where the roadway had been cut through the top of the ridge, a wedge of silver in the center of a thick circle of bronze. Around the upper part of the circle, a crescent of red and gold lowered steadily.

But for Pock it was anything but beautiful. The gold fist

in his forehead tightened steadily. He could see the flow change as the thick upper rim of bronze turned to meet the new attack. The red and gold of Gun Sub Runn's forces had flanked it on both sides and the tips of the crescent seemed to pinch in on the circle in the middle until it had cut the bronze circle into two parts.

Whoever was directing the rebels knew his business. The wedge of Dah Beel's troops expanded rapidly at its flattened end until it was a diamond with its point piercing into the upper arc of the bronze circle. When it touched the center of the red-and-gold crescent, the silver spearhead separated from the wedge at its lower end and began to expand to the side until it touched the tips of the crescent. The result was that the arc of bronze was cut in two again, and each half was sandwiched between a layer of silver and another of red and gold. Pock watched the two arcs shrink and form themselves into small, tight balls that got smaller by the moment.

The rest of Dah Beel's wedge re-formed into a much smaller and tighter triangle, keeping its flat edge tightly against the forces behind it to keep the bronze circle from closing around it again. If it hadn't been for the wave of blue moving up the slope, the outcome would have been inevitable. Once the small circles of bronze were eliminated, the wedge would have been re-formed and the crescent following it down the Wideway would have driven the rest of the First Barracks down the hill or enveloped it around the point of the wedge, if it resisted.

But the arrival of the Third changed everything. The diminishing crescent of bronze was gradually backed by a mass of blue that covered the Wideway from side to side. The sheer iron sides, where the mountain pressed in against it, made it impossible for the Third to be flanked and enveloped as the First had been.

The numbers were on his side again, but it would not be easy. The Blues of the Third had come up the last five hundred yards at a dead run when they saw what was happening, and they were winded. The Bronze had been fighting steadily for a long time, and it was all they could do to hold their ground against the forward drive of the wedge until the Third caught its breath. But more and more of the Third arrived with each passing minute, and the mass of troops behind the Bronze grew steadily thicker and more powerful.

The circle of the First had drawn back from the sides of the wedge and then disengaged even from the point to retreat fifty yards down the Wideway. The wedge hesitated instead of pursuing. It was a mistake. The Bronze re-formed as a band across the Wideway and then, given breathing space, opened in the middle to allow a river of fresh Blues from the Third to surge through.

The tight circles of Bronze farther up the slope had dwindled, but they still occupied the attention of half of Dah Beel's wedge and all of Gun Sub Runn's forces. By the time they realized that the smaller wedge was in trouble, it was too late. The Third did not make the same mistake the First had; they did not attempt to surround Dah Beel's wedge. Instead, they simply overwhelmed it with sheer numbers, blunting its point, flattening it out across the Wideway, and then remorselessly driving it backward up the slope until it collapsed between the circles surrounding the last of the Bronze.

The Silver half of the surrounding forces folded back from each circle to form an irregular line across the Wideway with the collapsed wedge. The Red-and-Gold tried to take its place by closing around the circles of Bronze from the First Barracks, but the contingent on the right formed a wedge of its own and fought its way out down the side of the Wideway until it slipped through the wall of Blues pressing forward to the attack.

The other circle was not so fortunate. Part of the Red and Gold freed by the escape of the other Bronze contingent turned its attention to the surviving circle and quickly annihilated it. That done, they formed in behind the Silver, and the band across the Wideway doubled. It was still far, far thinner than the mass of Blues that pressed steadily against it. And the fist in Pock's forehead began to loosen a little. It was only a matter of time before the combined forces of Dah Beel and Gun Sub Runn were forced back on the barricades.

The fighting would be tougher there, but the motley colors of defenders still behind the barricades told him they were indeed remnants of the mob, and the disciplined forces of the Fist would quickly overrun them despite the difficulty of fighting over the barricades. Before long, the hill would be his, and from the hill an attack could be mounted down the other side of CORPQ Hill to relieve the Annex.

After the Annex was secured, the Fist could be reassembled and the compound at the Little Door retaken. Once that was accomplished, a two-pronged attack from outside the Little Door and from the compound would squeeze the remnants of Yung Gun Runn's forces and their Obee reinforcements between the twin arms of a pincer movement that would annihilate them. Then it would just be a matter of retaliation and reprisals. For the first time in what seemed like days, Pock felt like the situation was in hand.

But his relief was short-lived. The thinning band of defenders was almost up against the barricades when an opening appeared at the center of their line and a thick column of reinforcements drove out into the center of the Blue mass. It was good tactics, and if the column of reinforcements had worn the Silver of Dah Beel's guard or the Red and Gold of Gun Sub Runn's forces, Pock would have been worried. But they were a motley crew, obviously made up of spontaneous recruits from the Upside mob.

The truth of their identity did not occur to him until the line penetrated to the middle of the blue band and began spreading outward. More reinforcements flowed out through the center of the barricade, and the flat tip of the thrust formed a triangular head. The head grew and began to swing slowly from side to side, carving a huge clearing in the body of the Third.

Pock was stunned. The entire center of the Third was crumbling before his eyes under the attack of ordinary

Granders. Only when he looked farther down the Wideway did he realize the truth. The Reds of the Fifth were being driven back out of the Offshoots by the same greatly outnumbered rabble. There was only one explanation; the new fighters were the caners of UWalk Wenn. The fact that the rickshaws had been a trap should have told him as much, just as he should have suspected a trap when the message from the Annex came from somebody other than the Fist. Now it was too late. The Third was being steadily driven back, and their rear was seriously endangered from the Offshoots. If Wenn's forces broke the line of the Fifth across the Wideway just above the turnoffs, the Blues of the Third and the survivors of the First would be caught between two forces they could not defeat.

The only reasonable thing to do was to order a retreat, but before he could do it, the head of Wenn's attack force cut entirely across the Wideway, leaving the Third divided into three parts. Two isolated islands of Blues were pinned along either side of the Wideway, and the solid but much smaller block of the main body was being pushed steadily back down the hill.

More troops flowed up the center of the spear shaft and into the head, which drove forward again into the main body of Blues. When it began to open a wedge even there, the field commander did the sensible thing and ordered a retreat down the Wideway to regroup with the part of the Fist holding the Wideway just above the Offshoots.

But UWalk Wenn's troops did not make the same mistake as Dah Beel's. They followed the retreat and drove the Fist down the Wideway almost in a rout. A large band at the tail end of the spear broke off and sealed the Wideway behind it, to prevent the islands of Blues from breaking free and trapping them from behind. The Silver and Red-and-Gold ranks that had taken the initial assault attacked the two islands of Blues who had been cut off. They were fresh, and the momentum was with them, and they made surprisingly short work of the demoralized remnants of the Fist that had been left behind.

The body that made it down to the Offshoots with Wenn's caners in hot pursuit were in little better shape. Instead of fresh reinforcements to fall back on, they found a tiring band of defenders, themselves hard pressed by the superior abilities of Wenn's forces from the Offshoots, who had driven them back onto the Wideway. The assault from behind was furious, and the Bronze in charge of the retreat did the only thing he could do. He formed a solid wall of Blues as a rear guard and pressed the rest of his forces forward in an attack.

The tactic worked and the Fist broke through the caners from the Offshoots and ran the rest of the way to the bottom of the Wideway and the safety of the door. Pock had given up any hope of taking the hill; the best that could be hoped for now was simply to save what remained of the force and get it back inside CORPQ. But what he saw at the bottom of the hill put even that in doubt. The Wideway was a mass of rioters, and an equally solid stream of them were already halfway up the winding path from the Wideway to the door of CORPQ.

He ordered the Sixth Barracks out the door to help the retreating survivors of the force that had gone up the hill with such arrogant certainty of success. The column of Bronze cut their way easily through the crowd on the approach road, but the mob was so thick at the Wideway that the best the Sixth could do was forge a small curving perimeter about fifteen yards into the Wideway and hold it as an entry point for any of the Fist who fought their way through from the bottom of the hill.

There were not many. When the main force hit the bottom of the hill, they were almost in a rout. The mob was like a wall, and the fleeing survivors from the Third and the First jammed into them and came almost to a dead stop. It was only a few moments before Wenn's combined forces from the top of the hill and the Offshoots slammed into the disorganized mass from behind. After that it was a massacre. Pock was dumbfounded. The mob fought with almost the same effect as Wenn's far better trained forces. He could not imagine what could have inspired them to such fury.

Certainly Corporation was hated within the League, but the Sphere was not Hardcore; no monomaniacal hatred of Corporation born of years of impotence against its power could unite them against it. What could have unified the whole of the Sphere in that kind of rage against the Fist was utterly beyond him. The only possible answer lay in the cases in his office, but the guns had not been used. Until they were, reports that they even existed within the Sphere would be nothing more than rumors, and rumors could not turn the entire populace of the Grand Sphere out of their homes in search of revenge.

Only a few small knots of Blues and most of the surviving Bronze made it as far as the entrance road to CORPQ. The Bronze of the Sixth held the entrance until they were safely on their way up the road to the door, but Wenn's caners had worked their way through the crowd by then, and after a brief but costly skirmish, even the Sixth was forced to form a suicide rear guard and retreat rapidly up the road to the door. When they were inside, the Battle of CORPQ Hill was complete. It was an absolute disaster for the Fist. Less than a fifth of the forces committed to the battle had survived, and many of the survivors were wounded or too exhausted to fight anymore.

The mobs were beginning to flow up the entrance road and up the grassy slopes that led to the steep walls of the first tier of CORPQ. The walls of the first tier would keep them out indefinitely, but if the door was breached and they got inside, it would be a massacre. Fortunately, the heavily charged fields of the door annihilated anyone who tried to force it. A few in the front line of the crowd were pushed against it and reduced to flaming ash in a matter of seconds. The mob drew back from it, but continued to mill around angrily along the lower tier, looking for an opening.

Pock had no choice; he ordered the Reds of the Fourth Barracks to fill the natural bottleneck between the corner of the second farm barracks and the wall of the tier. The space was small enough to hold with minimal force, and an entire barracks wedged into it could probably withstand even an attack by Wenn's caners. At least they might hold it long enough to get the forces under Ah Bir back, if only he could contact Ah Bir.

Instead, he got Standard again. The Exec's impatience was so intense Pock suspected he was being deprived of DeeBee until the crisis was over and wanted it over immediately. "Have you retaken the Little Door?" Standard demanded.

Pock simply shook his head. There was no point in hiding the situation. He made his report short and unmistakable. "The First, Third, and Fifth Barracks have been defeated by the combined forces of Dah Beel, Gun Sub Runn, and UWalk Wenn. The Sixth Barracks has also suffered heavy casualties. The entire populace of the Sphere is in the streets. CORPQ itself is under attack.

"The Second and Seventh Barracks under Silver Ah Bir was dispatched to the compound at the Little Door but cannot be contacted. The compound is probably under attack both from without by rioters from Downside and from within by the Obees. The compound has probably already fallen. The Annex cannot be contacted and has probably fallen as well. It is only a matter of time before CORPQ itself is surrounded, although it can be held indefinitely."

Standard's mouth dropped open. Even *he* was not expecting such a defeat. "You've lost the Sphere?! Are you telling me you've lost the Sphere?! A hundred guns, and you lost the Sphere?!"

"The guns haven't been used," Pock said.

Standard fluctuated between outrage and disbelief. "You Grander trai—"

Whatever else he had intended to call Pock was lost with his image. In place of it, the image of Tinker Manwalker and a view of Downside filled the room. She was almost as irate as Standard. "What have you been doing with this equipment?" she demanded. "It looks like someone took a hammer to it."

The revelation of sabotage did not even surprise him; compared with what he had just seen, it was nothing. "Is it working?"

"A minute...." He could still see Tinker, but the voice was not hers.

"Silver A. Bir reporting."

"Ah Bir, where are you?"

"In the Outer Fields just short of the compound. We've tried three assaults, but it's completely overrun. We'd need the entire Fist to take it back."

"Is your force intact?"

"Thirty percent casualties in the Second, sixty percent among the Blues. One of the rickshaws destroyed."

"Return immediately. Bring as many of the Fist as possible with you in the rickshaws and start the others back on foot."

"Yessir."

It struck him suddenly that Ah Bir could see what was going on in Upside. "Do you have a pair of close-ups?"

"Yes, of course."

"Look at Upside. What can you report?"

There was a pause. "The same as Downside. The Wideway is filled with mobs. There's a lot of activity in Dah Beel's Village and Tinker's Tor. A huge crowd near the Annex. I can't see much of it, but there are people all over the part of the first tier that I can see and clumps of them on the second."

"Can you see the notch above CORPQ?"

"Yes. What *happened*?! We have no one on the hill!"

"Routed. Three barracks decimated. There's a mob surrounding CORPQ. If you don't get back soon, they'll have closed the Orchard Gate. Can you see anything else of CORPQ? Do they hold the other notches?"

"I can't see the one above the Little Door, but it doesn't matter; they have the Wideway. Wait. The Crossways Upside are almost deserted. There are some people, a small body moving up the Crossway toward the Orchard Notch, but I can't see the far side of the hill from here."

"Good. Send four rickshaws loaded for speed to take the notch. Load all the others, but one with as many as they can carry, and have the rest of the Fist move down the Outer Fields Narrow and up the Crossway on foot. Keep the rickshaws circling back to ferry the rest. Get back here yourself as quickly as you can." He didn't wait for a reply. There was a quicker way. "Officer of the Door."

There was a long delay before he got an answer. The voice was out of breath. "Officer of the Door, sir."

"Are there any rickshaws?"

"Only one that was sent back by Silver Bir, sir. It's badly damaged."

"Send it to the Hexagon immediately." It was a dangerous gamble. With the guns and high ground, he might still rout the mobs. But there was also a chance that the mob surrounding CORPQ might come up behind him in the Orchard Notch. If a volley didn't put them to flight, there was still the possibility that he might be overrun. If he left two of the cases at the Hexagon, Ah Bir could use them to come to his relief if he was cut off, but there was no guarantee Ah Bir would get back in time. It was the kind of Risk a Grander would have taken without hesitation.

But merely staying where he was and using the guns to drive the mob from the door of CORPQ would not be enough to save him. Unless he used the guns in the Sphere itself and at least put the mob to rout and retook the Annex and then the Little Door, he was as good as dead. If he lost the Sphere, his life would be worth nothing. If the rebels did not kill him, Old Spence would have him killed when they retook the Sphere. If not, when the return of the Sphere to Corporation was finally negotiated, his head would be one of the bargaining chips, one Spencer LeGrange would gladly pay. He had seen it done before, more than seen it.

Pock was beginning to worry. The cargo shuttle was halfway back to Earth and no opportunity had presented

*itself. He watched Commander Swyn intently, waiting for
an opening. The Gold sat disconsolately in the forward
passenger area pondering his defense. Pock knew what he
was thinking. He was taking some hope from the fact that
Spencer LeGrange had not merely turned him over to the
mobs in the Sphere. He was consoling himself with the fact
that Old Spence had not yet relieved him of his command
or his rank. He was reassuring himself that he would not be
permanently relieved, that although Pock could run things
for a few months until the Sphere stopped whirling, no one
trusted Pock enough to make him permanent commander.*

*Pock could see his face change as he realized that there
was still no way to explain the death of Elgin Dah Beel;
Spencer LeGrange did not accept accidents. Nor would it
do any good to remind him that the wearing of guns
publicly had been a Corporate decision. Swyn had argued
too vehemently in favor of it to pass the buck. He did not
even have an explanation of why a Blue had been wearing
one, since his order had been that no one below the rank of
Bronze was entitled to a firearm, and admitting that his
own men did not respect his orders was almost the same as
a confession of incompetence. A lot of Corporate property
had been destroyed, and somebody's career was going to
have to pay for it.*

*Pock waited until Swyn's frown deepened toward despair
before he approached him. He stood formally erect and
gave the salute. Swyn returned it halfheartedly and
returned to his thoughts. Pock waited patiently. When he
did not either go forward into the pilot's compartment or
back to his seat closer to the cargo area, Swyn finally
recognized his presence. He nodded to the seat across from
his. "Rest it," he said. "And report." He doubted that Pock
had anything to report, and he did not want to hear any
consolation about the bad luck that was taking him
Earthside.*

*Pock sat but leaned conspiratorially close. "Sir, may I
speak without record?" Swyn nodded. "Sir, I believe there
is a way out of your predicament."*

Swyn smiled at the euphemism. If a man with a reasonably good expectation of being the scapegoat of Spencer LeGrange's lethal wrath was merely in a "predicament," he wondered what Pock called danger. "A way out?" He half expected Pock to suggest suicide.

"An explanation for what happened."

Swyn shook his head. "Corporation is not interested in explanations."

"They must be, sir, or . . ." He hesitated as if deciding how to phrase it until Swyn acknowledged the point.

"Or I wouldn't be going back," he said bluntly.

Pock nodded. "Did you ever wonder why a Blue was armed?" It was obviously one of the questions that Swyn had pursued relentlessly ever since the incident had occurred, but a nod was as far as he would go toward admitting it. "Because he wasn't a Blue," Pock said.

Swyn looked at him as if he were crazy. "Shall I promote him retroactively?" His voice was heavy with sarcasm. "Would things be any different if he was a Bronze?"

"They'd be different if he was a Grander."

Swyn laughed. "They'd be different if he was an Exec too."

Pock tried not to let his disdain show. Any Grander would have grasped the implications immediately. It astounded him that a man who thought on so few levels had managed to even live in the Sphere as long as he had without assassination. "A Grander disguised as a Blue."

Swyn considered it for a moment. He seemed to decide that they might accept it as possible Earthside, but he still did not see the point. "But why?"

Pock gave an embarrassed look. "Why, to get rid of the toughest commander they've had to deal with in a decade." He waited for Swyn's vanity to get out of the way of his intellect so he could see the out he was being given. It was the perfect argument for not even replacing him. If it were Pock, he would be preparing to go to the meeting demanding a medal just to show the Granders that their little ploy had not worked. But even the fundamentals of it were *beyond Swyn. It was a farfetched scheme even for a Grander, but Earthside would accept that kind of plot as typical of the Grand Sphere. Swyn should have grasped that from the beginning.*

"But the uniform . . ." he said.

To Pock, the uniform was a triviality, a detail a Grander would make up a dozen plausible explanations for on the spot and not come close to the truth with any of them. "Stolen from a new recruit." He didn't let Swyn get to his next objection. "It could have been any one of the Blues reported missing after the fighting." He hoped Swyn would note that he said "could have been" instead of "was." But it was too subtle a distinction for the Gold.

Swyn looked hopeful. "Do you think they'll believe it?"

"They have to, sir. It's the truth." Swyn seemed ready to accept any lie, however preposterous, if it gave some hope of saving him. Pock leaned conspiratorially close. "I have the proof."

Swyn raised an eyebrow. "Show it to me."

Pock looked toward the door of the pilot's compartment as if ears were listening on the far side of it. "Not here." He raised his voice and nodded toward the door. "I think you should inspect the cargo from Dah Beel's, sir. There are some irregularities." He gestured toward the cargo area, and Swyn nodded that he understood the need for the charade, although Pock was not convinced that he did.

"Let's go," he said.

Pock led the way back, through the empty passenger compartment to the cargo area and back through the towering crates into an alleyway formed between the last two rows. He stopped at the entrance to the dead end and gestured the Gold in ahead of him. Swyn shook his head as if he were humoring him and started down the narrow corridor. He was barely three steps in when Pock stuck him with his cane. The prongs made a slight mark, but Pock knew the "accident" would cover up any trace of it. Swyn went down hard; he twisted his head around to see what had hit him, but the sting of the cane had stolen his voice.

Pock could see the question in his eyes. It disgusted him. If the situation were reversed, he would have grasped it the moment the prongs hit him. The man was simply too stupid to live. He gave him an answer anyway. "Dah Beel," he said.

Swyn still looked at him blankly. Pock toppled the first crate onto him. It was almost too heavy to move, and he was afraid for a moment that the pilot would notice the impact, but Swyn's upper legs and pelvis cushioned its sound. The Gold tried to scream, but the paralysis still held his voice. Pock watched the pain screwing up his face. Sweat was pouring out of his forehead. It was a detail Dah Beel would hear and approve of.

Swyn still had a look of puzzled disbelief on his face. The look disgusted Pock, and he toppled the second crate with vigor. It crushed Swyn's shoulder and chest, not enough to kill him right away, but enough to kill him before Pock could be expected to come back from the passenger area to look for him. There was a great deal of blood and an even greater amount of pain. It was exactly the death Dah Beel had negotiated for.

Pock took the bag of jewels from his tunic and bent over the broken form of the done commander. He spilled a couple of the jewels on the deck and tucked the bag next to Swyn's unmoving hand. "A gift from Dah Beel," he said. The Gold's eyes were crazy with pain and fear, and yet they looked up at Pock for a reason. Pock shook his head. "It's a hard life for a Fool," he said. Then he turned out of the corridor and was gone without looking back.

Twenty minutes later, he was back. Swyn was dead. His face a mask of agony and bewilderment. The sight did not bother Nohfro Pock; he had seen worse, had caused worse, and been rewarded for it by Swyn. He waited a few moments and then ran forward to the pilot's compartment to get help. The third mate returned with him. There was clearly nothing either of them could do. Pock made sure the mate found the jewels, saw clearly that they had obviously fallen from Swyn's hand while he was examining them. If a witness was needed, the mate would make a convincing one. Pock took the bag from him and emptied it into his palm. He picked out Dah Beel's crest, looked at it, and put it back into the bag. "Make me a holo to Corporation," he said.

The mate led him forward. In a few moments his image stood before Spencer LeGrange himself. His report was short. Commander Swyn had been killed by falling cargo during the flight. He had apparently gone back to examine the contents of the bag found next to him. He answered all the questions easily. Swyn had sent him forward and told him not to return until called for. He had waited almost half an hour before daring to disobey the order, and by then it was too late. When Spencer LeGrange asked what was in the bag, Pock said, "Jewels," and showed him the Dah Beel emerald crest. He did not need to say they were Swyn's bribes, collected for betraying Corporation most of his career.

The true situation was as obvious to Old Spence as it would have been to a Grander. "You'll be in charge of the investigation, Pock," he said. "Consider it your first duty as the new Commander of the LeGrange Police." There was a pause. "And see to it that Dah Beel gets his crest back."

Pock had no doubt the same thing would be done to him by Ah Bir on his way back, assuming Old Spence didn't just turn him over to the mob, claiming Pock had gotten the guns on his own and used them without authorization. The best he could hope for would be for Old Spence to throw in Standard as well, as a gesture to satisfy Corporation's involvement. He regretted not throwing him out of the rickshaw when he had the chance. It was a chance that would never come again.

He went back through the wallway to his office. The cases sat side by side, not quite touching, near his desk. He thought for a moment that they had been moved, but he was not sure. They had probably been in the way when Manwalker and her crew had done their work. It didn't matter. He grabbed the nearest one and lifted it. It seemed heavier than before, and he checked the lock, but it was undisturbed. He grabbed a handscreen and touched it on. The Basecom's face appeared on it. "Have the Tenth stand ready at the Orchard Gate. I want anyone who's ever danced rickshaw, or used firearms, and ten of the best caners. And tell Standard I'm out." He touched the handscreen off and slipped it inside his tunic, then hefted the case and went out.

The rickshaw was standing ready at the door of the Hexagon when he reached the ground. It was in bad shape, and the Blue dancing it was inexperienced with it at best. Pock threw the case up onto the shortseat and climbed up after it. The Blue began almost immediately to run the rickshaw up to speed, but they were at the Orchard Gate before he got it going sufficiently to climb up onto the forks. The wheels wobbled and the forks were slightly bent, and the Blue's weight did not add to the momentum as much as it detracted. The rickshaw slowed, and the Blue had to jump down between the forks to get it up to speed again. Things were no better at the gate.

Of the four who had had some experience dancing rickshaw, none were very adept at it, and Pock ordered three teams of four to run the rickshaw up the hill instead. There were almost a dozen, mostly Blues recently Up from Earthside who could handle a pistol, but the rickshaw was too bent to carry more than Pock and four others. He ordered the rest to follow on foot, but before they got out the gate there was an urgent message from the Bronze in charge of the Second Barracks that he could not hold the bottleneck any longer without reinforcements. There was nothing to do but order all but the twenty best caners and the shooters to reinforce the Second. He and the four with their guns could secure the unprotected notch and hold it until the others reached the top, and Ah Bir's troops would be available shortly.

The rickshaw clattered out of the gate, and the Fist flowed out behind it. All but a fragment of the column promptly peeled off and ran along the wall to the aid of the Second. The rickshaw rode badly and all but stopped when the relays of pullers changed places, but he was most of the way out the Near Orchard Narrow when he heard from Ah Bir. It did not occur to Pock that the handheld worked well while all the communications at CORPQ were out of order. If it had, he might have realized that Tinker Manwalker was responsible for all the trouble, and that Tinker Manwalker was still behind in CORPQ. But he was too preoccupied with getting to the notch to notice. The Silver distracted him even more. There was a cut over his eye and he looked weary. Pock asked the inevitable. "What happened?"

"Ambushed," he said. "We saw a part of the mob coming across the fields to get behind us, but when we tried to outrun them, about twenty more came out of the Orchard and held the narrow against us until the mob caught up with us."

"Twenty men held up your entire contingent!"

"They were *not* ordinary men, and the two that led them fought like nothing I've ever seen. No one could stand against them."

Pock had the sinking feeling that it could have only been UWalk Wenn and Aerowaffen. "What did they look like?"

"A big, husky Obee."

"With a black beard and a white pleasuresuit?"

"No, clean shaven. Dressed like a heavy-equipment hauler from Hardcore."

Pock frowned. It was not Aerowaffen, but the other might have been Wenn. "What about the other?"

"Smallish, gray hair." He shook his head as if he still could not believe it. "The first rickshaw tried to run him down, but he clung to the forks, and they dipped and dug into the roadway. The rickshaw flipped over. It was unbelievable that he wasn't killed." There was a touch of admiration in his voice. "And the way he fought!"

"The smaller man, was he UWalk Wenn?"

Ah Bir shook his head. "No, I've seen Wenn. This man was much older."

Pock let it go. It had probably been Wenn who directed the defense of CORPQ Hill. It didn't matter where he was as long as he wasn't in the Orchard Notch. "What about the rickshaws?"

"Still with the main body. We fought our way out on foot after ours went. The two behind us were lost as well, and the others turned back and joined the main force. We're continuing on foot until the Fist can clear the road and send the rickshaws on along after us."

"Better do it at a run. If the mob spreads out around the Farm Barracks and comes in behind the Second, the Orchard Gate is going to be cut off before you get there." The Silver saluted wearily. "When you get back, you'll find two cases in my office in the Hexagon. Open them. If the Second gets overrun, use what you find in them. Stand ready to relieve us at the notch if necessary." The Silver acknowledged the command, and Pock cleared the screen as the rickshaw bounced out of the narrow and onto the Crossway.

The mountain was widest where it formed Orchard Hill, and the rickshaw had to be pulled along less than three hundred yards of level before it began the steep ascent of the hill itself. It was a slow process. Even with two Blues between the forks and one pushing the rickshaw from behind, it made poor speed, and the frequent changes of teams all but canceled the advantage of its sprints. Only the fact that the defenders making their way up the other Crossway were entirely on foot gave them any chance at all to succeed.

There was still nobody in the notch as the rickshaw neared the end of its climb. Pock looked back down across the curve of Outer Fields. The Fist had cleared the road and the rickshaws were moving again. He watched the foremost stop to pick up Ah Bir less than halfway to the Crossway.

He looked back toward CORPQ. The Second and the Tenth were still wedged in the bottleneck, but the mob was finally circling the Farm Barracks. He watched as a block of

Blues detached from the rear of the mass in the bottleneck and moved to meet the mob as it came around the nearest corner of the barracks. Pock still wondered what had brought the whole of the Sphere into the streets. He did not have long to wonder.

Ah Bir's face appeared on the handheld again. "The road has been cleared," he said. "Proceeding to CORPQ by rickshaw."

"I can see you," Pock said.

"Sir, we now know the cause of the riot." He didn't wait for Pock to ask what it was. "A member of the Pleasure Crew named Roger Count Aerowaffen and his rickshaw dancer, UWalk Wenn, were shot to death on the Downside Window by a man dressed as a Blue. The Fist is being blamed, and there is a widely believed rumor that firearms are stored in the Annex, CORPQ, and the compound at the Little Door."

Pock shook his head. Corporation would have been better off if the guns really had been sent to all three places. It had been a big mistake to keep them all at CORPQ; they would have made all the difference in the world at the Little Door and probably could have saved the Annex as well. It was a card he could play against Standard once he retook all Corporation property in the Grand Sphere.

It was not going to be easy; any movement ruthless enough to murder its own members to start a riot and organized enough to use the shooting to get so many Granders out onto the Wideway was a formidable enemy. Still, the fact that they had neglected the notch was going to turn out to be a fatal error, he was sure.

What he saw as the last team sprinted the rickshaw to the crest made him less confident. Less than a hundred yards down the hill, a small mob was running toward the notch. He had the rickshaw wheeled sideways and turned to open the case. The mob worried him less the closer it got. There were nearly fifty of them, but they were all from the Pleasure Crew. Probably not one in five could use a cane at all. He recognized the white hair of Vor Van Vast in the lead, but he doubted that there were five others in the whole bunch who could give even a Blue much of a fight. He worked slowly and deliberately with the lock mechanism, but it seemed stuck, and even when he finally fumbled it into place, the lid of the case did not fly open.

He shouted to the Bronze who had already jumped down from the rickshaw. "Get the caners out in front and form a wedge. Shooters stay close to the rickshaw." He redid the lock but nothing happened. He glanced down the hill and recognized Eleganza almost immediately. The rest were just a blur of angry faces. He turned his attention away from them again just as the spearhead of the mob clashed with the tip of the wedge. He tried to force the lid open, but it would not go. He checked the lock, but there was no reason it should not have opened. It dawned on him finally that Tinker Manwalker must have tampered with it after all.

He took out his cane and turned it to full force. The flash when he touched its tips to the metal of the locking mechanism made him flinch. There was a loud sound like a shot, and for an instant the fighting seemed to freeze. The caners seemed unsure the shooters weren't just firing indiscriminately into the mob, and their hesitation was costly. The mob flowed around them along the sides of the wedge. In an instant it was behind them as well. They were better caners than he expected, and the others, some armed only with their fists, were beginning to overwhelm the exhausted Blues of the rickshaw teams, who formed the base of the wedge.

Pock threw open the lid. The guns lay still neatly stacked inside. He smiled in triumph. If the wedge held on a few seconds longer, it would be all over. He lay his cane aside within the case and grabbed a gun to toss it to the first of the shooters, but it seemed stuck. His fingers slipped off it and it stayed where it was. He wrapped his fist around the barrel and yanked, but the gun did not budge. He grabbed another, but it too seemed welded to the gun below it. He grabbed at guns with both hands, frantically clutching one after another, but they were all stuck together. Not one could be separated from the others, making all of them useless. He clawed in panic at the weapons, but they could not be pulled apart.

He knew immediately who had done it, but he did not know how until he tried to pick up his cane. It too clung to the mass of metal beneath it. He had to grasp it with two hands to break it free, and only as it came unstuck did he realize that the guns had been magnetized while still in their metal case. They were as useless as if she had melted them together with fire. He turned his face toward the hill in despair. What he saw only made him feel worse. A stream of rickshaws loaded with Granders was starting up the hill.

Chapter Seventeen

Eleganza stood on the edge of the fountain, the Pleasure Crew crowded around her like supplicants begging to be made whole. It amused her more than anything she could remember. They were so totally committed to her whims now. Before, she had been only the one who mattered most, now she was the only one that mattered. They reached up their hands to her, laughing, yearning for her to give them what she alone had the power to give them now. She held the crystal chalice high above them. They worshipped it, worshipped her for having it, for having been so clever as to earn it or take it or tease it from Spencer LeGrange himself. Its possession made her indescribably beautiful, even to herself.

She luxuriated in their adoration. And she was kind. The myriad times in the past when they had run counter to her desires, sometimes only on whim, sometimes just to assert their own foolish and trivial wills, sometimes for the sake of sheer perversity, were forgiven. She did not hold against them the times they had done less than homage to her; when, knowing she was the best they could offer, they had spitefully refused to do whatever she wanted. She did not remind them of the times, however infrequent, when they had failed to treat her as they should, as the absolute center of their world. She was magnanimous in her deification. Even those few, jealous of her wit or beauty or appetites, who had maligned her, who had understated her virtues and invented weaknesses for her, were forgiven, were blessed, as she blessed all of those who gathered in her gardens, with the DeeBee.

The blue flakes in the chalice seemed to glow in the waning light. All hands stretched upward, begging silently, clutching and unclutching in anticipation. All voices adored her without reservation. And the adoration was genuine. She deserved it. Who else would have thought of more than themselves; who would have pried from the clutch of Corporation more than an unlimited supply of pleasure for themselves? Only Eleganza would have forced Old Spence to create such a huge supply of the ultimate pleasure for others of her class and kind as well as for herself.

The chalice was her triumph, filled with little blue dots, created by the sweat of Corporation technicians, to arouse and satisfy each of them individually. And although it was true that it had not been such a great task for Corporation to duplicate hundreds of blue dots from the patterns it already had stored in its computers for each of them, only Eleganza could have forced it to do so. In one brilliant maneuver, she had freed those faithful who had gathered around her gardens since they were children together.

It was true she had not so liberated the less than faithful who had always taken their pleasure at Tinker's Tor or Dah Beel's, while Elgin was still alive, or in the Halls of the Rickshaw King. But she could do so. And would, when they realized the wonderful thing she had done for them and worshipped her as everyone else did.

In the meantime, she had rewarded only the most deserving, naming them each to the nondescript technician who had loaded their identities into the great apparatus that had made such pleasure for them, making sure that none were forgotten, none left out. And when the chalice was empty, she had only to return Earthside to come back with more. Spencer LeGrange might still control the Grand Sphere, might still have the power of money and force the League made for him even Earthside, but Eleganza had in return the greatest of all powers in the only world that mattered to her, the world of her class, her kind, the Pleasure Crew.

It did not matter to her that she had purchased her power with Aerowaffen's dream of a Revolution. It was an idle dream at best, something that would take years if not decades to come to fruition. From the moment he had touched that white dot to her forehead, she had known everything. She did not need Spencer LeGrange to tell her what could be done with the power of pleasure. Given five years or ten, Aerowaffen and his Revolutionaries might have used the Universal Tickler to infiltrate the whole of Corporation. In a decade or two, they might have used the lever the need for DeeBee created to secure absolute allegiance to their cause, even within the Fist, and in the end they might even have succeeded. She did not care; she herself had freed the only part of the Grand Sphere that needed freeing, the Pleasure Crew. It was all that mattered. She was sure even Aerowaffen would come to see that eventually, that he would return and do her homage with the rest.

She had already determined to forgive him for his meanness to her. It was true she had hated him when he had refused to touch that liberating white dot to her forehead as she lay drowning in that terrible nightmare, but that was all behind them now. She had seen that undeniable look in his eyes as he had bent over her, the tender concern for her safety struggling with the necessity to destroy her. She had seen it before in Voorpenny's eyes, but she had been too young then to understand that Voorpenny would have to betray her *because* of what he felt for her. She had known in the instant that Aerowaffen bent over her that he was different only in kind, that he would betray her *despite* what he felt for her instead of because of it. She had only beaten him to the punch. And now she was willing to forgive him. She could afford it; she had won.

She did not even plan to tell him that he was alive because of her, that his life had been part of her bargain. She had no doubt that he would figure it out for himself eventually, and if it took him awhile, she was willing to wait. Time passed easily for her in the DeeBee. Ultimately, he would return and beg her forgiveness, and she would give it. He amused her so much, brought her so much enjoyment, added so much to the pleasuring. After all, even if he was not of their class, he was of their kind. Even in the DeeBee, there was a need for the kind of stimulation and excitement, the unexpected diversion only Aerowaffen could create. She could not stay angry with him for long. She was sure he knew that.

She dipped a hand into the chalice and withdrew one of the blue dots on the tip of her finger. She turned it toward her and read the code. When she announced the name, it was greeted with groans and laughter, and the lucky pleasurer struggled forward through the press of the Crew to kneel in front of her. She pressed it to his forehead, and the joy spread across his face. He rose and glided through the crowd toward the glistening colors of the pool. The others were already cheering for the next name and the next. Eleganza smiled regally and dug into the chalice again. She read and raised the dot, but she did not call the name. She looked instead at the figure who stepped from the entrance of the maze.

The Crew turned slowly to follow her eyes. There was no missing the man. His Skyshocker's cloak and flaming red hair were as out of place among them as the unheard-of seriousness of his expression. Skyshockers were always smiling, but this one seemed on the verge of tears. He came slowly toward the silent crowd; those nearest forgot the DeeBee for the moment and stood aside in anticipation of his passage. Only Vor stood in his way.

Vor cared nothing for the DeeBee or Eleganza's ritual, but he had good reason to want no interruption. His partsister had no desire for any power but the power over pleasure, but *he* knew what that power could bring. Viktor Van Vast was rapidly slipping into the apathy of old age, and the family would soon be his to govern, if only by default. He was clearly Viktor's intended successor, but it was a shaky inheritance. Since the opening of the Little Door, the Van Vasts had been gradually crowded from power by the Dah Beels and Gun Sub Runn's clan. Even the upstart Tinker Manwalker posed a threat to the family's fortune.

Nor would the Van Vasts be the first of the Original Speculators to fall. The peak that Tinker Manwalker now owned had once been the stronghold of a Speculator almost as powerful as Viktor Van Vast. The sooner and the more irreversibly the Pleasure Crew was bound by addiction to Eleganza's chalice, the sooner its rightful power would begin to return to the family Vor Van Vast would soon head. With that much power over the Pleasure Crew, he could restore the family to the position it had held when he was a child. He could control the Grand Sphere, and if the rumors about his parentage were true, even Spencer LeGrange's vast empire might one day fall to him. The Skyshocker started to pass him, but Vor stuck his cane in the man's chest. "You're intruding here," he said. He looked around disdainfully at the rest. "They have no time for ordinary entertainments."

"I have news," the redhead said.

Vor laughed. "Skyshockers don't *have* news, they make it." It was true, when the Skyshockers played the news, they made half of it up as they went along. It didn't matter; it still contained more truth than any news from the LeGrange Amusement and News Network.

"I have news from Aerowaffen."

Vor took the cane out of the man's chest and gave it a threatening twist. "Then we definitely don't want to hear it."

Eleganza lowered the chalice. "Wait. . . ."

Vor poked the cane toward the Skyshocker, but it never reached him. Push slapped it by in front of him and smacked Vor in the middle of the forehead with the back of his fist. It left Vor sitting on the grass, trying to clear his head. The Skyshocker stepped up beside Eleganza on the edge of the fountain. "Aerowaffen's dead," he said. "The Fist shot him on the Upside Window." He caught the chalice as it fell from Eleganza's hand. There were murmurs of disbelief and dismay.

Eleganza felt numb. Under its cobalt-blue cap, her finger began to throb. Her voice was foggy with bewilderment. "Shot?" she said.

"Gunned down in a rickshaw along with UWalk Wenn." The Pleasure Crew shouted denials.

Eleganza spoke without thinking. "Who?"

"A Blue." He spoke as if he had been there himself. "He stepped out of the crowd and shot them as they went by."

"Was it an accident?" She knew already it wasn't. Spencer LeGrange had played her for a Fool. The DeeBee in the chalice was all she'd ever get.

Push shook his head. "It was an ambush." Eleganza felt sick. "And it's not the only gun in the Sphere."

The Pleasure Crew roared with outrage. "But why?!" someone shouted. "Why would they murder the Panda?"

"Because he had the DeeBee," the Skyshocker shouted, "Because he was giving it away to *you*. Because Spencer LeGrange wants your pleasure squeezed tight in his fist!"

"Where are the guns?!" someone else shouted.

"At CORPQ and the Little Door and the Annex!" There was a great commotion, but he shouted over it. "Old Spence plans to use them to take back the Little Door and the Sphere." He waited for the significance of the threat to sink in. "Unless *you* stop him!"

Vor raised his cane in anger, but not at the Skyshocker. He knew immediately what the guns would mean for the Van Vasts, the end of everything. It was all-out war, and it could have only one objective, the complete subjugation of the League. Spencer LeGrange obviously meant to put the Grand Sphere under the absolute control of Corporation for the first time since it was built. It would mean a purge, with trials Earthside and executions for everybody with enough power to oppose Spencer LeGrange, guilty or not. The power of the Speculators would be broken forever. Spencer LeGrange would finally have his revenge.

The Skyshocker pointed straight up where the Sphere curved overhead. "Downside is already in revolt. We have the Annex! We have the Little Door! And before the night is out, we'll have CORPQ!"

The crowd shouted its rage and approval. The thrill of the Risk flowed through them and even the DeeBee was forgotten for a moment. "Take CORPQ!" they shouted. But Push handed the chalice back to Eleganza and raised his hands.

"Wait! Even Upside's in the streets. The Wideway is jammed. You're not needed *there*!"

Vor was the first to ask, "Then where?" His mind was already made up, but Spencer LeGrange was only partly responsible. All his life he had hoped for a Risk as big as the one the Original Speculators had taken. He had never really expected to get his chance, and now it was before him. The odds against succeeding were even greater than they were when Viktor Van Vast had sealed the hemispheres. But the rewards were greater as well. There were no limits on what a man like Vor Van Vast might do in a League freed of the domination of Corporation. Endless riches if he won, death if he lost. It was the kind of bet Vor had only dreamed of.

"Where?" he shouted again. But he already knew. If the Wideway was blocked and both hemispheres were in revolt, there was only one place of importance worth taking beside CORPQ, the Orchard Notch.

Push pointed toward it as he spoke. "There's only one way out of Downside, and that's over the Round Mountain at Orchard Notch. If the Fist takes that, it can take Upside back. Somebody has to hold the Orchard Notch!"

The Pleasure Crew hesitated. The thrill of danger pulled them toward the battle, the love of pleasure held them back. Only Eleganza could set them free of it. Push turned to her. "I was with him when he died," he said. "He left a message for you. He said he'd bet the digit with you if he could."

Eleganza took the chalice and turned it upside down. The

blue dots fluttered down into the Sauce. They sparked and crackled as they hit. "Free DeeBee or none!" she cried. "Death to Spencer LeGrange!"

Vor pointed his cane toward the top of the Crossway. "To the notch!" The Pleasure Crew surged toward it, possessed by the spirit of the game.

Chapter Eighteen

The Pleasure Crew poured down through the maze behind Eleganza and Vor, grabbing everything they could find to use as a weapon. Perhaps a dozen had canes, the rest picked up abandoned gardener's tools, or tore branches from the trees in the lower garden. Push ran alongside them to the bottom of the maze. They ran easily, and only a few straggled behind before they got to the bottom. They worked hard at their pleasure, and it kept them in top physical condition. They ran gleefully; the risk of death was no more to them than the most fascinating part of an exciting game. The thrill of being on the edge kept them from thinking about Aerowaffen except to think how splendid a Panda he had been to leave them such an adventure as his parting gift.

Vor glanced over at the Skyshocker as they ran. "You have a name?" He was certain the man had dozens.

The Skyshocker nodded. "I'm Push of the Cage."

Vor nodded. "Van Vast," he said. Only the head of the family would use the last name alone. They ran a little farther in silence before Vor asked the important question. "Are there guns in the notch?"

Push shook his head. "There's nothing in the notch," he

said. "They's why you've got to get there first." It didn't
exactly say that Pock would not have guns, but Vor let the
question drop. He himself was willing to go up against guns
if they were there, but he would not have told the others
anyway for fear of their turning back. When they reached
the lower arc of the maze, Push began to turn off. Vor looked
at him doubtfully, and Push answered the unasked question.
"You're going to need reinforcements. I have rickshaws in
Dah Beel City. I'll be back as soon as I can with help. You'll
have to hold off Pock alone until then."

Vor raised an eyebrow. "Pock?"

Push nodded. "Try to take him alive. He can get us into
the Orchard Gate at CORPQ." He handed Vor a small bag
of chewables. "These'll help," he said. "But don't give them
out until you reach the bottom of Iron Mountain." Then he
was gone cross-country toward the lower part of the Crossway. The Pleasure Crew went overland as well until they hit
Upper Vast Narrow and from there it was all hard road to
the Crossway. They exited onto it only a few hundred yards
from the base of the mountain. At the bottom Vor stopped,
and the rest gathered around him. He handed the bag to
Eleganza. "Bless everybody," he said.

She looked at the bag and cocked her head. Vor shrugged.
"Zooms, probably. Or Stings. Or both." He looked at the
Pleasure Crew waiting anxiously to start the Game.
"What'll this lot care?"

Eleganza scowled at his belittling of her congregation; she
took a handful and tossed them into her mouth defiantly.
Then she turned and went among her followers, giving each
a portion of what she had. Although some had thrown
themselves into the fountain after the DeeBee, the rest
seemed confident that they would triumph over Corporation
and obtain unlimited stores of it anyway. Most secretly
suspected that Eleganza had more stored somewhere and
was only testing them to see who would love and follow her
even without the DeeBee. Not even Vor believed that she
had really thrown it all away.

She did not disillusion them, but what she had thrown

into the pool had been all that she had for them, including most of the dots programmed specially for her own brain. It did not matter; that high, clear note had begun to sound the moment she turned the chalice upside down, and it was ringing still all around her. She had more than a finger at risk, and the exhilaration of it swept through her continuously. It was stronger than her grief for Aerowaffen, stronger even than her rage against Spencer LeGrange. Stronger even than the DeeBee. For the moment, it was all she needed.

Vor watched them take their chewables and waited impatiently for the effects to begin, but no change in their mood or their stamina was visible. Eleganza came back and handed him the bag, all but empty. He looked at what she had left him and closed the bag untouched. Only a Skyshocker, he decided, would give the Pleasure Crew drugless drugs. It was a great joke. When they began to run, he was not so sure.

The crowd that had run behind him all the way from Van Vast's Peak suddenly started swinging up abreast of him and darting ahead of him from time to time before falling back, more out of deference than fatigue. By the middle of the hill, he was beginning to feel the strain of the steep uphill run, but the rest were bursting with energy and kept pushing him to go faster. Eleganza was running backward in short sprints to see if everyone was keeping up, and whenever she did, she pulled away from him steadily and always gave him a disdainful look before turning around and letting her pace drop to his.

The third time she did it, reason overcame arrogance and Vor pulled the bag from his pleasuresuit and crammed a handful of chewables into his mouth. It was the rational thing to do; however enthusiastic Eleganza's playmates were, he was still going to have to do most of the fighting, and Pock's forces would be stoked on every Zoom and Sting available. He would be foolish to go up against them with less help.

Almost immediately, they took the dryness from his

throat and the ache from his muscles. By the third step he was fresher than he had been at the beginning. The threat of bullets seemed absolutely insignificant to him, and the power of Pock's forces seemed trivial, even when he saw the first of them crest the hill and take up position in the notch. It did not even worry him when he saw Pock fumbling to open a large case on the rickshaw, even though he was certain it was the guns. After that, they had closed with Pock's small advanced guard, and it was all fighting.

For Vor, it was pure joy. He hit the point of the Fist's wedge, sidestepped a lunge, and knocked the lead caner back into the rest with an elbow that was all shoulder and follow-through. Somebody beside him went down in a blue flash that meant they would never get up again, and he half expected the rest to turn and run, but they didn't. One of the unarmed ones threw herself into the wedge right on the points of a cane aimed for Vor. There was another blue flash and the smell of charring meat, but she dragged the cane down with her and opened the Blue to Vor's thrust to the throat. There was no blue flash from Vor's cane, but it left the Blue too stunned to hold his weapon. No sooner did the cane drop that it reappeared in the hands of one of the attackers. The attack rolled over the fallen Blue, and when it had passed, someone with hedge shears did what Vor's cane couldn't.

Everywhere one of the Pleasure Crew fell, two more seemed to appear, and their ferocity put the Fist on the defensive even more than their numbers. He could not believe they were the same people who had giggled and languished beside the pool. Out of the corner of his eye, he caught sight of Eleganza ducking a lunge by a huge Bronze and throwing herself on him in an embrace that was all fingers and teeth. She had the Bronze's cane arm pinned, and somebody reached down and pressed the point of a cane between his eyes. There was a blue flash and an upcurl of smoke, and Eleganza was up and advancing with the rest.

The wedge buckled in a storm of red flashes that came from cane tips striking insulation suits, but it re-formed

itself and retreated steadily up the hill until it was almost to
the rickshaw. Vor was a blur of parries and lunges down the
side of the wedge to intercept canes meant for others. Of the
seven caners who had gone down out of the wedge, four had
fallen under Vor's thrusts. There was a trail of bodies down
the short stretch of hill. At least three pleasurers were down
for every member of the Fist. Some of the Granders were
only stunned from glancing blows; some were burned and
writhing on the ground in pain, and some were dead-burned,
but not one of the Fist would ever rise again.

But it was not merely the violence of the Pleasure Crew's
attack that demoralized the Fist, it was their laughter. To
the rickshaws coming up the far side of the hill, it sounded
like a party was being thrown just beyond the crest. Even
those who fell from the stings of canes went down in a shriek
of laughter, and those who sat on the roadway cupping their
wounds closer to themselves seemed to chuckle as they
rocked with pain. Once one of the Blues broke and ran, but
from the moment he left the tight knot of the wedge, he was
doomed. He got halfway around the rickshaw, heading for
the downhill, before he disappeared under a ball of howling
pursuers. In a moment his cane was yanked out of the pile
and in another his suit was ripped away and he was just
another smoldering corpse.

They were almost to the rickshaw when Vor saw the lid of
the case fly up. He knew instantly what it meant, and he
knew that he was too far away to stop it. He jabbed and
swung, but he was pressed against the wedge and there was
no breaking away in time. He waited for the first shot,
knowing he would be its target, but the shot did not come.
The fighting was too fierce for him to look up again until the
last four of the Fist were pressed back against the side of the
rickshaw. When he did, he saw Pock trying to yank something out of the case with both hands. He saw Eleganza
come leaping up the far side of the rickshaw. Pock caught
sight of her over his shoulder at the same moment.

For Eleganza, the struggle up the hill had been one
exciting game after another. When she had thrown herself

on the Blue, she had gripped him with a passion that was not satisfied until the flash exploded near her ear like the sound of her release. And when she leapt to her feet, quivering with pleasure, she was overcome by a doubled hunger for greater risk, greater danger. It was not the sharp, gnawing need she had felt with DeeBee; it was hardly a need at all, just a growing momentum of passion that peaked and peaked and continued to rise.

Wherever there was Risk, there was pleasure, and Pock's rickshaw seemed to glow on the peak of the hill with desirability. She had tried to run for it even before the Fist had been backed up into it, but there had been a shove from the crowd milling past her to the attack, and she had been knocked off her feet. The rickshaw seemed to rise from the center of a great fountain of light as she picked herself up from the roadway.

There was no passing the mob, and she waited for it to flatten against the Fist and the rickshaw, and when it did, she saw her chance and took it. She was around the rickshaw before anyone even noticed her. It did not occur to her that if Pock managed to raise one of the guns and fire it into the crowd, the whole attack would fall apart. For her, Pock's struggle with the case was only the light at the center of the light, and she was drawn to it by the irresistible callings of desire.

She went up onto the shortseat in a single leap; Pock was only a little beyond arm's reach when everything slowed down. She watched him catch sight of her over his shoulder and start to turn. She threw her arms wide to wrap them around him and bear him over the side of the rickshaw into the mob, but she never got the chance to close them on him. She expected the roar of a gun and an impact in her abdomen that would fling her dead out over the forks. It did not seem to matter. All the finality of it added was a thrill, like the instant before the bet. Her finger seemed still to be in the tight, unforgiving hole of that little gray box on the Wideway. Everything shone with unimaginable delight.

And then everything snapped back into motion. Pock wheeled, and everything went black.

Vor watched Pock turn with a despair that hit him like a blow. He expected a terrifying explosion, an orange flash, a spattering of blood. Instead, Pock wheeled, not with a gun but with his cane. The butt of it caught her alongside the skull and rocked her head to the side, even as her body kept falling forward. Her hair spread out from her head and wrapped around the cane. There was a flash of blue and a flare of orange flame as the force of the blow swept her out over the side of the rickshaw. Gun or cane, that flash had meant fatality, he was sure. She landed in a heap on the far side of the rickshaw. Vor gave a strangled cry of rage and despair.

He took a lunge on the forearm and let it burn him. The insulation on his pleasuresuit was far less than on the uniform of the Fist, but it was enough. The flash was reddish purple. He used it to throw the cane aside and step inside the arm. His kick doubled the Bronze, and he used the crumpling defender as a step to mount the side of the rickshaw. Pock had followed Eleganza's fall and had not turned his attention back to the fight before Vor was on him. His jab was aimed at the slice of neck exposed above Pock's insulated collar, but Pock turned in time and caught the shaft of the cane with a sweep of his hand. He yanked as he turned, all in one motion, and the cane came free. It did not save him.

The hand swept across the momentum of Vor's body to catch the cane, but it had passed well out of the way of the rest of Vor's lunge as he hurtled forward. The flat of his forearm caught Pock in the face and toppled him backward. They both fell from the rickshaw without a chance to break their fall, and they lay stunned on the roadway. Pock hit on the back of his head, and the fingers of his fist flew open, releasing his cane. Vor landed on the side of his forehead, his right cheek and eye. Both of them fought to rise but couldn't shake the dizziness and nausea. Pock lay staring up at the lights of Downside. The Wideway shone only in flecks and speckles where no Grander was standing. The Downside Window glowed around its circular island; the cross of roadway between the four bridges was dulled by the crowd of bodies blocking its light. It occurred very vaguely to Pock that it might be all over. He rolled to his side.

His head ached as if the fist had grown until it could squeeze his entire skull. He tried to stand, but the fist squeezed him to his knees again. He saw his cane beyond the back wheel of the rickshaw, but it seemed so far away he did not think the fist would even let him crawl to it. He watched Vor struggling to push himself up from his knees. Vor raised his head and looked toward him, but one eye was swollen shut, and he had to swing his head from side to side to see anything.

The sound of the rickshaws coming down over the hill turned them away from each other. Vor groaned. The rickshaws were filled with a contingent of Bronze. If the whole of the Pleasure Crew had studied electric cane as long as he had, it would have been a fierce battle; instead, it would only be a massacre. The numbers that had once been on the side of the Pleasure Crew were now on the side of the Fist. Everything was on their side. They was attacking downhill. They had ridden up the far side of Orchard Hill instead of running, and they were fresh. They swept past him and around the rickshaw, intent on slaughter.

The Pleasure Crew had no sense of tactics, but the Fist came flowing around both sides of the rickshaw and compressed them into a wedge. It shrank their perimeter to a size they could defend. They were hopelessly outclassed, but it did not seem to matter. They threw themselves at their attackers with a maniacal joy that stunned the Fist and made it give way. The Pleasure Crew pursued; it was a tactical mistake. Their enthusiasm spread them out and made them more vulnerable. Clamped between the encircling arms of the Fist with their back to the rickshaw, they had been able to hold their own, but as they spread out, it was easy to retreat from their wild, individual charges and then close in around them as they attacked. Vor could see that in a matter of minutes they would be picked to pieces.

He forced himself to his feet, but he could not find his cane. His right eye was swollen shut and his left was watering too hard for him to see anything. He wiped it with the back of his hand and peered under the rickshaw. The cane he saw was not his, and it was too short to be a Police cane, but it would do.

Pock was on his hands and knees, crawling toward his own cane. When he forced himself up and staggered after it, Vor made a run for the rickshaw. It was not much of a run, but it seemed like miles. His vision was blurred and his body felt as if he had fallen all the way across the Sphere. Pock picked up his cane and turned to look for him; Vor dived and rolled under the rickshaw.

Pock turned in two short, bewildered circles. He stepped away from the rickshaw and looked around. Bronze poured past, adding to the forces pressing in on the Pleasure Crew. He thought for a moment that one of them had driven Vor past him down the hill, but he looked under the rickshaw and found him. Vor had a cane by then, and he came out from under the rickshaw on all fours, a perfect target if Pock had been close enough to touch him. But the distance was too great and Pock was still hazy. He lurched toward Vor; his thrust was ill-timed and missed by a half a yard, but it put him on Vor's blind side and he was safe.

Vor slashed a backhand into the darkness on his right. The motion turned him, and he saw that he had missed. Pock dodged a second lunge and backed away, circling to his left, always into Vor's blindness. Vor turned sharply in a little circle, trying to keep Pock in view. Shouts and cries and crazy laughter sounded from the far side of the rickshaw, but they paid no attention to them. Pock's circling took him close to Eleganza's body, but he glanced down at it only enough to keep from getting his feet tangled up.

The hair on one whole side was frizzled and singed. Her eyes were closed and, except for the dark swelling around her left eye, she might have been asleep. Vor's cane lay near her, and he thought for an instant of picking it up and attacking with both hands, but he did not want to risk bending down for it and giving Vor a momentary advantage. He was much larger than Vor, and anything in close was as much to his advantage with one cane as with two. Vor looked at Eleganza and made his lunge. He did not see her eyes begin to open.

Eleganza's eyes opened on Downside. The little points seemed like assurances that everything would be all right. She half expected to see Aerowaffen's face looming over her, talking her back to the light and the beauty. She wondered where he was for a moment, how she had fallen into that darkness without him hovering protectively near, and then she remembered that he was dead. It seemed to plunge her into darkness again. Her head throbbed, and her sight cleared and blurred. Two figures circled in her vision, one so close that at first it seemed only a pair of large, muscular calves. The calves fascinated her. The thick muscle bulged through a rip in the gold of the uniform. It seemed to thrust itself into the light as if unafraid of its vulnerability outside the safe insulation of the suit.

Only gradually did she realize that it was Pock and Vor, and as soon as she did, she tried to rise. She got to one knee and had to put a hand down for support. It fell on the shaft of Vor's cane. She looked down at it without comprehension. Only when the picture carved on its handle came into focus did she realize what it was. She was afraid for a moment that Vor was unarmed, but when she looked again, she saw him make an attack and knew that he was not. She stood shakily, the cane dangling loosely from her hand, and started toward them. She was almost to them, the cane coming slowly up for a sting, when her legs gave out and she fell to her hands and knees.

Vor and Pock were almost within reach until Pock's fist hit him in the chest and sent him staggering backward. Pock followed it up with a lunge, but Vor parried it and answered with a lunge of his own. But his lunge carried him too close to Pock again. The Fist stepped into the shadow of Vor's vision and punched him hard to the side of the head. Vor stumbled to his left and slashed backward into the blackness with his cane. Pock leaned back and the tips cut an arc inches from his face. He made his own strike after it went by, and the prongs of his cane touched Vor's suit. There was a bluish-purple flash, and Vor flew away from it as if he had been kicked in the chest.

He landed in a heap, tried to roll, and flopped over again. He strained to lift his head so he could turn his good eye toward Pock but fell back on his face. Pock stood looking down at him, waiting for him to rise. His head ached and he wanted to get it over with and sit down, but he seemed too tired to step forward and put an end to it. The standing made him unsteady, and he took a wide step backward to catch his balance. It was the biggest mistake he had made in a long series of mistakes.

It put him within reach of Eleganza, and she did not miss. The tips of Vor's cane touched the exposed flesh of his calf, and his head snapped back as the voltage shook his body. His knees buckled and he sagged to the ground. Eleganza sank back to her hands and knees again and tried to let her head clear. She had never known real pain before, and it fascinated her. She was surprised at how sick it made her feel and how weak. She sat on the backs of her legs with her head dangling until someone came and tried to lift her up. It occurred to her too late that she should have tried to revive Vor and sneak away in the heat of the battle. She knew capture meant trial and execution, but she was too tired to care. She looked up into the face of her captor and started in surprise.

Instead of a Blue, the hands that helped her up belonged to Push. He smiled at her with the kind of ironic smile Skyshockers were famous for and lifted her to her feet. "Had enough pleasuring for a while?" he said.

Strong hands from Dah Beel City were helping Vor to stand. He looked at Eleganza as if she were a hallucination and reached to touch her as if he expected his fingers to pass through her. "I saw the flash. . . ." He did not need to say what he thought. Eleganza stroked his cheek.

Push pointed to the mass of frizzled and singed hair that made up one side of her head. "The points must have discharged in her hair and the strands caught fire and shriveled up instead of carrying the charge."

Vor looked down the hill for the Bronze, but there were only the dead and wounded. Push shook his head. "Fools came right down around the Pleasure Crew and turned their backs on us. They were so intent on annihilating the rest of you, they forgot we were coming up the hill behind them. Until the rickshaws rammed into them." He laughed as if he could still see bodies flying out of the way like tossed pebbles. "Of course, it didn't hurt that a third of them were our people to begin with. When they came over to our side, the rest broke and ran."

Vor gave a disappointed sigh. "Then it's all over."

Push laughed. "Not quite. We still have CORPQ to take." He gestured toward Pock. "But with a little help from our friends, it won't take long."

Chapter Nineteen

They had Pock awake and talking in ten minutes. The calf of his leg was knotted solid as Iron Mountain and he kept rubbing it, trying to knead it into straightening out. His toes were flexed upward, and he pushed them forcibly down every few seconds, trying to loosen the knot behind his leg. He was still in a lot of pain, but he did not mention it. For a man so close to death, it seemed too trivial to be worth saying anything about. He sat in the rickshaw on the long-seat opposite Push, close enough to reach out and take him by the throat if he was dumb enough to try it.

But Pock was far from dumb, despite his circumstances. He waited for Push to speak, feigning a dizziness that had long since left him. Vor Van Vast and Eleganza sat in the shortseat, half turned toward him. Eleganza's left eye was swollen shut, Vor's right. Side by side they made a complete uninjured face. It was not smiling. If there was a vote on his execution, the only argument would be over who got the pleasure. Push was smiling. Pock was not sure what it meant, if it meant anything.

Push opened the lid of the case and shook his head at the guns. The smile seemed about to break out into laughter.

"Bought a bad case," he said. It had a number of meanings besides the obvious one that the guns did not work. It meant everything from catching a venereal disease on the Wideway to buying in quantity what nobody would have bought individually. In the Fist it was even a synonym for going undercover, and in that regard it ridiculed Pock for "buying" Push's cover as a Blue.

Pock had been in the Sphere long enough to know that it probably had a meaning he couldn't even guess at. He shrugged. "It was a gift."

Push nodded. "You're lucky Old Spence likes you." The sarcasm was hardly noticeable. He did not need to say that Pock would be the scapegoat for the loss of the Sphere. "He'll be glad to get you back."

It was as much a promise as a threat. At least Earthside, he would get to live through a trial, and even if Old Spence arranged him an accident or a suicide on the way back, it would be better than being thrown to the mob on the Wideway, or being sent to Hardcore. There were a lot of ugly ways to die in Hardcore. Whatever Push wanted from him, it was a buyer's market. He tried to act as if it weren't. "He likes his own back," he said. It was a useless bluff, and they both knew it. The only thing Old Spence would want him for was public execution.

"So do we," Push said. There was no doubt he meant the Sphere. "All of it."

"Talk to Old Spence about it." It was something a Grander would say to indicate he had nothing to do with whatever was being discussed, or that somebody might as well ask to talk to Spencer LeGrange as ask for whatever they were asking for.

Push's Skyshocker grin widened as if they were on the brink of striking a bargain. It worried Pock more than the frowns on Eleganza and Vor Van Vast. "So we will. So we will," he said. "If you'll lend us your private holo."

The exchange of exactly those words took place on the Sphere a hundred times a day. The futility of trying to get through to Spencer LeGrange, and the outrageous pretense that someone had a private channel to him, were a traditional part of Grander humor. Said the wrong way, the last phrase was an accusation that the listener was a Corporation spy, and in the right situation was as certain to provoke violence as "Drop a mountain on it." But Push was not joking, and the private holo next to Pock's office was the only direct way to contact Spencer LeGrange to negotiate.

The ramifications were obvious to Pock. The holo was in CORPQ; to use it they would have to get inside. Push was asking that he surrender CORPQ, and yet he was sure Push was not such a Fool as that. As long as the Fist held CORPQ, the Sphere could be retaken. The guns might have been destroyed, but the next time they would come carried by the Fist and not in a case. Giving up CORPQ meant giving up the only hope Corporation had, and there were no guarantees that he would not be returned to Old Spence after he did it.

To have lost the rest of the Sphere by incompetence was one thing, but to give up CORPQ was something else. For a thing like that, Spencer LeGrange would have teams of doctors keep him alive forever just so Old Spence could burn his brain a dozen hours a day. Next to years of brainburn, being torn apart by a Grander mob seemed like a reasonable alternative. Pock snorted. "You don't suggest I give you CORPQ."

Push looked hurt. "Certainly not," he said. He gave it a Grander pause. "Only the Orchard Gate."

Pock laughed despite himself. "Would you rather the Universal Tickler?" It was meant as a joke, the Grander equivalent of asking for the impossible.

Push shook his head. "We already have it," he said, "thanks to Spencer LeGrange."

Pock's face fell. He looked at Eleganza. It suddenly struck him what had been wrong with the skinner on Standard's thighscreen. The dot on her forehead in the pleasuresuit's recording of Standard's first trip to the Sphere had been *white*. It should have been blue! And the dote in the second skinner was white as well! It could only mean that Corporation had invented the Universal Tickler years before, and that Standard had brought a prototype Up for testing on his first trip to the Sphere. It was why Old Spence had only laughed when he saw Standard too overdone to stand upright.

But if the Universal Tickler had been around for even a year, half the key positions in Corporation and in the Fist could be in the hands of the Revolution. He had never had a chance of stopping it. The League had been as good as lost before he even heard about it, and it was all Old Spence's fault. The sheer irony of it made him laugh out loud.

Push nodded as if Pock had finally caught on to the joke. "That's right," he said. "Old Spence had it invented to destroy the Pleasure Crew, and when he sent a prototype Up to the Sphere, we stole it for a while and copied it." He smiled at Eleganza, and Pock understood when it had been stolen. He groaned at his own stupidity. It had been right under his nose. He'd even been there when Wenn passed on the news of their success. A snatch of rickshaw song came floating back to him. "He be DeeBee, Slick and Slide, Elle took he tongue-o, tickee for a ride."

"Then we returned the original and used our copies to infiltrate Corporation's Research team." He shrugged as if it were no fault of his. "Their prototype developed problems, and they've been trying to get it working again ever since." He shook his head in mock sympathy. "And when they finally get it to work, it's too late."

Even Eleganza looked surprised. Push grinned and nodded. "Yes," he said, "that whole chalice was full of Universal Ticklers. Old Spence made them blue so you'd think they had to be renewed." Eleganza winced at the thought of them fluttering down into the pool. But it did not matter; if they were Universal Ticklers, the ones she'd saved for herself would keep both her and the Pleasure Crew in DeeBee for a long, long time.

Push shook his head. "And poor Slick was the only one they had good data on, so every time they thought they had a working model, they had to try it out on him." It explained why Old Spence had been so tolerant of Standard's addiction, at least until the Tickler was perfected and it wasn't useful anymore. No doubt Eleganza's visit had been an opportunity for a final field test.

Pock could figure out the rest. While Corporation's efforts floundered, the Revolutionaries went into mass production. With even a dozen models, they could have infiltrated half the Fist or more. With two years of the Universal Tickler and who knew how many years before that, preparing for just such an opportunity, he was surprised *anybody* was still on Corporation's side. No wonder Old Spence had sent guns; he was desperate.

If he had known that much before, he might have headed off the revolt, or at least held on to the Annex or the Little Door. He cursed Standard for withholding the information; he cursed Spencer LeGrange for letting Standard withhold it. There was no doubt he had bought a bad case, and he had bought it from Spencer LeGrange.

It did not occur to him just how bad the case was until he realized *why* Spencer LeGrange had sent the guns and *why* they had kept him in the dark. He was supposed to be Corporation's Fool. With the structure of Corporation subverted, both in the League and Earthside, Old Spence needed time to purge his empire. He had planned to buy that time with Pock. Given the guns and an order to use them, Pock would either stop the Revolution with a massacre or make himself hated enough to be a symbol Old Spence could offer up to the Granders during negotiations for the return of the Sphere. It did not occur to Pock any more than it did to Spencer LeGrange that the Granders intended to keep the Sphere. Just as it had not occurred to Old Spence that the Revolutionaries would strike early.

But Push and his kind had anticipated them at every step. Pock admired that kind of cleverness. It would take a good deal of cleverness of his own to avoid being its victim. It might be too late to stop the Revolution; it wasn't too late to join it. "He won't let you keep it," he said finally. "He'll blow it up first."

Eleganza and Vor looked at each other as if they hadn't considered *that* possibility. Push just laughed. "Not while we have hostages," he said.

Pock scowled. Certainly Push couldn't think Old Spence would hesitate for an instant to blow up every Exec and Fist in the League if the alternative was giving up control of the habitats. "There isn't anything on Earth Spence LeGrange cares *that* much about."

"There is above it," Push said. Pock almost laughed out loud at how obvious it was. Everything on Earth depended on the energy satellites the League had built. Without them, Corporation and Earth were both finished. If the Revolutionaries controlled them, Old Spence would have to capitulate. For the first time since he saw Push's rickshaw's start up the hill, Pock had hope that he would come out of it all alive.

He conceded the point. "But he won't even talk to you if you don't hold CORPQ." He saw his own leverage clearly. They could not take CORPQ without him. Push had admitted as much when he asked for the Orchard Gate.

Push cut the ground from under him with a smile. "We can take CORPQ anytime we want. We have it surrounded. The guns are unusable. Half the Blues inside are ours, and Tinker Manwalker can open the front door whenever we knock."

If Pock had not been in the Sphere so long, he would have accepted it all without argument. But he knew how Granders worked. The first thing a Grander did when he wanted something was to tell its owner why he didn't really need it. Some parts of the argument were almost certainly true. The guns had all been disabled, and it was likely that Tinker Manwalker could get to the circuits that would open the wallway in the front of CORPQ. CORPQ might even be surrounded; the Fourth had certainly been in trouble when he left. It was likely that some of the Fist had been subverted. The First could not have been defeated so easily in the Offshoots unless part of the Fist had turned against the others and aided the ambushers.

But he doubted that as many as a third of those who remained were not loyal. If half the Fist had gone over, there would be no reason even to talk to Pock. Still, it was likely that Push's boast was true. They *could* take CORPQ without him, but even without the use of guns, a great deal of blood would be shed. Push obviously wanted to take it without casualties. For that, they would need Pock. His cooperation ought to be worth at least his life. It might even be possible to convince people he had been in on it all along. How long he would last in the Grand Sphere after the fighting stopped was another story, but Pock had learned to narrow his focus to the present crisis at the cost of future ones. "What'll you give for a gate you don't need?"

Push seemed to ponder it as if the thought were completely new to him. After a suitable pause he said, "Well, for the gate and your holo, I'd say your life and an eight-hour start." It was the kind of Risk any Grander would have approved of.

It was the best Pock could hope for and he knew it. If the hundreds of enemies he had made over the years found him afterward, it would be his own mistake, and he would pay for it. "Done," he said.

A half hour later CORPQ had laid down its arms without a fight and the holopad next to Pock's office was crowded with people.

Chapter Twenty

Standard looked shrunken despite the size of his image. Need seemed to be making him smaller by the minute. Eleganza's battered face and Vor's swollen eye made him think the mob in the holo chamber were prisoners instead of conquerors. Need made him believe it.

It was true that the Skyshocker beside Pock was grinning and the blond in the green cape, who looked like his twin sister, was smiling also. But Skyshockers were crazy. They were always grinning. For them, the illusion of defeat was no less amusing than the illusion of victory. They would have kept those same enigmatic smiles if Pock were about to execute them.

The feelings of the Obees and Catchers scattered throughout the crowd were less easy to read, but Standard needed to see the faces of defeat, and everywhere he looked, that was what he saw. His own feelings about Pock's apparent victory were mixed. Much as he hated to see Pock do the impossible, he was willing to accept anything that ended the crisis and returned him to the bliss of the Glow.

Pock wondered what Old Spence would do with Standard when he found out that everything was lost. Nobody credited the old man with either justice or sentimentality, and Pock doubted Standard was going to be retired to a short but blissful life of unlimited DeeBee. Corporation might be responsible for Standard's addiction, but he doubted Old Spence was going to feel disposed to take responsibility for it when he found out what had happened. With Pock out of reach, Old Spence was going to need a scapegoat, and Standard was the only Exec handy who was important enough to make a good one. It made him glad he was in Push's hands instead of Old Spence's.

But he had no illusions; Push might let him go, but he was going to be on the run as long as he was alive. Probably the only thing Old Spence and the Granders would agree on was that he ought to die. A lot of people both Earthside and in the League weren't going to rest until he did. Still, he was a lot better off than Standard.

Standard looked at what he thought were the prisoners with contempt. "You should have used the guns to begin with," he said.

Whatever sympathy he was beginning to feel for Standard vanished. "If you'd been in range, I would have," he said.

Standard gave him an arrogant scowl. "Don't think it's going to change anything. A lot of Corporation property's been damaged because of your incompetence, and—"

Pock cut him off. "Shut up and get me Old Spence."

"Spencer LeGrange gives the orders here."

It almost made Pock laugh. "He doesn't give them *here*," he said.

The answer stopped Standard short. He was sure it was some Grander saying that meant everything but what it said, but he had no idea what its true meanings were. He couldn't imagine that it could be literally true.

Pock gave him no chance to ponder it. Knowing Granders, he was sure he would find out shortly that the clock on his eight-hour head start had been running since they left the Orchard Notch. He was going to need every minute he had left, and he had none to waste on Stefan

Standard. "Get him!" he said. The command rang with the threat of pain and death. Even some of his captors flinched at it. Standard reacted without another word. His image disappeared.

There was a long pause before another image materialized above the holopad. Pock turned to go. Two Obees and Vor Van Vast moved to block his escape, but Push waved them aside. "He still has more than seven hours to run," he said.

Vor looked at him steadily. The closed eye twisted his smile when he spoke, "A Chase, then," he said. The members of the Pleasure Crew in the room began the Starting Chant; they kept it up until Pock was gone. They would probably have kept it up until they started after him, but the flickering ball of light above the holopad distracted them from it.

The ball shaped itself into the outline of a gigantic head, faltered, and disappeared. The ball was replaced with a dazzling ring of light. The whole room cheered as if it were the Ring itself, taking the measure of their Risk. Push smiled. No doubt Old Spence's new Perscom was having trouble with the image. There was another dancing haze of light and finally the gigantic head formed before them.

Every fist in the room punched toward the sky, all voices shouted as one, "Live free or die!"

Old Spence recognized the slogan immediately. He even recognized Chancey, the blond in the green Skyshocker's cape, who had made it a fad throughout the League. He knew exactly what was going on the moment he heard it. His face was stern as death. Little shadows of outrage and vindictiveness played across it like interference patterns. He glared at the crowd and made his decision. "Return control of the Sphere to Corporation, or die," he said.

Push cocked his head as if he hadn't heard him right. "Repeat that," he said, ". . . slowly."

Old Spence looked at the Skyshocker as if he thought they were all beneath his contempt. But he repeated it anyway, slowly, a word at a time. In the middle of "control," the power went off all over the Western Hemisphere like a curtain of black running from north to south. Like an exclamation point after "Corporation," the Eastern Hemisphere shut down from south to north like a machine with its plug pulled. "Or" was as far as Old Spence got because there wasn't enough direct electricity on the planet to say any more. When the power came back on, it was Push's turn to talk.

"*We* don't need power satellites," he said. "We're self-sufficient. You have nothing to offer us, and we've long ago paid back the Corporation loan. The Grand Sphere, Hardcore, Catchcage, the Big and Little Wheels, and Henson's Tube are now free members of the League of Independent Habitats."

It wasn't exactly true, but it was as close to the truth as a Grander could be expected to get. There was still a good deal of arguing and infighting to do before the habitats would be able to unify themselves into anything as coherent as the League of Independent Habitats, but they had always been independent, and they were finally all free.

The declaration alone did not make them free. Even control of the habitats couldn't do it. Only power could make them free, and Push let Old Spence know just what power they had. "If any object whatsoever passes above the ionosphere, we will destroy two of the energy satellites." Old Spence didn't even blink, even though the threat meant a forty percent reduction in energy, planetwide. It was a reduction in power that would weaken the Corporation. Much more would cripple it. With four or five satellites gone, the Corporation would plunge back into the Dark Ages, taking the rest of the world with it.

The image of Old Spence disappeared for two minutes. When it returned, it said nothing. The dark, malevolent eyes looked around the room for recognizable faces that could be singled out for special punishment. They stopped on Eleganza and Vor and Push's twin sister, Chancey. They searched vainly for Aerowaffen, Wenn, and Pock. Twenty seconds later the head disappeared again. In its place was a satellite's view of the planet with a flight of launch vehicles coming up through the ionosphere to recapture the habitats.

Push shook his head as if Old Spence were an even bigger Fool than he thought and blew the first satellite. Before he could blow the second one, there were four flashes and the launch vehicles were gone. Old Spence's face reappeared; it looked decades older. "Terms," he said.

Push just looked at him and blew two more satellites.

Old Spence screamed. "What the hell are you doing?!"

It was Push's turn to look stern. "We told you. One attempt, two satellites."

Old Spence looked like his blood pressure was strangling him. The veins at his temples throbbed in the image like huge ropes being twisted. "THREE!" he shouted. "YOU BLEW *THREE*!!!" It was only one satellite from the end of everything.

Push looked at him as if he were surprised, then shrugged if off as if it weren't the difference between weakened and crippled. His Skyshocker grin seemed to go from ear to ear. "Well," he said, "the first one was to get your attention."

Spencer LeGrange looked for a minute as if he was considering blowing the habitats out of the sky and letting the Earth go down into oblivion with them. But there were still two satellites left, and he hesitated.

Push did not give him long to consider. "From now on, your affairs are the affairs of the planet. Ours are the affairs of space. Keep to your affairs, and we'll keep to ours." There was no need to say what would happen to that last two energy satellites if they didn't.

Old Spence had only two choices, capitulation and planetary suicide. He chose capitulation. There were still two satellites. The game would go on. It was not the same as surrender. Still, his voice broke when he said it. "Done."

Push nodded. "Done," he said. But it was not quite clear whether he meant that he was finished blowing up the satellites, or that the negotiations were over, or that Corporation was as good as dead. The grin, as always, seemed to say that he knew a lot more than he was ever going to tell.

Chapter Twenty-one

The Wideway was as packed for the Second Annual All League Rickshaw Races as it had been the evening of the battle they were intended to celebrate. Everybody was dressed up like one of the heroes of the Revolution. For three days the heats had been run and little or no useful work had been done in the Sphere. The festival was expected to go on officially for another two days, until the final eliminations had reduced the contestants to a field of twelve.

Cynics said it would be at least another week before the Sphere was sufficiently recovered from its fun to compete with the more sober habitats, like Henson's Tube, in the business of the League. Nobody in the Grand Sphere particularly cared. It was still the resort habitat of the League, and its business was still pleasure. The number of Fools allowed Up from Earthside had gradually increased in the months since the death of Spencer LeGrange, but they were not common.

Nor were they as popular as they had once been as a source of income. Contrary to expectation, the Sphere had found more than enough takers for its amusements, diversions, subterfuges, and swindles from within the League itself, and, at least until Spencer LeGrange died, there was a strong paranoia about a counterrevolution that made any-one from Earthside less than welcome. Among the ones who had come Up especially for the Races, few were made up to look like Earthside's chief participants in the piece of his-tory being celebrated, Stefan Standard, Nohfro Pock, and Spencer LeGrange.

Not that grotesque caricatures of them were not in abun-dance; Spencer LeGrange's face, with an exaggerated demonic cast, was visible everywhere, and white wigs were one of the most popular disguises among those who didn't want to go to the trouble of being Refaced. Those who were tall enough and on the skinny side anyway usually had themselves Refaced as Stefan Standard, and were invari-ably accompanied by someone in an Old Spence wig. Out of sheer perversity, most of the bigger males from Hardcore came as Nohfro Pock, and young Corehards even shaved their heads to look more authentic. Imitations of the League's 'three biggest villains were as commonplace as masks of the devil had once been in the old religious festivals Earthside.

It was said that all women became more beautiful during the five days of Race Week, although cynics insisted it was due more to the heavy use of Godsbreath and untold other recreational pharmaceuticals than it was to any actual change in appearance. Nevertheless, young and beautiful women, and a good many who were neither except during Race Week, undressed as Eleganza, and the sale of cobalt fingercovers was second only to the sale of wigs in general and dark black beards.

Eleganza had spent the first Race Week in seclusion mourning the Count, but had presided over a grand reopen-ing of her gardens on Halfyear Day and had been the official starter at First Race wearing the blond wig and green cape made famous by Push's twin sister, Chancey. It had all the makings of a tradition, since Chancey had started the *First* Annual All League Rickshaw Races dressed as Eleganza.

Young men from Upside generally wore white wigs and carried ornate silver canes like Vor Van Vast, or had themselves Refaced by artists on the Wideway to look like Yung Gun Runn for a week. Push's red hair and the uniform of a Blue were more popular in Downside, and anyone big enough, or fanatical enough, to wear sufficient padding watched the races and celebrated as Roger Count Aerowaffen, complete with black beard and white pleasuresuit. Among the older generation in both hemispheres, Dah Beel and Gun Sub Runn were the favorites, and artists used up tube after tube of Liquibrown turning women of all ages into Tinker Manwalker.

No one, however, appeared as UWalk Wenn, partly out of respect and partly to avoid a severe caning from the cult that had grown up among his former followers. Wenn's caners wore no disguise and always formed the bulk of the top two hundred rickshaw racers who qualified for the Annual. Rickshaw racing was popular everywhere, and thousands from Hardcore and Catchcage, where it was impossible, turned out weekly for races elsewhere in the League. Betting on the races was even more popular, and those who did not lose everything they had on the official races had the chance to lose it on the side races run on the twisting narrows of Downside.

During Race Week, the Downside Bridge was jammed with rickshaws waiting for a challenge. Most of them belonged to rickshaw racers from other habitats who had been eliminated earlier in the week and wanted a chance to redeem themselves. They hung out in flocks, complaining about the terrible starting positions, bad turns, breakdowns, and intentional fouls that had cost them their rightful place in the Last Race. The rest were hustlers preying on wounded pride and the universal inability to walk away from ridicule or a sizable bet.

Among the hustlers was a man who looked remarkably like Roger Count Aerowaffen, except that his beard was gray instead of black and he was somewhat smaller than most of the Aerowaffen pretenders on the Wideway. His

white pleasuresuit was more gray than white and looked
sadly in need of repair. He sat on the longseat of a dilapi-
dated rickshaw that looked like the Original rickshaw Pock
had all but dragged up Orchard Hill. He was half turned on
the seat, listening to another man bragging about what his
rickshaw racer would have done if it hadn't been for a loose
screw.

The man looked a good bit like the real Nohfro Pock,
except that he had a head of thick brown hair and a nose
that was considerably different from the holos of Pock that
sold on the Wideway. He wore no costume except the extra-
long cane of the LeGrange Police and an obviously painted
gold fist in the middle of his forehead. There was just the
tiniest hint of Earthside in his accent. He was on his third
repetition of the injustice that had cost his rickshaw racer
his chance when the slightly less than gigantic Aerowaffen
finally baited his hook. "If he can dance like you sing, he
must be UWalk Wenn."

The man stopped leaning on the forks of his rickshaw and
turned. "And who must you be?"

The man in the faded pleasuresuit looked as if he was
injured at not being recognized. "I might be Roger Count
Aerowaffen," he said, "but I *must* be Dealgrog Dooming."
He didn't wait for the other man to declare himself. "And
who must you be, if you're not Nohfro Pock?" The implication that the man was a villain was the way any Grander
would ask the name of a stranger if he wanted an argument
or a fight.

The hangers-on began to form an interested crowd
around the rickshaws, waiting for either a fight or a race to
bet on. The smart money would not have been on Dealgrog
Dooming. He was no small man, but the other man was a
head taller and a muscular fifty pounds heavier. The bigger
man seemed to favor canes over rickshaws for a moment,
but he chewed his anger into swallowable pieces and chose
the attitude that would lead to a race. "Justice T. Waitte,"
he said, "manager and trainer of Yung Sun Wenn." He
nodded toward the muscular young man between the forks.

Dooming gave a snort of derision. "Not UWalk Wenn?"

Waitte took the insult with a smile. "He learned to dance rickshaw under the great master UWalk Wenn."

Dooming gave a laugh. "Saw him shot on the Crossway too, no doubt." If he thought his listener was a Fool, every Grander in the Sphere claimed to have been on the Downside Window when UWalk Wenn was shot.

Waitte gave him a look of withering contempt. "No, he was in the Offshoots at the time." Few rank-and-file members of the Revolution were more respected than those who ambushed the first contingents of the Fist on CORPQ Hill.

"Then perhaps he saw my friend there." He nodded toward the small man leaning against the forks of his rickshaw. "Shot Lung Whee." Whee looked at Dooming as if the name were an intolerable alias.

It was Waitte's turn to be skeptical. "Did he learn rickshaw under UWalk Wenn as well?"

Dooming nodded. "He took Wenn to CORPQ once in this very rickshaw."

Waitte looked at the rickshaw. "Was Wenn a child then?"

Dooming gave the rickshaw an affectionate pat. "This is a fine wheel," he said.

Waitte looked at the rickshaw dancer. He looked remarkably like UWalk Wenn, if Wenn were perhaps a dozen years older than he had been when he died. "And that's UWalk Wenn's father," he said.

Dooming nodded at Waitte's rickshaw dancer. "And is that Wenn's daughter?"

The young man glared at Dooming but said nothing. Waitte answered for him. "He'll leave Whee and your wheel choking on the uphill."

Dooming laughed and waved the idea out of the air as a flight of fancy. "I could beat him myself," he said.

It was exactly the kind of boast a hustler like Waitte would have been waiting for. "What will you risk on it?"

Dooming gave a shrug. "Rickshaw for rickshaw and twenty thousand."

Waitte looked at him disdainfully. "Can you borrow that much?"

Dealgrog Dooming smiled. "On a sure thing."

Waitte struggled to pin him down. "Up the Crossway, down the Ripple, around the Heart, and back. First rickshaw on the bridge takes all." It was the standard race; up the curve of the Crossway, through the center of Downside, a right into the dozen or so sharp curves of the Ripple, another right onto the upper curve of the heart-shaped tangle of narrows that looped around the housing hills of Lighter Downside.

From there, the course curved toward the Tip and then curved away again onto the Downside Main, where it ran erratically along the edge of Iron Mountain before looping back to form the left hump of the Upper Heart. After a sharp reversal of direction at the point, the narrow looped back to form the upper right hump of the Heart from which the Ripple twisted back to the Crossway again. There were a lot of turns in the course, and the ability to weight the wheel was far more important than size or strength.

"You sit the longseat?" Dooming said.

Waitte nodded. "If you dance the forks."

"And who weights my wheel?"

Waitte nodded toward Dealgrog Dooming's rickshaw dancer. "Shot Lung Whee," he said. The relatively light weight of the passenger seemed like an advantage, but there was no steep uphill in the race where Dooming's superior size would have been an advantage and Waitte's bulk as passenger a definite liability. Waitte would be all momentum for his dancer to work into the wheel, while Dooming would have to create all the energy himself, probably by running the rickshaw up to speed time after time. He didn't expect Dooming to accept the handicap without a price.

Dooming wouldn't. "Eighty to twenty, rickshaws even up."

Waitte had expected to have to give even bigger odds. It didn't matter. There were few big rickshaw dancers who were any good, and none, he was sure, who could beat Yung

Sun Wenn. He tossed his money to the Worthy who held the stakes, certain it would still be there when the race was over. "Done," he said quickly.

But he was not quick enough to keep Dooming from adding another condition. "Double if we beat you by at least three lengths." It meant another eighty thousand, more than he had intended to risk, but it was so unlikely to happen that he leaped at the chance. "Done," he said.

Dooming tossed his money to the Worthy. Before they wheeled the rickshaws back to the edge of the bridge for the start, he leaned close to the stakes holder and handed him another thirty thousand. "Take all the bets you can at ten to one when we're at the Tip of the Heart." The Worthy nodded. The rickshaws lined up with Dealgrog Dooming between the forks and Shot Lung Whee on one longseat while Justice T. Waitte sat the other longseat and Yung Sunn Wenn worked the forks. With the drop of a hand, they were off.

Chapter Twenty-two

The rickshaws stayed even for about thirty yards up the Crossway, but over the half-mile distance to the turnoff, Justice T. Waitte's dancer slipped out to a half-wheel lead. Waitte looked surprised that the big man could manage to stay that close for so long and that he had not had to get down between the forks oftener. But the look of worry left his face as the rickshaws entered the twisting roadway of the Ripple.

The narrow left barely enough space for two rickshaws to pass, and the lead increased to a full wheel and then widened further as the rickshaws rounded the right-hand loop of the Heart. When they passed the exit to the Wideway halfway down the side, Dealgrog Dooming was a rickshaw and a half behind and seemed to be tiring. He had to get down between the forks twice to get the rickshaw back up to speed, and by the time the rickshaws reached the Tip, he was trailing by three lengths.

Reports from spotters at the Tip had Waitte's rickshaw increasing its lead, and the Worthy found easy takers for Dealgrog Dooming's thirty thousand, even at ten to one. It was a sucker's bet. From its point, the Heart swung upward around the middle curve of the Downside Main. The Main followed the irregular curve of the mountain base, zigging and zagging wherever the mountain jutted out or retreated. There was a slight uphill grade to the first half of it, and an equal downhill coming out of it as well. By the time they had finished both, Dooming's rickshaw had closed to within a length, and Waitte was beginning to look worried again.

The small man on the longseat of Dooming's rickshaw was frowning as well, but for a different reason. Dealgrog Dooming climbed back from the shortseat and sat beside him. "We've been a long time dead," he said. The rickshaw dancer knew he meant that they had been holding back their rickshaw long enough, but it was equally true in another sense.

"Too long," he said. The rickshaw began to pick up speed.

UWalk Wenn fed the last bit of momentum into the wheel and turned the rickshaw off into the Outer Fields Upper. His chest no longer hurt, and even his arm and his thigh had decreased to a burning soreness. He assumed he was merely becoming numb with approaching death, and he brought the rickshaw to a stop at the side of the narrow. There was no one there to meet them, but he did not worry about that. There was no telling what use the Skyshockers had for their bodies. He suspected they would be taken away and buried secretly, and a legend spread that they would return if ever the Revolution was in jeopardy. The making of legends was a Skyshocker preoccupation, and he doubted they would waste any opportunity for it.

He had no regrets except that he would never dance rickshaw again. The Revolution was well under way. The cane and the rickshaw had taught him that there was a momentum to events which could not be resisted and that the true power over things came with going with the flow. He closed his eyes and waited patiently to die.

Aerowaffen's voice startled them open again. "Have we been dead long?" he said. Aerowaffen pulled himself up and sat on the longseat. He worked his shoulder in a circle as if it had become stiff with being slept on. He looked around at the fields. "Just where we should be, I see." He looked at Wenn. "You didn't plan on staying dead, did you?" Wenn said nothing. "A revolution needs martyrs," he said, "but there's no point in getting yourself killed for it." His laughter almost shook the rickshaw.

He peeled the bullet wound off his forehead and rubbed the skin. The one at the back came off easier; he wiped the back of his head and his hand came away bloody. He reached into the cape of his pleasuresuit and peeled off a towel-sized sheet of the tissue-thin absorbent the very nature of pleasuresuits made necessary. He tossed it to Wenn and peeled another for himself. "Get cleaned up," he said. "We have work to do yet."

He rubbed his chest and felt inside his pleasuresuit. He shook his head and pulled out one of the packets. "Earth-side workmanship," he said and tossed it to Wenn. The liquid made it flop in the air, and Wenn almost dropped it. "Didn't go off," Aerowaffen said. "Must be the one you were playing with. Probably bent the micropressor." He looked at Wenn and began to laugh again. "You didn't think you were really shot, did you?"

He did not wait for Wenn to deny it. "Feel the stiff part in the middle?" Wenn squeezed the packet and nodded. "It's a multichannel receiver. Every time Push fired, a transmitter on his wrist gave off a different frequency signal that set off a small charge in one of the packets." He raised a fist to his forehead and let his fingers explode outward. "Charge blows the blood out, packet bursts just like skin, looks just like the real thing."

"But the shots," Wenn argued.

Aerowaffen shook his head. Like most Granders, Wenn's abhorrence of guns was surpassed only by his ignorance about them. "Blanks," he said. "Cartridges with wax tips. The bullet explodes, but nothing comes out." Wenn looked dubious. "The sound sets off the explosion in the packet, not something hitting it."

Wenn rubbed his chest. "Something hit me," he said.

Aerowaffen looked as if it were all too simple to keep explaining. "That was the explosive charge in the packet."

"It knocked me back onto the longseat." Wenn rubbed his chest again and looked at *Aerowaffen* as if he believed it could have been done with a lot less force. "I couldn't get my breath."

Aerowaffen laughed again. "The shot-lung wheeze," he said. Wenn did not find it funny and *Aerowaffen* shrugged. "What's true is what you believe is true. If you didn't feel shot, you might not have been convincing."

There was no arguing the point, but it raised a very disturbing question. "What happens when they find out we're not dead?"

Aerowaffen looked a little sheepish. "They won't." He let it fall as gently as he could. "I'm afraid we're going to have to stay dead," he said. "Our part was to be martyrs."

Wenn thought of what it would mean to live as someone else. Dancing rickshaw was the only thing he cared to do, except electric-cane defense, and earning a living at either would expose him to discovery anywhere in the Sphere. It meant nothing to *Aerowaffen*, who had changed identities so often he barely remembered his original name, but to Wenn it sounded like a living death. "How long?" he asked.

Aerowaffen smiled as if it were an opportunity for endless adventure. "Permanently," he said. "Unless the Revolution needs us again." He did not give Wenn time to think how long that might be. "Which it will shortly."

Wenn had a good idea where. "Orchard Notch?"

Aerowaffen shook his head. "No. Push should be on his way to *Eleganza's* to tell them about our murder." He looked up at Iron Mountain. "That ought to fill the notch."

There were not many places they could go without someone recognizing at least one of them. Wenn was about to say so when *Aerowaffen* opened his cape again and withdrew a small, flat case. Wenn recognized it as a Skyshocker face kit. It was a legend throughout the League that the Skyshocker face kit contained a hundred thousand disguises a Skyshocker could use to become anyone he *wanted. There were even ribald stories on the Wideway about Skyshockers impersonating brides and bridegrooms undetected.*

In truth, it contained only a few vials of basic color and a small, flat spraying apparatus for laying down layers of filament on the skin. Deftly used, it could build up cheekbones or noses or foreheads that a little color could transform into a new face. It was an art few outside the Skyshockers had any mastery of, and it was as good as magic to the rest of the League.

He put a hand on Wenn's chest and said, "Keep still a minute or you'll end up looking like Nohfro Pock." He moved the sprayer deftly, changing the nozzle several times. "Close your eyes," he said finally and moved the nozzle over Wenn's head. Wenn felt a thin mist on his ears and his forehead just below the hairline. When Aerowaffen was finished, he looked like a different man, a man a decade older, with gray hair and high cheekbones and narrower eyes. Even Wenn could hardly recognize himself. The disguise was not uncomfortable, and it might be possible to go through life that way if it meant he could continue dancing rickshaw and practicing electric-cane defense.

It took a good bit longer for Aerowaffen to become someone different, but a few changes in its tightness and the pleasuresuit looked more like a pair of coveralls and without his beard, Aerowaffen looked more like an Obee than a member of the Pleasure Crew. A few more changes in coloring, and they were ready to go. Aerowaffen leaped from the rickshaw and began to kick its wheels until they were too bent to track properly. Then he came around to the front and laid the forks on the ground and jumped on them until they bent. Wenn hated to see good equipment abused that way, but he knew as well as Aerowaffen that they could not let the rickshaw fall to the Fist in working order, and a properly damaged rickshaw would cause them more trouble if they took it than if they left it alone. They started across the field at a run toward the cover of the orchard that ran along the base of Iron Mountain.

"You have to die to come alive," Aerowaffen said. They rocked in unison on the edge of the flywheel. Wenn leaned forward to keep the forks down as the rickshaw shot ahead. It seemed a bad time to be picking up speed; the top of the Heart dipped to a sharp point, and Waitte's rickshaw had cut its speed in half to make the turn. It was almost stopped when Wenn's rickshaw flew past, still gaining momentum. They seemed certain to crash, but Wenn lifted the far wheel and the rickshaw cocked to its right in a tight lean that took it around the turn without flipping over. By the time Waitte's dancer turned the corner, Aerowaffen and Wenn were well up the last curve of the Heart.

Aerowaffen looked back over his shoulder and laughed. "You should have waved to your son," he said.

Wenn did not laugh. "Dead men have no sons," he said. The rickshaw began to slow down.

Aerowaffen gave a sigh of exasperation. "What do you want, then? Things the way they were. Spencer LeGrange and all." It was an irrefutable point. Their lives were the cost of the Revolution. "Life is what it is."

Wenn had been willing to lose his life, but he had not expected to have to live through losing it. He did not like dancing rickshaw in every habitat but the Grand Sphere, and teaching electric-cane defense to Corehards whose idea of defense was a stiff kick to the groin. He did not like his new identity, and much as he liked Aerowaffen, he did not like coming home only for Race Week so Aerowaffen could win enough money for his endless pleasures. He had waited twenty years for the time to be right for the Revolution, so it was not difficult to wait six months for the time to be perfect for his own revolution. The moment had come, and both he and Aerowaffen knew it.

"Changes," was all he said or needed to say.

Aerowaffen looked back. The other rickshaw was well behind them, but it would not stay there forever if Wenn kept working the wheel against him instead of with him. "Done," he said. "What do you want?"

"Shot Lung Whee." Aerowaffen looked hurt. The alias

had been his idea of a joke, and he seemed to get endless fun out of using it.

"What about him?"

Wenn gave him a murderous look. "He's lived too long."

The rickshaw behind them was beginning to catch up. Aerowaffen looked back and then at Wenn again. "Done," he said. "Who do you want to be?" Wenn started to answer but Aerowaffen cut him off. "And don't say UWalk Wenn."

Wenn smiled. "Dealgrog Dooming," he said.

Aerowaffen looked appalled. "My *grandfather* was Dealgrog Dooming." Despite all Aerowaffen's shifting on the longseat, the rickshaw slowed further. "That's my real name!" Aerowaffen insisted. Wenn only shrugged. Aerowaffen looked back again. "Done," he said.

"And the betting," Wenn said.

Aerowaffen shook his head. "It's the only thing that keeps you from being suspect. Everybody knows UWalk Wenn never bet on rickshaw dancing. As long as you bet, no one will suspect you're you." The other rickshaw was hardly a length behind and coming under full power. Wenn slowed the rickshaw even further and Aerowaffen had to jump down between the forks. "This is the last," he shouted over his shoulder.

Wenn shifted to multiply the force going into the flywheel. "Done," he said.

Aerowaffen hopped back up onto the shortseat. The other rickshaw passed them like they were just starting out. It was only a hundred yards to the Ripple. "If we win," he said.

"Done," said Wenn. The rickshaw shot forward. It was a full length in front again when they turned into the narrow turns of the Ripple. Their speed should have slowed in the Ripple, but instead they seemed to pick up momentum. They took the turns on one wheel, then the other, and the forks were continually lifting and having to be forced back down. But they were almost ten lengths in the lead when they came out of the Ripple onto the Crossway. The Worthy was already standing where Aerowaffen expected him, with his winnings in a bag ready to grab as they flew by. The other rickshaw was not even in sight when Wenn lifted the forks and spun the rickshaw on its wheelbase.

"What else?!" Aerowaffen shouted.

It was Wenn's turn to laugh. "*Your* new name."

Aerowaffen looked at the finish line and the Worthy holding up their winnings. "What is it?" he said.

Wenn tried to keep a straight face. "One Long Laff," he said.

"Done," Aerowaffen groaned. UWalk Wenn dropped the forks, and the rickshaw shot toward the finish line. They took their winnings on the fly, and the rickshaw disappeared into the crowd on the Downside Window. Above them in Upside, the finals of the Second Annual All League Rickshaw Races were just beginning. Eleganza dropped her hand to start it. She thought of Aerowaffen when she did. Most of the rickshaw dancers thought of UWalk Wenn.